W9-DGR-778

PETER ASHLEY

PETER ASHLEY

by DuBose Heyward

FARRAR & RINEHART
INCORPORATED
On Murray Hill   New York

PETER ASHLEY

CHAPTER I

HIGH noon of December twentieth, eighteen hundred sixty. Pierre Chardon walked north on Meeting Street until the crowd became so dense that to proceed farther would have required the incentive of a definite objective. And Chardon was going nowhere in particular. At least not consciously. He had let his steps carry him where they would, and now he realized that it was inevitable that he should find himself here.

Over the densely massed heads of the crowd, his gaze took in the familiar row of buildings that lay opposite the spot where he had ceased to resist and had surrendered to the inert pressure of the crowd. The five buildings that fell within his range of vision had, he found, lost all sense of the familiar, as though the momentous hour that was passing over them had broken them loose from all their past associations and was endowing them with a new significance, a new group of associations that in future would make them something quite different.

Starting from the north, he noted first the large brick building which contained the beer garden and dance hall, quieter now than he had ever known it. Next to the beer garden stood a small, nondescript brick building. It had always been a blank spot in the landscape, but he wondered now who occupied it and for what purpose. His glance traveled south and was relieved by the tranquillity and space of the Circular Church yard. It alone,

3

he thought, continued definitely to signify the past, with its tombstones gathering their lichens in the deep shade of the live oaks. Above the oaks the spire of the church, springing sheer through the ceiling of dark polished green into the clear winter sunlight, seemed to Chardon a sustained and courageous gesture in the face of a known and hostile destiny. Directly opposite the spot where he stood, Institute Hall reared its imposing façade, and beyond it to the south the puritanism of the bourgeoisie flung a futile challenge in the direction of the beer garden from its broad signboard: "Teetotal Restaurant, N. Fehrenbach, Prop."

Chardon's glance returned to the hall. It was strangely quiet. Even the crowd that waited jammed in the street had muted its voice to a pervasive buzz which, more emphatically than words, expressed a mood tense with excitement and anticipation. The silence, Chardon thought, probably signified that the signers were attaching their names to the Ordinance. That would take about an hour, and then it would all be over. Well, in reality it had all been over on November the seventh, when the news of Lincoln's election had reached Charleston. That day the attitude of the whole city had expressed itself in the action of Judge Magrath, who, turning the key in the lock of the Federal Court on Chalmers Street, had washed his hands of the Union and stepped down into the waiting crowd.

The judge had been wearing a French rose in his buttonhole, Chardon remembered. His lapel with its unfailing boutonnière was as dependable as the calendar: camellia, violet, azalea, crimson rambler, oleander. One could almost date one's letters from the judge's buttonhole. Chardon thought, that every year thereafter when the French rose sent its late crimson to throb in his spent rose garden and sing of life in the very moment of death, he would always remember the locking of that door; and he wondered why, as we grow old, the things that we love most are one by one poisoned for us by new and painful associations.

He supposed that he would not be minding this so keenly if it had not been for Mexico. He might even have been one of the hotheads in there now, busy with pen and ink. But having fought under the flag made it different. Human loyalty was a strange paradox. It was given most unreservedly in return, not for favors, but for scars. The war had flung him back broken in body. Tragedy had piled upon tragedy. It had drawn a keen blade across his life, dividing that part we call youth cleanly and irrevocably from the rest. And in return he could not look at the flag without a surge of pride, a sense of complete identity with it and all that it signified.

The Union and his nephew, Peter Ashley—the two things that mattered. Within the next few minutes the slender tie that bound South Carolina to the Union would be severed. There would be war; he no longer doubted that. Within a fortnight Peter would arrive from England. Well, they should not have the boy. He knew his sensitiveness, his fine-drawn nervous temperament. For these others war was a game—for Peter it would be deliberate suicide. He knew now that all during the years that Peter had belonged to him he had realized that this moment must come. Under his conscious care of the boy there had always been this fear that had guided him almost without conscious planning. His schooling in the North—his years abroad. Everything that could tend to broaden an inherited provincialism into a spirit of nationalism. He saw it plainly now, and he was glad.

His hand, thrust deep into his pocket, encountered a card. He drew it out and looked at it. It was an admission to the floor. His brother-in-law, Thomas Wakefield Ashley, Peter's father, had sent it to him. Thomas was a delegate from his parish and he could not imagine any member of the family not being eager to attend and witness him, grown suddenly to heroic proportions, in the act of signing.

On an impulse Chardon started forward, shouldering his way between the bodies that were pressed so closely together that they seemed to cohere in a solid mass. Chardon, always intensely fastidious about his person, resented the close physical contacts. He had the feeling that he was submitting his person to an indignity. He had brought out of the army a theory, in which he was quite sincere, that he was democratic; confusing personal friendship for a few individuals of the lower orders with a general principle. But this theory always broke down when subjected to elbow-rubbing with the mob.

At the steps, however, he found that a small area was held clear by a line of police. He was passed at once upon exhibiting his card, and ascended the steps to the entrance. Everyone in Charleston knew Chardon, at least by sight, and the doorkeeper was no exception. He was standing outside the door, peering through a crack. He turned and touched his hat.

"You're late, sir. There are only a scant half dozen left to sign."

Chardon surrendered his card and entered. Limping

slightly, he climbed the broad low stairway that ascended from the ground floor to the convention hall. At the door of the large apartment he paused, struck as he always was by its vast and pretentious ugliness. Built only four years previously, it belonged to what his old friend Gilchrist characterized as the parvenu school of architecture, although it was beginning to be spoken of as Victorian, in order to differentiate it from the Georgian period with its simple and dignified beauty. "Victorian!" he scoffed. As though anything could be less British in spirit than these misplaced borrowings of Italian grandeur. The Hall, Chardon remembered, had been designed to foster the agricultural and mechanical development of the state. Its present usage caused him to smile ironically. But this feeling of irritation over an old grievance was soon forgotten. The silence in the great hall was intense. Near Chardon a north window stood open and through it came the low tense buzz of the crowd, and, shocking in its irrelevance, an oath and a burst of coarse laughter from the beer garden beyond the church yard.

The capacity of the auditorium was three thousand, but he guessed that it contained nearer four with the delegates on the stage and the standers ranked along the walls. Half the floor was reserved for the state legislature, while representative citizens from all parts of the state filled the remaining chairs. The shallow galleries that flanked both north and south walls were crowded with gaily dressed ladies. Mr. Jamison, the president of the Convention, stood at the table in the center of the stage—the table, Chardon remembered suddenly, upon which the Federal Constitution had been ratified—and in his deep resonant voice called the name of the delegate who was next in order of signing. At first there had been cheering as each signer went forward, but the solemnity of the occasion had silenced the demonstration, and now there would come only the name, boot-heels loud and measured on the bare boards of the aisles, the scratching of the pen, plainly audible to the occupants of the stage, again boot-heels, silence, and another name.

The last signer returned to his place. The silence quickened. Mr. Jamison rose to his feet and lifted the document between his two hands. The gesture was strikingly like that with which a priest elevates the Host. For a moment he held the large parchment before him. The great seal of state, struck deep in the crimson wax, stood out against its pallor like a prophecy.

Then full-bodied, deep and resonant, the voice of the President filled the hall:

"The Ordinance of Secession has been signed and ratified, and I proclaim the State of South Carolina to be an independent Commonwealth."

For a moment after the proclamation the silence persisted. It came to Chardon suddenly what awful power lay in the spoken word. An utterance as ephemeral as the breath that gave it life, and a nation that had been in the building for two centuries had ceased to exist. But to the serried mass of humanity that filled the hall it was a signal, not of an ending, but a beginning. The State of South Carolina, an independent commonwealth. With a concerted roar the sea of heads that filled the floor of the hall rose before Chardon as the men leaped to their feet. In the galleries the women lifted suddenly in opposed waves of color and sound. One almost expected to

see them sweep together over the heads of the men—
meet like toppling breakers, and dissolve in multicolored
foam. Their shrill clamor cut across the heavy cheering
from below, then merged with it in a deafening volume
of sound. All about Chardon staid and respectable citizens were behaving as though demented, wringing each
other's hands, slapping backs, brandishing canes and
hats. Outside, the crowd caught the contagion and a
refluent wave of sound roared back upon them and smote
the outer walls of the building.

Chardon turned his back upon the pandemonium that
reigned in the hall and made his way to the door. From
the low stone steps that descended to the street he witnessed the commencement of the celebration that would
last far into the night. For several blocks in either direction the street was a dense mass of humanity. From the
direction of the Citadel came the measured boom of a
cannon in a first official salute to the flag of the independent state. The rhythmic detonations cut through the
steady cheering, dividing it into well-defined intervals.
Somewhere near by, a brass band crashed into a martial
air that at once foundered in the sea of sound. Pitched
high above the babble the chimes of St. Michael's released a burst of bright, clear music, that Chardon heard
distinctly from the steps but lost in the general discord
as soon as he descended to the pavement.

Behind Chardon the hall commenced to disgorge its
horde of jubilant Secessionists, and the police forced the
crowd back, urging them to disperse. A resounding slap
fell on Chardon's spare shoulder blade, almost throwing
him off his balance. He always discounted the slight
limp in his right leg that still carried a fragment of a

Mexican shell, and the blow made his lameness at once apparent, filling him with embarrassed irritation. He turned and looked into the flushed and excited face of Thomas Ashley. But his brother-in-law was too absorbed in his own affairs to note his victim's discomfort. Slipping an arm through Chardon's, he directed an energetic and effective assault against the crowd. When he could make himself heard, Ashley exclaimed, "This is a great day, Pierre. Not only in the annals of the state but the family as well. You were there when I signed, of course."

Chardon realized that this was a statement and not a question, and that no reply was expected of him. Ashley hurried on:

"And you must celebrate with us at dinner. We are stopping at the Planters Hotel. It's just a step, and Emily will meet us there. She attended in the gallery with the Saint Clairs, and will join us presently. And of course Wake will be on hand, and will want to see you."

An instant realization of what that dinner would be like came to Chardon. The surging throng of guests, servants, delegates and militia officers, Governor Pickens and his staff. The stupendous dinner—the one topic of conversation, secession. He decided that much as he wanted to see Emily it could not be faced. What he needed now desperately was the ordered quiet of his own home—a chance to think.

He made his excuses and was about to turn away. Then he hesitated and swung back toward his brother-in-law. Ashley, in the act of going, paused and waited. Chardon said, "Thomas, I want to ask you a very especial favor. I want you——"

A wedge of sound drove between the two men, breaking Chardon's speech off short. Down Meeting Street raced three fire companies. The volunteer firemen, clad in their red shirts and rubber helmets, tugged at the engine ropes and cheered at the top of their lungs. The engine, jerked at high speed over the rough paving, rattled and bumped, bells clanged, and firemen's rattles whirled deafeningly.

When Chardon could make himself heard again, he took up his plea. "Peter has been away a long time. He has been out of all this. And now he'll soon be home. He's a man now, Thomas, and should have a will of his own. If there should be war, promise me that you won't coerce the boy—let him decide for himself."

Ashley looked as though Chardon's words carried no meaning to his brain. "Why, bless my soul, Pierre! Why should I coerce him? He's a South Carolinian still, isn't he? He's an Ashley. His tastes are strange, I'll admit. I haven't always understood him. But this is a different matter. Of course I won't have to, as you say, coerce him. His brother Wake is already talking about recruiting a company from our neighborhood. No, you need entertain no alarms on that score. I am perfectly safe in saying that the boy shall do as he pleases."

Chardon watched the well-set-up, confident figure of his brother-in-law receding down Queen Street in the direction of his hotel. Suddenly he realized that he was envying Thomas Ashley profoundly. He was so utterly free from doubts and hesitations. He was in such perfect adjustment with the life to which he had succeeded at Wakefields Plantation. Life had been handed to him with complete plans and specifications. Success had consisted largely of duplicating the career of his father down to the most minute detail, and in turn to pass the process on to his eldest son, Wakefield. Thomas Ashley at fifty, with the appetites of the flesh keen, undiminished and held in nice control by the tenets of good taste that prevailed in his class. A full busy life that provided the wherewithal to satisfy these simple and uncomplicated desires. A crack shot—a good seat in the saddle—a kind master—a born host, with his house continually crowded with guests—and a watchful factor in town who could be depended upon to keep him out of bankruptcy.

But Peter—certainly more Chardon than Ashley— Emily's child, born with the destiny of going perpetually hungry in that land of plenty. Born with the appetites of the spirit. Born to question rather than to accept. Chardon concluded that when all was said and done humanity could be divided into two general classes—the gregarious and the solitary. Thomas and his first-born were of the former—Peter, like himself, of the latter. Between the two there could never be any real fundamental understanding. Thrown together, they would perform the conventional grimaces. Employing the same spoken language they would hail each other across the void. But at parting there would never be a looking back over the shoulder—a final moment of regret.

At the intersection of Broad and Meeting streets, Chardon's progress was arrested. He had been loitering along, lost in his speculations, and now he had been overtaken by a parade. Three militia companies in dress uniform, preceded by a band, passed the historic corner. He recognized them all at a glance—the Vigilant Rifles, the Zouaves, the Washington Light Infantry. They swung before him in successive waves of gray—red—blue. He supposed they would all be in new uniforms of the independent state as soon as the frenzied activity of the tailors could accomplish the metamorphosis.

At last he reached home. His castle. A colonial residence set behind a wrought iron fence, and overlooking White Point Gardens. The shadowed quiet of the library drew him in, and Cæsar, sensing his need of solitude, brought him a decanter and glasses and retired to the kitchen to tell the cook to hold dinner until the master called for it.

A sound penetrated the somber curtain of Chardon's thoughts—carriage wheels that crunched to a standstill on the crushed shell of the drive. The house waked to the peal of the front doorbell. There was a moment of alarm. He couldn't see people now. He had to be alone. Then Cæsar's tread on the piazza reassured him. Cæsar could be depended upon to understand his master's mood and say that he was not at home. He was pouring himself a thimbleful of brandy when the drawing-room door opened and Damaris Gordon paused upon the threshold. She made a vivid picture against the shadowed hall. Her small figure, wrapped in a gay barcelona that covered her from chin to the hem of her hoopskirt presented a perfect cone surmounting which her face, under a small close turban, showed with the color, the lift and the freshness of a morning rose.

"I knew I'd find you hiding in here, Uncle Pierre," she said. "If Cæsar had just said that you were out, I'd have believed him. But when he told me the hour you left the house, the name of your club, and added that you were well and happy, that was too much, so I came in and invited myself to dinner." She turned back toward the shadows where the servant hovered in embarrassed silence. "You may tell Daphne to take up dinner, Cæsar. It is after two and I'm famished."

Chardon stood regarding her in silence, his grim foreboding forgotten for the moment, wondering as he always did what she was going to do next. He knew that it would be direct, decisive. It was that quality in her that always fascinated him. Her impulses were purely feminine, but there was an almost masculine quality in the directness with which they were acted upon.

Damaris threw off her wrap and advanced upon her host with an air of bravado. She was small and beautifully made. Her high corseting and the revealing snugness of her bodice accentuated the virginal curves of her bust, and when she walked her limbs moved with a grace that shimmered through the masking bell of her skirt. She came directly to Chardon and held up her face to be kissed, then seated herself and smiled up at him.

"Cæsar thinks I'm a hussy," she announced, "coming in and ordering dinner as though I were a real niece instead of an adopted, but I shan't mind and I will eat very little. What I'm really hungry for is a talk with you."

Standing before the fire and smiling down at her, Chardon felt a little bewildered, and rather ridiculously young. She always affected him that way, shocking him out of habitual attitudes of mind by her direct attack, then provoking an almost forgotten youth into a giddy and not altogether comfortable sentience. He said: "Then you have remarkable endurance, my dear. It is— let me see—at least six months since I was last honored.

You dropped in then and cured my touch of gout, and ever since I have been sedulously cultivating a recurrence in the hope of another visit." He raised his glass and smiled at her over the rim.

Cæsar appeared and announced dinner. Then, separated by the square of snowy damask bright with afternoon sun, Chardon regained sufficient balance to wonder as to her motive for coming. He remembered that she was sponsor for one of the militia companies—the Dragoons, or was it the Washington Light Infantry? He knew how she loved excitement. Her father, Proctor Gordon, would certainly be assisting at the entertainment of delegates at the Planters Hotel or Mills House, and she would have been invited. It would have been her native element, with its surging color, its martial music, and a score of dashing gallants offering themselves as willing victims to her charm. Only one sure of her position as the undisputed belle of her set could have afforded to retire and leave the field to her rivals.

But why had she elected to come and dine with a disgruntled Unionist who was a contemporary of her father's? He hazarded a leading question. "Of course you were at the hall for the signing?"

She nodded. "It was tremendous, wasn't it?" She was addressing herself with youthful enthusiasm to Daphne's well-prepared dinner. Her frank enjoyment of food was one of the things that Chardon liked about her. It was typical, he thought, of the unaffected and at times almost ruthless gusto with which she took the good things that life brought to her.

"I must have known that Daphne was going to give you cooter soup today," she remarked as she put down her spoon, and Cæsar appeared to remove the plates. "There isn't her match in town." Then she leaned forward and regarded her host with wide, earnest eyes. "I saw you at the hall, Uncle Pierre. You weren't happy about it, were you?"

"Hardly, Damaris. You know how I feel about the Union. I won't deny it was an ordeal."

"If it's not asking too much, I want you to talk to me about it. Father is for secession, you know, but he is bitterly opposed to war, and then there are my own friends—they are for whipping the Union at once and having done with it. But you are so much wiser than they are. I want you to tell me what you think."

Cæsar set a pair of wild ducks upon the table and departed. Carving was one of Chardon's small vanities, and while his hands moved dexterously over the birds, he commenced to put his feeling about the whole distressing business into words. Damaris had a gift for listening that amounted to genius. Her eyes gave him an eager intelligent sympathy that led him on, and eventually made him lose himself utterly in his subject.

The square of winter sunlight left the table, slid across the broad polished planking of the floor, and commenced to climb the paneling behind Chardon's chair; but the girl's attention never seemed to waver. Cæsar had removed the dishes and brought coffee. Chardon lifted his cup and looked out over the rim at a flag advancing across a plain strewn with rocks and bristling with cactus, trying to put into words the inexplicable emotion that the picture always quickened into being.

He said: "It's useless to try to explain what we call patriotism. It is like trying to explain the Holy Ghost.

And I'm not even sure that my feeling springs wholly from a love of the Union. That, after all, is an abstraction. No, it's the sight of the flag that does it to me. Perhaps it is because when I was fighting under it I had everything—Bella and the children—youth. Perhaps it symbolizes that for me, and not a group of Confederated States at all."

He became conscious of the room again, of the girl with the wide, intent gaze, and he gave a short embarrassed laugh. "I apologize, my dear. You came to have me expound a cause, and instead of that I have been indulging in an emotional housecleaning that has nothing whatever to do with the actual issues."

"I don't care a fig what you think about it, Uncle Pierre. I wanted you to tell me how you felt. That is what matters with people we love. And somehow I wanted to be with you today. That was why I left Father's party and invited myself to dinner."

With a swift decisive movement, she rose from her chair and came to him. He raised his head and she pressed it impulsively against her breast. "I have to go now," she told him, "but I just wanted to say that whatever happens, whatever people say, I'll always love you, and so will Father and Mother. And the latch-string is always going to be on the outside for you. Always—will you remember that?" She kissed him then, and before he could follow her, had gotten into her wrap, and had her fingers about the knob of the big front door. Chardon, bewildered as he always was by her swift transitions, murmured apologies for keeping her and insisted that she wait until Cæsar could get the carriage; but she protested that she would rather walk, and before he could remonstrate further, the door opened and closed, and she was gone.

The closing door waked a dismal reverberation in the empty house. Chardon stood in the hall listening to it, and feeling the atmosphere chill slowly back to normal. It had been good to have a woman in the house. None had lived under that roof since Bella had died fourteen years before. And it was flattering to have the most sought after young lady in town drop in to dinner.

But why had she done it? Why had she left her world on this gala day to bring comfort to a lonely old widower? He insisted on considering himself old, although he was just past fifty. And then suddenly he realized that she had come to give, and not to get, and that it was just like her to have come when he needed her.

He remembered that she had started to call on him just after Peter had gone away. She had come one day all alone. He saw her again, in her short skirt and long pantalettes, wide attentive eyes fixed on his face. He had wondered then what had prompted her to come, and had learned later that she had overheard Proctor remarking that he would be lonely without Peter.

She still had an uncanny way of knowing when she was needed, and she would gaily toss away an engagement that another girl would have given her hope of heaven to secure, and devote an hour or two to an adopted uncle, or, Chardon had to admit, even to less attractive and more ancient relatives. It was, he concluded, her roundabout way of evening scores with a sex among whose younger representatives she was notoriously callous with her heartbreaking.

Quite let down by this unflattering conclusion, Chardon returned to his drawing room and his decanter of brandy, and reëntered upon his solitary vigil.

The afternoon passed, and as the early winter night drew in, the excitement in the vicinity of Secession Hall became intensified. Barrels of tar were rolled into the middle of the street and set ablaze. The heat burst the barrels, and the tar flowed out in rivulets of fire to lap the street in flame from curb to curb. Crowds that had cheered until their voices refused longer to respond to the demands of patriotic fervor amused themselves by throwing Indian crackers into the blazing street. With the fall of night the sky had become overcast, and now, taking its color from the conflagration, hung low over Secession Hall, lit to a sullen and prophetic red. As the night advanced, the beer garden and adjacent saloons disgorged crowds of excited cavaliers who shouted furiously for their mounts, then raced at high speed through the streets, firing derringers into the air, and proclaiming at the top of their voices, "The Union is dissolved!"

Only in the deep residential section in the south of the town was there comparative quiet. True to character, the ultimate stronghold of the aristocracy was expressing its emotions, whether of joy or regret, behind barred front windows and firmly latched street doors. Occasionally a carriage would rattle to a door, the occupants would be admitted, and the world again shut out. Occasionally a slave would pass on some mission, his face an expressionless mask over the conjectures and alarms that must have been seething beneath.

And in his great Georgian drawing room Chardon sat alone. His thoughts turned to his old friend Alfred

Huger. Today's business would be a blow to him, he knew, none the less distressing because expected. But, unlike himself, he reflected, Alfred was a man of strong character. Instead of hanging morbidly about Secession Hall, he had doubtless remained in dignified isolation on the plantation.

Later he thought of calling for cloak and stick and going to see James Petigru. That staunch and philosophical Unionist would, he thought likely, be staying late in his law library in St. Michael's Alley, and could give him comfort in this moment of doubt. With his unfailing wit he might even extract some humor from the situation. But at the last moment he gave it up. The day had taken more out of him than he would have thought possible, and, too, his accursed leg was beginning to throb again.

CHAPTER II

THE bond that existed between Pierre Chardon and his nephew, Peter Chardon Ashley, was one of such extraordinary understanding and interdependence that in the comparatively small circle in which they moved none ever thought of one without an instinctive realization of the other. In the lives of both there had come a moment of supreme need, and Emily Ashley, Peter's mother, had effected one of those apparently divine adjustments in human relationships by the simple and heroic act of virtually giving her youngest son into the keeping of her bereaved brother. Her generosity probably saved Pierre Chardon his sanity. And the older man requited her by bestowing upon the moody and bewildered boy of ten a sympathy and understanding that could have been made possible only by a similarity of temperament so close that it amounted to a spiritual kinship.

Those who were romantically inclined in the old city liked to tell the story to the chance visitor who, in the course of time, always asked the inevitable questions about the distinguished-looking middle-aged man and the extraordinary lad with the high forehead and vivid unresting eyes, who were such inseparable companions.

Pierre Chardon's story, though briefly told, contained all the essential elements of romantic tragedy. Of independent means and aristocratic French Huguenot lineage, he had early in life married a woman for whom, since childhood, he had entertained an almost fanatical devotion. Following the marriage they had spent a year in travel and had then returned to settle down in the large high-ceilinged residence that overlooked the White Point Gardens and had been left to Chardon by his parents, who had died within a few months of each other when he was a lad of twelve, leaving besides himself a sister, Emily, two years his junior.

At the time of their parents' death, the plantation upon which the Chardons had risen to affluence had been sold by the children's guardians and the proceeds conservatively invested. The town house and the house servants were retained, and a rather ineffectual aunt was installed, bulwarked by a succession of nursery governesses and tutors. Fortunately, however, the evolution of an infant Chardon into an adult member of Charleston society had only to proceed along certain preordained and definite lines, and the process was neither materially helped nor seriously hindered by the shadowy and vacillating discipline of the administrative aunt. Lessons, dancing school, riding lessons, soirées, the début, were the events that carried the brother and sister forward by pleasant stages, and finally landed both into early and apparently entirely satisfactory marriages: Emily to Thomas Ashley of Wakefields Plantation, and Pierre to Bella de Veaux.

Since he had been deprived of the logical vocation of a Chardon by the sale of the ancestral rice fields, it was inevitable that the neighborhood would speculate as to the career Pierre would select for himself when he returned from his wedding tour and settled in the big house facing the lovely gardens. But to the blunt question of what he proposed to do with his future, which is always the unpleasant prerogative of one's relatives, he replied with perfect seriousness, "Marriage," and added, "Bella and I waited years for our marriage; we are utterly happy and we know that happiness cannot last always. We shall devote ourselves to each other."

That was in 1840. There was a lyric quality to the six years that followed. The Chardons entertained lavishly and graciously. But even in their home their friends experienced the feeling of being exterior to their lives, and moving about the outer orbit of a circle of which their hosts' absorption in each other was the incandescent core. Even his own sister, Emily Ashley, the mother of Peter,—for whom Chardon had always entertained a deep affection,—felt little better than an outsider when she, with Thomas, came down every February for the races and balls. Two children were born to the Chardons. A boy and a girl.

Then suddenly in 1846 Pierre Chardon did a quixotic thing. He joined the South Carolina Volunteers, imprinted a farewell kiss upon the stricken face of his wife, and boarded a transport for the Gulf and the first stage of the journey to the Mexican front.

It may have been that to his senses came a faint premonition of that satiety which is the inevitable climax of passion and that he hoped to forestall it by a temporary absence. It may have been a tardy awakening to the hereditary obligation to the state which was a tenet of his class. There was no understanding the obscure actuating motives of Pierre Chardon. He was certainly a romantic—with a touch of the poet, inarticulate, but nevertheless an essential part of him. At any rate he was living up to the best traditions of the Chardons. The relatives consigned him to the hell of war with expressions of extreme self-appreciation. Blood would tell. Chardons could be counted upon sooner or later to be Chardons.

Two years passed and Chardon returned. He walked with difficulty and was wasted almost beyond recognition from the ravages of camp fever. No one had the courage to tell him, so he limped painfully up the steps of his home, and opened the door into the tombed silence of the house. The servants looked into his face and burst into a loud blubbering.

Then he knew. His wife, Bella, and his two children had been carried off in one of those brief up-flares of yellow fever that came intermittently, like thunders before the storm, and culminated in the decimating epidemic of 1858.

When the news of Pierre's return reached Wakefields plantation Thomas Ashley was off on a hunting trip and Emily made the only completely independent decision of her life. Tying the strings of her bonnet decisively beneath her chin, she called Peter, bundled him with a small leather trunk containing a hastily assembled wardrobe into the carriage, and ordered Ephram, the Wakefields coachman, to drive her at once to town.

Six hours later they were sitting together in the appalling emptiness of the huge Georgian drawing room, Emily with an arm about her son's shoulders, the lad himself,—wide luminous eyes in a white bewildered face,—and Pierre Chardon crumpled deep in a huge mahogany chair, apparently incapable of movement under the appalling pressure of the silence and loneliness.

Peter never forgot the brief interview. Its imprint lingered on his senses in a series of sharp indelible impressions. The great room shuttered against the afternoon sun, latticed by rays of white light in which the dust motes vibrated against the damp cool gloom—a shaft falling across his uncle, bringing out in startling contrast his white stricken face with its prominent Huguenot nose. His mother, clad in some soft white material and sitting with exaggerated erectness in her straight chair, was utter beauty—strength—and, when he touched her, the source from which a flood of tenderness lifted and broke over him, causing his eyes to sting and the tendons back of his knees to go suddenly slack.

In the enormous quiet their voices sounded to him like the sounds mice make in an empty house. His mother said, "You will really be doing us a great favor, Pierre. He is not happy on the plantation, and he is a disappointment to his father. If I had more time to keep him by me I would not let him go, but with the plantation and the negroes, I cannot. Thomas expects a great deal of me, you know."

The figure in the great chair had looked up. "You are doing this for me, Emily. He is the apple of your eye, and you are doing this for me."

Then Peter's mother had said, "Nonsense!" and the trivial little word had broken under the emotion that it had to bear. But in a minute she went on. "The truth of the matter is that he's like you, Pierre. You will understand him. You will bring him through."

After a while his uncle had said, "God bless you, Emily." Then Peter had torn his body from that of his mother, and the pain had broken his manhood. But he had cried only a little while. And then his mother had gone, and Uncle Pierre had taken him upstairs into a bright sun-filled room that looked out across White Point Gardens and on over a blue expanse of water, and had told him that it was his room, and he had suddenly thrown his arms about his uncle's neck and felt comforted.

When Pierre Chardon took up his life with Peter, it was as though he had entered into a reincarnation. He had lived romance to the hilt. He had known its heights, and in sorrow he had paid the full measure for that knowledge. That phase of his life was over—done with. Now he would become a philosopher.

Although scarcely of what is called middle age, and with many of his contemporaries still good for a day in the saddle or their tenth julep of an evening, he nevertheless gave the impression of being of an older generation. His attitude toward the many pleasures of his city and time was detached, musing, philosophic. His lusts and physical excitements he was content to satisfy vicariously through youth, as is the way with age. And although possessed of a caustic wit that could bite and sting on occasion, he had already learned that upon the whole it is less exhausting to the vitality to be kind rather than clever.

It was as though, with the sudden tragic termination of Chardon's own romance, he had deliberately assumed the rôle of spectator at the drama that was being enacted about him, viewing it with an amused and exaggerated tolerance and feeling it throb with life only when it touched Peter, and through Peter his own emotions.

There were those who thought his attitude an affectation, for, as the years drew out between the periods of the Mexican and Civil wars, and the mode in men's attire became more drab and hideous with its elaborate affectation of masculine carelessness, he clung obstinately to the snug, military lines of the coat, the flaring coat-skirts, the peg-top trousers strapped under the instep, and the claret stock that he had worn during his brief idyllic marriage. But this was not an affectation with Chardon. It was not an attempt to be different, or to "date" himself as a survival of a glamorous past. It sprung quite naturally from character. He had always been fastidious in his dress. He got a sensuous enjoyment from form and color. In a word, he was still a Frenchman in spite of the century and a half that had elapsed since the first Chardon had turned his back reluctantly upon a France that was inhospitable to Protestants.

In a society that was renowned for its cuisine, his table was famous. He himself always ate sparingly, delicately, yet with great relish. Three juleps were his invariable number—either morning or evening. That amount of alcohol produced exactly the proper degree of philosophical detachment. The cumulative effect of four in succession, he had found, tended to infuse life with too painful a degree of reality, so that it at once repelled, attracted and tempted him to some rash act that might plunge him again into its fevered stream. Having eschewed the fiercer passions, Chardon derived the most exaggerated pleasure from the æsthetic aspects of his daily life, arranging and rearranging the mundane details through years of patient experimentation until its whole developed that pleasing variety within complete unity that characterizes a finished work of art.

The fifteenth day of May was always a notable date in the calendar of the Carolina Low Country. There was a universal conviction that plantations were safe from the dreaded visitations of malaria until that night. But the following night, and thereafter until the first autumn frost, the pestilence would be abroad in the land. And so the estates were abandoned for town houses, pine-land villages, Saratoga, Hot Springs or the Grand Tour, and the broad acres were left to the ministrations of the negroes who were immune, and the supervision of over-seers, who docilely accepted fever as an unavoidable inci-dent in the thankless lot of their class.

And in town Pierre Chardon, sensing the stir of mi-gration in the air, would enter upon his summer morn-ing ritual. He would awake at seven o'clock and lie with his gaze fixed through the open window, with its frame of crimson ramblers, upon a square of open har-bor. This would be crossed from time to time by a ship, glorious in the early sun, or an owner's barge from one of the sea island plantations, manned by chanting oarsmen and moving across the area of vision like a great many-legged water beetle. From below would come subdued laughter and a great splashing, where three small negroes were drawing water from the cis-terns for his bath.

St. Michael's chimes would sound the half hour, and the door would open to admit Cæsar with dressing gown and towels. A moment later a strange procession would leave the side door of the mansion and proceed toward the rear of the garden. Under the successive rose trellises went first a small negro with a pail of steaming water to take the chill from the bath. Then Cæsar, black, massive and important, towels over arm. And last—Chardon in a flowered silk dressing gown, very erect, very eager, as though each repetition of the routine were a fresh adventure, pausing now and again to plunge his great Huguenot nose into the heart of some particularly fine blossom, then lifting his head to inhale the soft air perfumed by the flowers and heavy with the pervasive salty tang of the sea.

At the extreme rear of the garden, covered by a grape arbor and surrounded by fig trees, stood the bath. Chardon was very proud of it and had acquired it in Italy when he and Bella were on their wedding tour. It was hewn from a block of Carrara marble, with a frieze of grapes chiseled just below its rim as its only decoration. Its cream-white flesh was laced with a network of faint blue veins, and in it the water lay deep, clear and tranquil in the heavy shade. Left to himself, Chardon would lie in the limpid element while the outer world commenced to steam under the mounting sun, and would listen to the loud boom of the "figaters" in the trees about him, and to the chatter of the birds getting slow and drowsy in the heat.

Later, on fine days, Peter would join him and they would breakfast leisurely in the garden. It was during these long breakfasts that the mass of factual matter that the boy had received during the winter school term was subjected to that selective process which is the basis of true education. His uncle would sort it over with him, then leave him to decide for himself what he would accept and what reject. Frequently they would read and discuss the morning paper, and from their discussions Peter gradually developed a code of ethics. "There are two sides to every question," the older man had said on one of these occasions. "It is a curse to our class that we inherit only one, as we do the family plate. But it is a fine and manly adventure to discover the other side for ourselves."

The years that he passed in the big house that looked out over the White Point Gardens and the bay were extraordinary ones for Peter. His uncle treated him always as a contemporary. And presently the older men who came to dine with Chardon accepted him on the same basis. He met Gilmore Simms, and the author, responding to the frank idolatry of the lad, carried him often with him on his visits to Russell's Book Store on King Street near Wentworth, which served as a club for the literary group. There, sitting entranced by the fire, with his thin nervous fingers locked about his knees and his extraordinary eyes devouring the faces of the men, Peter heard the discussions that crystallized into the editorials which appeared later in *Russell's Magazine*. He heard Simms, with his magnificent gusto, thunder his dictums at the group.

Later he met there Henry Timrod and Paul Hayne, also protégés of Simms, who had chosen letters for their career and were proud of it, young Basil Gildersleeve who was just leaving to complete his studies at Heidelberg, the poet J. M. Legare. Under the stimulus of these contacts his own vague aspirations took form. He wrote his first poem, burned it, and announced to his uncle that he had decided upon his career. He would become a man of letters.

Chardon accepted the decision with a gravity befitting the occasion, and journeyed to the plantation to win the parents' consent. At first Thomas Ashley demurred. He had realized before the boy was five that he would never make a planter. But even for a bookworm there were dignified alternatives—medicine, the law, statecraft —"But great God, Pierre, not a poet! I have done nothing to deserve that!"

Pierre for once had forgotten his rôle of onlooker at life, and cried passionately: "My God, Thomas—look at the boy. You're blind, I know. But open your eyes now and look. Can't you see that he's not like you— not like me? Can't you see in his face that sooner or later life will have her claws in him and that she is going to tear him to pieces? If he is to have happiness he must be about it. He must choose his own way. I don't know whether he'll make a poet or not, but that's not of the least importance now. The boy must be free. He's got to be given a chance." In his intensity he had risen, his face working, his cane gripped in a shaking hand.

Emily Ashley had been sitting a silent auditor at the conference. Now she spoke, her cool syllables falling into the momentary and sultry silence that enveloped the two men. "This is a matter, Pierre, that Thomas will want to discuss with me at leisure. It is not a question for a hasty yes or no. Suppose you leave it with us until tomorrow. That will give Thomas an opportunity to decide. And in the meantime I imagine that he will want you to join him in a toddy before dinner."

The following morning when Pierre set out on his

return journey he had his answer. The discussion had ended with Ashley executing eloquent hand-washing gestures, and Pierre assuming full liability for Peter's career.

Peter's response to this adjustment was immediate. There were frequent visits to the plantation and these, with the old sense of frustration gone, became a delight. He was now accepted as an individual by his father— an individual of inexplicable tastes and habits, but one for whom the older man was no longer responsible. He could see his fill of his mother, and he could ride alone for hours with the rhythm of one of his father's thoroughbreds beating between his gripped knees. And best of all, he was no longer expected to go whooping after the Wakefields hounds in a fox or deer hunt after the joyous and exemplary manner of his brother, Wake.

Once when Peter was sixteen a discussion took place that illustrated the unique quality of this relationship that had crystallized between his uncle and himself, a relationship in which the separate individualities stood apart and strongly marked, yet in which there existed in each an awareness of the thoughts of the other, so acute that at times the bond seemed psychic.

It started one morning while they were breakfasting in the rose garden. Peter looked up from his perusal of the morning *Courier* with a puzzled frown.

"Well?" queried Chardon, and waited, watching the face of the boy. Its expression wore the quick, yet absorbed, look that the older man recognized as indicative of some ethical perplexity.

Peter read:

"For Sale: At Slave Mart on Chalmers Street, intelligent girl nineteen years of age, a superior house servant. A likely and intelligent woman thirty-five years of age, a good cook. A prime man forty years of age, splendidly trained house and personal servant. A likely and intelligent girl twenty years of age, a superior washer, clear starcher and ironer, and seamstress. *And at private sale only to a known and responsible city resident, a remarkably likely light mulatto girl fourteen years of age, of good character with privilege of repurchase at future date.*

"ARCHIBALD HOLCOMBE."

There followed a moment of silence. Then, "Uncle Pierre, what does that mean?"

Chardon replied in the didactic manner which he employed when pointing a moral lesson, and which under the direct precocious gaze of the boy always made him feel spurious and unconvincing. "It means that Archie Holcombe has always been a waster and a gambler. The time has come when he must reap his reward. He is being sold out. That is all."

The boy kept his disconcerting gaze full upon his uncle. "Fiddlesticks, Uncle Pierre," he said. "You know what I mean—the mulatto girl. Why the distinction?"

Chardon clutched at the opening word of the sentence. "Fiddlesticks, eh? Do you consider that a proper word to employ to your uncle, sir?"

But Peter smashed through the flimsy obstruction. "I know," he announced. "It means that Holcombe's the girl's father. But why has he got to come out and prac-

tically admit it in the public press? I can't understand
it. He's no gentleman!"

Chardon reached across the table, took the paper and
read the brief notice through for himself. It plunged
him into such a current of excitement that he forgot his
rôle of moral instructor.

"Why, damn it, boy," he cried, "this is colossal. In a
way it's superb. Read this advertisement seriously in all
of its implications, and suddenly this mulatto ceases to
be an act of God performed miraculously without the
assistance of the Caucasian race, and if she ceases to be a
miraculous creation, why, so probably do thousands of
others. It took a peculiar type of courage to do that, my
boy. It is a gesture of defiance at the society that bank-
rupted Holcombe. It will probably result in virtual os-
tracism, but he has had his revenge."

He fell silent for a moment, turning the idea over in
his mind; then his manner changed to one of ironical
amusement. "But why perturb ourselves? It is a simple
matter merely not to understand it. To consign the
paragraph to the oblivion which will await its rash author. It will not be referred to. It will not even be
thought about, and presently it will become non-existent.
And so, rash boy, will Archie!"

For a moment he sat musing. Then, "Archie Holcombe. I never cared for him. He has taken our virtues and by his excesses has made them vices. He has
caricatured us and made us seem ignoble. I always
thought him a braggart and a waster, but now he
emerges as a revolutionary, and a revolutionary may be
an even more vital factor in life than a gentleman. I
want to know more about him. I want to get at his

motives. We must have him to dinner some day, Peter. We ought to get his side of the question."

Peter had nothing to say in reply. He sat looking abstractedly before him. Presently he got to his feet, absently excused himself and returned to the library.

The next day at dinner Peter looked up suddenly and said, "I wish you wouldn't, Uncle Pierre."

"But why not, boy? We know now that he is honest and fearless—two virtues to start over with—and probably a diabolical sense of humor. Let's hear what he really thinks of us all."

"I don't want to have him here," Peter said with a tone of finality. "He's not our kind."

Chardon bowed over the board with mock humility. "I accept the rebuke," he said. "But I still have the last word. If you are going to write, you must see life impartially. You must be more than merely a spokesman for your class. Dr. Gillifant tells me that you are sufficiently advanced in your studies to enter college. We will go North next autumn. I must write at once and make the proper reservations."

CHAPTER III

PETER ASHLEY leaned against the starboard rail of the brig *Kiawah* thirty days out from Liverpool with a cargo of general merchandise for Ravenel & Company, factors of Charleston, South Carolina, and strained his gaze out beyond the dipping bow into the shrouded west.

Peter Ashley, twenty-three years old now, B. A., with Harvard and Oxford behind him and his sheepskin in his leather steamer trunk tucked safely away under his berth. Pictures of Paris, Berlin, Cairo, Rome, Vienna and a thousand other places, caught on the grand tour and fixed in the kaleidoscope of his mind, ready to fall into lovely and surprising combinations in answer to his mood. Under the thick, unruly chestnut hair, behind the forehead that he had, with secret delight, discovered to resemble that of Poe, theories. Theories on the Tariff, Slavery, Democracy, Literature—English and American, War. The years of preparation over. Now for his serious apprenticeship. Now for long hours of writing. Simms, Timrod, Hayne, no longer denizens of a remote and unattainable star, but fellow craftsmen. Peter had recently received news of the demise of *Russell's Magazine,* which, in spite of its favorable critical reception at home and abroad, had languished for want of popular support. Its revival would be the first task he would set himself. He knew that he could count upon his Uncle

Pierre for financial backing. They would make it a magazine for Charleston to be proud of.

He had awakened that morning to the twittering of land birds outside his porthole, and the monotonous chant of the leadsman as he called his soundings to the mate. In a fever of anticipation he had dressed and raced for the deck, only to find that a low mist clung to the surface of the sea, obliterating the horizon and effectively concealing the approaching shore line. Restraining his impatience, and substituting a cup of coffee on deck for the breakfast that awaited him at the bountiful table of Captain Ferguson, he had stationed himself in the starboard bow and commenced his watch.

Overhead the mist thinned. A faint lemon-colored sunlight bathed the upper air and flung the taut curves of the topsails into relief against the thin far blue of the sky. There was a cutting edge to the January morning, but Peter, with the damps of an English winter still in his bones, felt immediately under the morning chill the faint touch of languor, the promise of a gracious acquiescence to the power of the sun, that marked their presence in southern waters. "By noon it will be clear and warm," he thought. "God! It is good to be home again!" He opened his arms in a wide characteristic gesture and filled his lungs to their capacity.

Across the soft drumming of the sails a hail fell clear and sharp from the lookout. "Steamer on the starboard bow." Under Peter's feet the brig gave slightly to port, throwing him lightly against the bulwark. He remained there, his body rigid, his hands gripping the rail in eager anticipaton. The peremptory blast of a steam whistle smote his ears, and a vessel loomed sud-

denly before him. The hull presented a strange two-
dimensioned apparition in the low mist, but the belching
funnel stood out above it, and the flattened fore-and-aft
sails slashed through the sunny upper air like bronze
blades. While he watched, fascinated, the hull assumed
length. In a smother of foam the soaring cutwater
came, trampling down the mist, leaping clear and sharp
at the green rollers. Then the vessel thundered abreast
and hurled a succession of vivid impressions down upon
him. He gazed across the narrow aisle of water into a
low open deck crowded with black faces fixed woodenly
into terror, laughter, child wonder. Above them the
sheer lift of the superstructure, the pilot house and the
ruddy face of the quartermaster, the saloon, its windows
crowded with white faces, gay, laughing, a fluttered
handkerchief or two. The air shook to the tumult of
the paddles' snatching at a momentary purchase in the
water, hurling it behind them, threshing the sea between
the vessels into a maelstrom of foam, and driving the
great hull past. A deluge of coal smoke, acrid in Peter's
nostrils, and through it, hanging high on the ship's coun-
ter, the name *James Adger of Charleston, South Carolina*. For a moment the letters stood out in sharp relief,
then the suction of the hull pulled the smoke and mist
in upon its wake in a swift obliterating wall.

The impact of the familiar name started a succession
of memories in the boy's mind, detonating them one
after another like a sequence of soft explosions. It had
been upon the Adger that his Uncle Pierre had carried
him North on the first stage of the journey to England.
He remembered the captain distinctly. A jovial little
man, inordinately proud of his vessel. "Pride of the

coastwise fleet, my boy—forty-eight hours Charleston to New York. Tell the Yankees to beat that if they can."

Then came a picture of his Uncle Pierre—listening eagerly to all he had to say—talking things out with him man to man—not battering him into silence like his father with bursts of hearty laughter. And his brother, Wakefield, so like the older Ashley, like all foregoing Ashleys for that matter. The perfect scion of the house. Sitting his horse like a cavalier. Hallooing after the hounds in an ecstasy of animal spirits.

Then with a throb, part love, part pity, came the thought of his mother, maintaining the exterior serenity demanded by her position, while under the tranquil surface vibrated the taut nerves that could never slacken under the burden of her husband's enormous hospitality —the importunities of the slaves—the exigencies of an uncertain income. He was glad that he would be living in town with his Uncle Pierre. There would be quiet there—and books, and, at last, a chance to write.

"Land on the port bow." The lookout's voice cut short Peter's reverie and sent him scrambling over the coiled hawsers and anchor chains to the port rail. The mists were thinning and rising, revealing the low white line of Morris Island. With a heightening excitement Peter saw the line take form, rising from its bright thread of surf to a rampart of naked wind-sculptured dunes. Then at the extreme northern point of the spit his gaze stopped, arrested by an alien formation that rose abruptly from the dead level of the beach and, even at that distance, suggested some sort of fortification. He stood regarding it in complete mystification. The letters that had reached him in England bidding him return had been written only two months before, and while they all predicted secession as an inevitable result of the election of the "Republican rail splitter," not one had taken the idea of war seriously. Each of the three who had the direction of his destinies in their hands had disposed of it in a manner most characteristic.

"We shall certainly leave the Union," Uncle Pierre had written. "The partnership into which we entered under the Constitution has ceased to function to the advantage of the Southern states, but in spite of the widespread insanity of the abolitionists in the North, and the bloodthirsty talk of our own hot-heads, it is inconceivable that in exercising our right as a sovereign state we should have to resort to arms. Plans are already under way by which we hope to negotiate the purchase of the forts, custom house, and other government property, and then South Carolina, whether alone or in a confederation of other Southern states, will take her destiny into her own hands. Of course, you know my views. I believe that we are making a tragic mistake. But the fact remains that we are in for it."

In marked contrast had been the letter from his father: "The Black Republicans have had their way at last. Now they shall reap the reward of their own folly. In forcing us to secede they will kill the goose that lays the golden egg. We shall leave them to their just deserts. With our warehouses bursting with cotton, we can make our own terms not only with the Yankee manufacturers, but with the world. Once we are free of the Union we have only to place an export duty of a few cents on each pound of cotton that is shipped, and with this revenue we can presently equip a fighting force which will exact that respect which the Union is now loath to concede. No, my boy, the Yankee's heart is in his pocketbook—and cotton is king. When the moment comes we shall make the terms. The future lies glorious before us. It is time that you returned to take your place in that future."

And his mother: "There are some who think that Mr. Lincoln will try to hold us in the Union by force, but this will mean war, and war is impossible. It will mean such misery—such suffering. I look at Wakefield strong and gay, and already so successful with the plantation, and then I think of you with your dreams, and your odd lonely ways, and my thoughts turn into a prayer to God to spare you to me and to spare all sons to their mothers North and South, and then I am comforted. And something in my heart tells me that there will be no war."

Peter heard an exclamation behind him and turned to find Captain Ferguson—his long thin legs, placed wide apart, alternately flexing and stiffening to the roll of the ship, his spare figure erect, and a brass spyglass to his eye. After a long scrutiny he removed the glass and looked at Peter. "Well, my lad," he said, extending the glass, "we're none too soon. Take this and have a look at that sand pile yonder."

Peter raised the glass and brought it to bear on the strange formation that had attracted his attention. A gasp of astonishment escaped him. From the vague shore line a bright disk leaped into vision, its small compass crowded with detail. The slight eminence stood revealed as an earthwork with the sullen muzzles of cannon projecting from embrasures of stacked sandbags. To the west of the fortification, tents stretched away in a precise serrated line.   The elfin notes of a bugle reached him, and black specks that were scattered about the area milled for a moment against the white sand and fell into an immobile square.

"Steamer dead ahead." bawled the lookout, and the excitement in his voice charged that psychic current which all mariners know, and which in a moment of tension seems to make a vessel a sensate thing.   Behind Peter the call was repeated along the deck.   Up the forecastle companionway came the thump of sea boots, the padding of bare feet.   Then, abruptly, from noise the *Kiawah* fell into tense silence.   All hands stood watching the channel ahead.   The mists had broken over the sea and their tattered fragments were being whipped this way and that by a fresh wind out of the southwest.   There would be moments of unobstructed view, followed by periods of obscurity.   Suddenly, not a mile ahead of the brig, the vessel sighted by the lookout stood clearly revealed.   She was steaming forward at normal cruising speed, and was evidently a merchantman, as she showed no cannon under Captain Ferguson's scrutiny.   But in spite of her commonplace appearance, the tension among the watchers on the *Kiawah* persisted.   Captain Ferguson stood gripping his glass, growling interrogatory profanity into his grizzled beard.

The last of the fog wraiths disappeared.   Peter's gaze traveled landward, and his excitement was submerged by a wave of nostalgic longing.   It was so incomparably lovely—so exactly as he remembered it all.   Off the starboard bow lay Long Island crowned by its palmetto forests, and dead ahead Sullivan's Island with the bulk of Fort Moultrie an ominous note at its center.   To port

lay Morris Island, and beyond, Fort Sumter, with the
town on the horizon behind it, showing in faint gleams
of light, where the sun caught the spires. It was all a
part of him, as he was flesh of its flesh. God! It was
good to be coming home! And then he was struck by
something odd. The landscape lay fixed—static. The
harbor was without movement. The few boats that
could be seen in the distance of the inner harbor lay at
anchor. Over the broad flat country and the still bay
the sky arched vacant and enormous. All life seemed
gathered up in the steamer that preceded them into the
waiting silence. In search of some explanation, Peter's
gaze turned toward the fortification on the point of Morris Island. In that moment he saw a flash of orange
light at the muzzle of one of the cannon. A fountain of
spray broke the blue of the water before the bows of the
advancing steamer, then a second splash, and third, as
the ricocheting projectile lost velocity. Across the
water came a rumbling detonation.

The steamer lurched like a shying horse, giving a point
to starboard. Then a bugle rang out. Peter saw a flag
soar to the masthead. The breeze snatched the bundle
of meaningless color and flattened the Stars and Stripes
smartly against the empty sky. Across the distance that
separated the two vessels came the sudden thunder of
the paddles as the helm was put over and the steamer
driven at full speed ahead towards Fort Sumter.

"Hell!" ejaculated Captain Ferguson. "We've done it.
We've fired on the flag."

For perhaps three minutes the paddles beat their frantic
tattoo—the bow foamed, the flag preëmpted the sky.
Then the Island battery burst into flame—spray flew in

half a dozen places about the racing craft. The detonation, heavy and menacing, shook the air, and with it came a rending crash where one of the projectiles had found the steamer's hull.

Peter felt the captain's fingers rigid about his arm. The older man was thrusting the spyglass into his hand. "Look, boy," he commanded, indicating the battery. "Look—the flag."

Peter's hands were trembling so violently with excitement that he had difficulty in finding the fortification—and when he did, the smoke of the discharge had it shrouded, but above it a flag was snapping bravely in the breeze: the palmetto tree, yellow on its bright blue ground. Pride swelled within him, but almost instantly a hideous, premonitory tremor shook the pit of his stomach. What did it all mean? His state, yes,—but there were the Stars and Stripes at the steamer's masthead. He heard Captain Ferguson's, "By God, they're turning tail," and turned to find the steamer in the act of putting about for the open sea.

Silence had fallen again. The harbor lay like an amphitheater, quiet, attentive, watching the movements of the vessel that held the center of the stage. Reversing one paddle and steaming ahead with the other the steamer pivoted in the narrow channel, picking her way with meticulous care; then with the beckoning Atlantic before her bows, she came to life, a torrent of smoke gushed from her funnel, and she flung the harbor water behind her in her leap for the open sea.

The *Kiawah* drew a point to port to let her pass, and in the narrow channel one could have almost thrown a biscuit from deck to deck. For the brief moment of her passage, she stamped an unforgettable image upon Peter's mind, as he stood gripping the rail and staring up at her. There was dignity, almost a touch of grandeur, he thought, in her going. She reminded him of some great lady who has been insulted and who, gathering her skirts about her, sweeps majestically from the ballroom. She had about her a thoroughbred look—the jet black of freshly tarred rigging, the glitter of brass, the fleckless white of deckhouses, and above her the flag in a bright splash of color against the sky. The flag that had epitomized home to Peter during his years of exile in England. It gave him the familiar thrill. A cheer rose to his lips. Then a recurrence of that odd tremor shook his solar plexus, snapped the spell, and held him silent.

Captain Ferguson stood at the rail, trumpet in hand. "Ahoy!" he shouted. "What craft?"

"*Star of the West,* supply ship, United States Navy," came the reply; and a grizzled sailor with a sea-bitten visage and a voice like a Caribbean hurricane amplified the stark statement of fact with: "Yes, and Goddam ye, ye're in for it now."

The remainder of the voyage to Charleston was a memorable one for Peter Ashley. Excitement had so sensitized his faculties that the sights and sounds that impinged on them remained with him for life. The channel took them first past Fort Sumter. The fortress, which had been under construction during his long absence, had been the subject of many an item in his letters from home, and was, he knew, considered impregnable. Her upper tier of guns, ranged almost sixty feet above the water, frowned down upon the low levels of marsh and sea island, and gave her a tremendous advantage over any earthwork that might be erected within range of her guns. His gaze followed the sheer lift of the walls, then was caught by the flag pole and swept on up to the colors. The impression that he got was one of almost limitless height. As the channel drew the brig past the fortress, a bugle rang out. Peter saw the familiar blue uniforms as a squad of artillerymen appeared for a moment upon the parapet, then dropped from view.

An exclamation from the starboard bow caused Peter's gaze to travel to the east. Sullivan's Island stretched its length of sand and myrtle thicket before him. The low expanse jutted sharply up at its center into the grim mass of Fort Moultrie, from the parapet of which floated the palmetto flag. A considerable body of men were encamped in the area about the fort. But the blue uniforms were gone, and in their stead the movements of the troops upon the parade presented shifting patterns of a deceptive blue-gray color that merged with the background and made it difficult for the vision to distinguish and separate them. On the *Kiawah* the air was wild with conjecture. Was there actually a state of war? In the brief month of the journey, had their world lost its moorings and gone drifting into the cataclysm?

The *Kiawah* bore to the northward, and, riding a strong flood tide, swung into the inner harbor. Aloft the men were shortening sail, leaving only enough canvas to carry her to the dock. Now the subtle, indefinable odor of the place assailed Peter. It had eluded his memory during the years abroad. One could recall sounds, sights, but this emanation was something that could not be carried away to live over. He drew a deep breath, filling his body to the point of saturation. It was more than an odor, he thought,—or less. It was an essence distilled from the strong sulphur breath of the mud flats when the tide was out, wind broken myrtles on the sea islands, the hard white cleanness of the beaches, and finally that faint indefinable suggestion of languor that was, more than anything else, like an emanation from the broad, sun-drugged land itself. In a word, it epitomized home.

The air of watchful yet detached attention that from a distance had seemed to prevail, had either ceased or had been an illusion. Now the harbor was the scene of hectic activity. The sea wall of the White Point Gardens was a mass of humanity. A small side-wheeler, loaded to the guards with gray-clad soldiers, came threshing up the tide toward them en route to one of the new sea island batteries, a palmetto flag at its masthead.

Then Peter witnessed a strange occurrence. He saw the taciturn personality of Captain Ferguson break to pieces before him. The self-contained, middle-aged Scotch-American dissolved—and something boyish and reckless surged up and took its place. He stood for a moment, his long legs spread caliper-wise, his face red and working. Then in a mad scramble he tumbled aft. Head and shoulders disappeared in the flag locker. Geysers of bright bunting flew out about him to lie neglected on the deck. Then he found what he was searching for, jerked it out, tied it to a flapping lanyard, and, with his own hands, sent the Palmetto Tree soaring to the masthead.

The troop steamer was in the act of passing as the colors ran up. It responded with an involuntary shout, followed by three resounding cheers. The transformed captain jerked a derringer from his hip pocket and emptied it into the bright January sky. From where they were—high in the rigging, forward at the anchors, aft at the helm—the crew of the *Kiawah* burst into a single wild cheer. The tension that had gripped Peter snapped, leaving him suddenly cold, remote, detached. Then the premonitory tremor that had warned him earlier in the morning swept up and invaded his whole being. He looked at the frenzied men about him, the fresh laughing faces of the boys on the troop ship. He wished to God he could be like that, forget himself utterly, succumb to the mad contagion, but instead there was a sudden lump in his throat.

The faces on the pier-head steadied him, gave him something definite to think about. Certainly there were no dark forebodings there. All was excitement and glad anticipation. The *Kiawah* drifted closer, and individuals became distinguishable from the mass. Then Peter saw the little group that was waiting to receive him: his mother, Thomas Ashley, Wake, Uncle Pierre, Saby and Pemba, two of the Wakefields' house servants. Wake was a man in body now, but with a face singularly unchanged, he seemed like a larger edition of the boy whom he remembered.

Then Peter was going ashore. The two servants swarmed over the rail for his boxes. He was in his mother's arms. His father was telling him that it was high time he was coming home. Uncle Pierre looked definitely older, and Peter knew that he was worried. He had none of the conventional words of greeting for his nephew, but his fingers closed about those of the younger man in a grip that made him wince.

There followed introductions in voices that had to shout to be heard above the turmoil of the debarkation. There were names that, like the air in his nostrils, were redolent of the Low Country. His cousin Bull-Smith, who, with several of his ten children in tow, and his bass rumble sounding over the general babble, reminded Peter more than ever of the singular appropriateness of his hyphenated prefix. René Berrenger, one of Peter's few boyhood friends, a man now, slender and dark, with smoldering Latin eyes. There were Warings, Gadsdens, Rhetts, Elliotts, names that sang in his memory like old tunes. The lovely girl in the scarlet turban and modish barcelona, who dimpled up at him and wagered that he'd never guess her identity, turned out to be his cousin, Alicia Pringle. The chill "Mr." and "Mrs." that had marked the measure of his British intimacies were gone with the London fogs. Everywhere now it was Cousin this and Cousin that. "You must dine with us at once, Cousin Peter." "You haven't seen Mulberry since we added the ballroom." "We'll expect you within the week, sir." Then suddenly Cousin Bull-Smith: "By God, sir, we knew you'd be among the first to come. Count on an Ashley." And had he heard that Tom Broughton had resigned from West Point, and had arrived the day before? And that Wilmot Gadsden and Dessie Parker had both resigned their commissions in the regular army, and were coming back to Carolina, "Where they belong, by God, sir!"

Over by the gangplank of the *Kiawah* some incident out of the ordinary was taking place. The noise gave way to a curious silence. The crowd opened to permit the passage of an official who proved to be Mr. Colcock, the collector of the port. Ah, this would be well worth watching. You could count upon Captain Ferguson to give as good as he got. The lanky form of the captain appeared at the rail. He advanced with hand extended, his seabitten visage wreathed in an ingenuous smile of hospitality. "Come aboard, Mr. Colcock, come aboard, sir. This is indeed an honor, sir. An honor worthy of the opening of the bottle of old London Dock that is awaiting your pleasure in the cabin."

The official accepted the proffered hand. His face was set in the stern cast of a man who has an unpleasant duty to perform. But those who stood near were prepared to swear that when his eyes met those of the captain, one of them closed solemnly, then reopened as he replied: "It is a matter of regret, Captain Ferguson, that I come upon official business, and not a social call. It becomes my duty as the United States customs officer in authority at the port of Charleston to demand that you present the manifest of the *Kiawah* at the exchange for the levying of the proper duty upon her cargo."

The captain bowed formally: "But I am reliably informed, sir, that I am in a port of the Independent State of South Carolina, and that the commonwealth imposes no duty upon imports."

Mr. Colcock replied with dignity, "As an officer of the United States of America, I have had a duty to perform."

"And you have performed it like an officer and a gentleman. My compliments, sir. And now, there is still the London Dock. And I don't believe that I mentioned the fact before, but it was born in eighteen-twenty-two."

The crowd burst into good-natured laughter. It closed behind the official, cutting off his retreat. He yielded to the inevitable, but declared that he boarded the brig under protest. On the forward deck the mate bawled an order. Off went the hatches. In the bright warm sunshine the crowd milled and jostled. Down with the tariff! Three cheers for an open port. Three cheers for the Palmetto Flag at the *Kiawah's* masthead. And around Peter Ashley a circle of faces, hands, eyes, that said more eloquently than the shout of a crowd: "Three cheers for one of our own. One of the first who has come home to fight."

CHAPTER IV

PETER paused upon the threshold of the big Chardon drawing room and looked about him with that impersonal appraisal that only a protracted absence can render possible. He saw now in the familiar apartment with its Adam decorations, its mellow portraits, its dim, warm brocades, an intrinsic beauty that enhanced immeasurably his natural pleasure in the familiar setting. Grandfather Chardon was still an ancestor, but he was also a Romney; and the two stiff little girls who had looked down upon his adolescent wonderings with prim disapproval were not only great-aunts Katherine and Amanda, but also Thomas Sully at his best. The warm transparent loveliness of the flesh tones seemed to endow the wooden little figures with an incongruous and deathless vitality. It was strange, he thought, as he stood looking up at them, how much more alive they were, fixed there in paint, than they had been as the two wistful and virginal shadows that he dimly remembered, and that time had absorbed by so gentle a process that their final passing left not the slightest impression upon his mind. Their biographies and their epitaphs were complete in the sentence that his mother had spoken when he finally remarked upon their absence. "Your poor aunts, my dear, they were very unfortunate. They never married."

Cæsar appeared with a julep, and unwilling to disappoint him, Peter yielded to local custom and accepted it. He wandered from object to object, smiling familiar greetings between drafts of the fragrant drink.

But when he arrived at one of the broad south windows he stood, arrested at last by the new and unfamiliar note. The old untroubled quiet of White Point Gardens was gone. Groups of people streamed constantly across the park toward the Battery wall, where a view of the harbor could be obtained. Upon the promenade itself a solid block of humanity was massed, and over their heads could be seen the constant march of funnels and mastheads as noisy, crowded dispatch and troop boats threshed their way to and from the harbor defenses that were being hurled up with feverish speed. The steady, blurred, disconcerting sound of the crowd penetrated and disturbed the habitual tranquillity of the room.

A slight sound caused Peter to turn, and he found that Chardon had entered and was sitting, watching him with quiet approval.

"Where do they all come from, Uncle Pierre?" Peter asked with a graphic gesture toward the window.

There was a vague resentment in Chardon's voice. "For the most part, rowdies from uptown, I suppose. War or no war, we are already ruined by an army of invasion. There is no such thing as privacy any more. They act as though the city belonged to them. Upon my word, Cæsar has to spend half his time dislodging them from the front steps."

The smile that Peter gave his uncle was quick, amazed, tender. It was strange, but before that moment he had never thought of Chardon as being definitely of an older generation. "And these people," he thought suddenly, "whom Cæsar is kept busy driving from the door, will presently be expected to die for the perpetuation of the status quo!" He wondered whether it was an invasion of his country, or his class, that represented the ultimate horror of war to the old aristocrat, and decided that it was probably the latter. He remembered his uncle's often repeated assertion that he was interested in the point of view of those of an inferior class. "Both sides of the question," he would say. This attitude of Chardon's had influenced his own outlook profoundly. He could not believe even now that it was merely sophistry. His uncle had sincerely believed himself to be a liberal, but when it came to a practical expression he had always reverted to type. There had been certain days when he had awakened in the morning and said: "Now I shall be one of the people." Race Week, for instance, when he always served on the committee that had in charge the public stands, and when he even exchanged modest bets with his barber. But there had always been the big house with the high iron fence to return to after Race Week was over.

While these thoughts were passing through his mind, Peter turned back to the window and let his gaze rest abstractedly upon the bustle of the street. He stood at right angles to Chardon, his glass poised lightly in his long sensitive fingers, with the clear winter sunlight beating directly in upon him.

Chardon, sitting deep in his armchair, took advantage of the opportunity to study his nephew. He told himself that even with the rush of pride that whelmed his senses when he looked at the boy, he was still philosopher enough to subject him to a cool and impersonal estimate.

He had deliberately refrained from crossing during the four years that Peter had been abroad. He had wanted the boy to go it absolutely alone, and now he was being repaid by the discovery of an altogether new and highly individual Peter.

Across his mind flashed his statement to Thomas, when he had won for the boy the right to choose his own way: "Life will have her claws in him, Thomas,—mark my words, and sooner or later she will tear him to pieces." Now he wondered about his pessimistic and rather hysterical prophecy. Physically he had come through rather well. That would have been the rowing at Oxford, Chardon thought, and the riding, for which the boy's passion had never abated. He followed Peter's movements as he turned back to the window, the unconscious flow of resilient power that broke his inertia, swung the body around in a slow, suave, continuous movement and brought it to rest lightly on the balls of the feet. There was a nervous energy, a complete coördination that would realize the utter limit of muscular power. He noticed with pride that he was taller than his brother Wakefield, probably as tall as Thomas, and would tip the scales at a good twelve stone. His English homespun was well cut, and actually achieved the effect of studied casualness that was just missed by the local tailors. He wore a low, soft collar, and his loose scarf, God bless him, was not the conventional black, but a bright, hard blue.

But when Chardon shifted his gaze to Peter's face, his old misgivings returned. It was a face made to bear the wounds of singularly vulnerable emotions; to be scarred by a warfare between the heart of a romanticist and an intellect that would be relentless in its destruction of illusions. There was more than a suggestion of the sensual in the large, beautifully formed, mobile mouth and the wide nostrils, but the sternness of the ascetic in the straight brows and high, intellectual forehead. The eyes, large and of a deep brown, were unusually expressive. The nose, Chardon decided, was the feature that most pleased him. It had nothing to do with the Ashleys. It was high-bridged, long on the face, pure Huguenot. It rescued the face from a too pure, too feminine beauty. It gave it a definite male distinction, and it linked Peter inevitably with the successive Pierre Chardons who had stood where he was standing at that moment and had watched a century and a half march past under the wide windows.

Chardon, when he spoke, was surprised to find himself a little in awe of his strange nephew. It annoyed him to detect an almost timid note in his matter-of-fact inquiry. "You're glad to be at home, I hope, Peter?"

Peter turned with a swift, yet almost immediately arrested, impulsiveness. Chardon was to learn that this was his most striking characteristic of manner.

"Yes," he said warmly. "Yes, but I'd have liked to wait for the race with Cambridge. It will take place a week or ten days before Easter, you know, and Easter is early this year. I was only a substitute. If I had made the crew I would have had to stay. But it was wise of you to send, and I have been wanting to get seriously to work." He stopped speaking for a moment. "This"—he added, with a wave of his hand toward the window—"it is all so new and unexpected. I was coming home to write, you know."

"I know, my boy. 'The best laid plans——' "

Peter said reassuringly: "It's nothing to worry about. I'll feel better when I get orientated. And then there's you, sir. It's splendid to see you and Mother and everything again. When I saw you two on the dock yesterday in the midst of all the hullabaloo, it was like—well, like finding port in a storm."

The glances of the two met. There was a moment of self-conscious confusion. The old faculty of sharing an unvoiced emotion had survived the separation. They were both men now and there must be no sentimentality between them.

Chardon said: "You haven't told me yet how you liked yesterday's performance. Everybody is envying you your view of the encounter."

Peter dropped into a chair, drained his glass, and placed it on a table beside him.

"Another?"

He shook his head, and Chardon saw the old, puzzled, absorbed look come into his face. "That's something I've been trying to decide for myself, Uncle Pierre—my feeling about it all. Perhaps it will help me to talk. The whole business has thrown me into terrible confusion. You see, I hadn't expected war. From the other side it seemed utterly incredible. And while I was in England, without quite realizing it, things happened to me. I've sometimes wondered if you had that in mind when you sent me to Oxford. Whether I was one of your experiments. You're damned devious, you know, sir."

Pierre answered the wry smile that accompanied the accusation with a rather guilty grin.

"At any rate, it worked. Harvard made me more of a Carolinian than ever. I could have stood the usual jibes at slavery, and all of that. But their assumption of a monopoly of intellect was unendurable. You see, I knew what we had here. I knew that, given a little time, we'd have a Southern school of literature that would make them all stand and listen." His voice trailed off into silence and his eyes had an expression that Pierre remembered well. They had ceased to focus on the object before them, as though they were looking out into another dimension.

"Yes," Chardon prompted, "and what about England?"

"England was different. You see, they've never got over thinking of us all as their own raw provincials. They are beginning to read our books, but that doesn't mean anything. If they are good, it is because they taught us how to write. If they are bad, they are typically American. It gets your dander up, I can tell you, sir. North, South, are all one to them. We are all stewed in the same skillet. But it worked, Uncle Pierre, that experiment of yours. In the second semester of my first year I took a most awful mauling because I wouldn't admit that Tennyson was a better poet than Longfellow. It was funny, wasn't it?

"And once on a holiday the boys in my form went down to Plymouth. It's warmer, you know, and there's a legend that the sun shines there. I wanted to get the mildew out of my bones. We were down on the Hoe. And then we saw that something was in the air. There was an official stand with a band in it. And a lot of gold braid and bunting. And a steam frigate was rounding the mole into the inner harbor. As soon as I saw her I got a shiver down my spine and I knew where she came from even before she broke out the Stars and Stripes.

And then—you won't believe me, sir, but the sun *did* come out. Then I saw a palm tree growing near. It must have had a most superior constitution, but anyhow, there it was—and it looked like home. And suddenly everybody started to cheer and the band struck up 'The Star-Spangled Banner.' I felt then the way you ought to feel when you're drunk—but somehow never do.

"Then that night Bobby Chavers, who just misses being a gentleman, thought he'd bait me. And he said that 'The Star-Spangled Banner' was a good song because, like pretty much everything else, we'd stolen the tune from the English. I answered that we were at least clever enough to disprove one of his good old proverbs, then, because we had made a silk purse out of a sow's ear. Of course, I pronounced it 'air'—I was still that much of a Charlestonian. Bobby was solemn and fuddled and a little more than tight. He shouted that we could steal the air for all he cared but that he'd be damned if any American was going to call England a sow.

"I hate fighting, you know, and the sight of blood still makes me sick. You remember my first and only fox hunt, when I got in at the death and disgraced the family by losing my breakfast at the sight of blood. The fight was fast and furious. I had rather the edge, I think, but his nose bled and I vomited. It was awfully humiliating. But anyhow I had fought over the flag and all that. And you'll be glad to know, sir, that I came out of it a nationalist."

Chardon said that if it was the result of an experiment on his part, and he wasn't admitting that it was, he was afraid that he had done the boy a poor service.

"I had those weeks at sea to get used to the idea of

disunion," Peter replied. "Your letters calling me home hadn't left any doubt on that score. I thought I had got it pretty well rationalized. Patriotism is only a broadened love of home, I said. Carry it to its farthest limit and you become an internationalist. Contract and intensify it and it narrows to your own hearthstone. And after all, I said, I'm going home. That's what counts.

"But you see, the idea of war had never occurred to me. It was too preposterous. And then suddenly, without warning, I was in the midst of it. And it wasn't at all as I had imagined. I saw Captain Ferguson and the men on the *Kiawah* go suddenly mad. And those boys on the troop ship—they were so damned young, Uncle Pierre—they were singing, and they had their servants with them as if they were bound to town for Race Week. And I wanted to break loose and whoop with them. I wanted to feel again as I had that day at Plymouth when I saw the flag, and took a thrashing. And instead of that I went as cold as a corpse. I had come home to my world—the one that I remembered, the old life, the crowd at Russell's Book Store. I was going to get down to work. I was going to capture all of this. And like that" —he made a graphic gesture—"my world was gone."

An impulsive movement took Peter to the window. He stood with his back to his uncle, his face turned toward the street.

"You jump to conclusions," Chardon told him. "Even after this there may be a peaceful adjustment. Even in the event of war, hostilities may be brief."

Peter turned and met the older man's eyes squarely. "Do you believe that?"

"No."

There was a silence, then Peter said: "What I can't understand is the suddenness of it all. From the other side, the idea of an armed resistance seemed absolutely incredible. Then by the time I arrived they were at it hammer and tongs. What brought it to a head so quickly?"

"Anderson's occupation of Sumter," Chardon told him. "A beautifully executed tour de force, but, I believe, a fatal blunder and one that will lead inevitably to war. It happened on Christmas Eve night. The holiday spirit was in the air. We have a way, you know, of forgetting our troubles when we go to a ball. Major Anderson very cleverly spent the early night in town, dining with friends. No one had the slightest suspicion that there was anything in the air. Then when we got up on Christmas morning we discovered that under cover of darkness the Yankees had spiked the guns at Fort Moultrie, and had moved over, lock, stock and barrel, to Sumter. It unquestionably put them in a better position to defend themselves in the event of an attack, but the secret nature of the evacuation, and the dismantling of armament at Moultrie, came perilously near to being an act of war. At least, the Secessionists interpreted it in that light, and the fat was in the fire."

After a moment Peter asked, "What's the book store crowd doing?"

"It no longer exists," Chardon answered. "Simms has developed into a military engineer. It is said that the plan for the ironclad battery on Morris Island is his idea as well as Stevens'. He was a rabid Secessionist, you know. Timrod has done a war poem or two, but he told me that he was enlisting. He is probably in uniform by now. Hayne has been commissioned on the Governor's staff. With his gallantry and charm, and his new gold braid, it will be a miracle if the women don't ruin him. No, it is all gone. You might as well make up your mind to it. You'll hear of nothing but war."

Peter said, "They'll all be expecting me to rush in. On the wharf yesterday, everybody assumed that I had come home to fight."

Chardon looked up sharply. Now they were upon the moment that he had been dreading. "Yes?"

"I can't, Uncle Pierre. I've got to have time to think it out. To get my bearings. Ever since I returned I have felt that I was looking on from another star. Yesterday when the crowd cheered, for a moment I seemed one of them. Then something perverse took possession of me and I was back outside of it all again. I've got to be a part of it. I've got to feel it here inside of me. It isn't a question of the Union. I haven't even that excuse. It is just that if I went in now, feeling as I do, I'd be an alien in either army. I'd be breaking faith with myself!"

Chardon said, "I'm to blame for that. I have taught you to think, and that is fatal in time of war."

After a moment he got to his feet. "Your position will not be altogether pleasant," he said. "You must be prepared for that. But you'll not be hurried, and you'll not be coerced by the family. Thomas has promised me that. But if you do not enlist at once he will probably suspect me of practicing Unionist black magic upon you. You will have to exonerate me."

Peter smiled and assured him that he would.

"And now," consulting his watch, Chardon said, "I've an appointment for you. Is the carriage at the gate?"

Peter replied in the affirmative, and presently they stepped together out into the unwonted bustle of the street. The barouche rounded the corner into East Bay Street and headed north. Now they were in the thick of it. The crowds had preëmpted the roadway and impeded their progress. Perched above them on the high box, Cæsar had difficulty in controlling the restive and high-stepping bays. Peter leaned back against the cushions, feeling conspicuous and a little ridiculous. Whatever his uncle's mysterious engagement was, the distance could not be great. They could much better have walked. He eyed Chardon sitting beside him, his body held very erect, his hands resting one on top of the other upon the gold head of his stick, his gaze fixed upon the two brass buttons in the small of Cæsar's back. It was that fastidious horror of the multitude, Peter thought. But he was mistaken, for presently Chardon said:

"You're not enjoying this, Peter. Well, neither am I. But we are sure to meet friends on Broad Street, and in here we are at least free from embarrassing questions. When your plans are made it will be different."

Peter said, "Thank you, sir." Then, tentatively, "Plans?"

"I haven't told you. You have a dangerous way of jumping to conclusions, and I want you to be in full possession of the facts before you decide. But if you want to write, you shall have a chance. My friend Willington of the *Daily Courier* and I have been plotting together and he has promised to receive us this morning."

Peter had to be content with that meager intimation of his prospects, and presently even the conjectures that it aroused were crowded from his mind by the drama of the morning streets. He was amazed at the temper of the crowd. There was an infectious and gay excitement in the air. He had conceived of yesterday's incident as a preface to the grim business of civil war. But here it seemed as though the whole population were engaged in some new and thrilling game. The atmosphere was more comparable to that of Race Week than to the prospect of imminent death. He had always thought of his native city as being predominantly English in temperament and tradition. But now, fresh from England, he saw it suddenly as Latin in its moods.

At Broad Street the carriage was caught in a jam of other vehicles and pedestrians. Across the babble of voices came the high-pitched, thrilling music of fifes. A company of soldiers swung into view. The uniforms fresh from the tailors made a brave show—gray pea-jackets trimmed with red, gray pants, and on their heads smart kepis with the initials Ae. G. in gilt. The familiar insignia started Peter wondering—then he remembered. This was the old Aetna Fire Company metamorphosed into the military. The Aetnas passed and were followed by a company of Zouaves bound for the debarkation docks. The high, colorless January sunlight fell full from the noon sky and the street seemed to split it into all of the colors of the spectrum. The red of the baggy breeches, the snapping blue of the flag, the ocher, orange, yellow, of the stuccoed buildings, and the tiers of bayonets that flung ripples of light up into the windows to play upon animated faces under secession bonnets.

"By God," thought Peter, momentarily swept out of himself, "we're not even European. We're tropic—Morocco—Egypt!" The crowd burst into wild cheering.

About Chardon's carriage the confusion was noisy, continuous, ecstatic. A group of young women in hoops became hopelessly involved with a rear guard of shouting pickaninnies that trailed after the Zouaves. Two youths in uniform rescued them, cuffed the ears of the small negroes soundly, and ordered them to go home before they were sent to the jail-house for a thrashing. Everywhere there was excitement, color, sound.

A wave of cheering broke over them. It caught at something that was young and boyish in Peter, and lifted him to his feet in the carriage. Then the cheers swept past him down the street. For a moment or two they came back to him in brief bright gusts like foam snatched from a receding breaker. Then the parade turned a corner toward the wharves and the street dropped swiftly back into the commonplace. For a moment Peter had almost lost himself, had almost been one of them; but now the spell was broken, leaving him to wonder. This strange and apparently carefree exuberance! Was it all forced gaiety, covering the hideous premonition of war? Or was it the voice of a people still living in a happy dream which they had endowed with an illusion of imperishable reality, and of which this bright pageantry was merely a part?

Chardon directed Cæsar to the newspaper office on East Bay, and presently the vehicle drew in to the curb and stopped before a handsome building with an imposing marble front. They were received by Mr. Willington, the owner and senior editor of the *Courier*. Mr. Willington was eighty years of age, and a cataract had deprived him of the sight of one eye; but he conveyed an impression of mental vigor that was extraordinary, and he seemed to possess that intuitive faculty which is given in compensation to those with impaired vision, for his face was quick to answer and even to anticipate the moods of his visitors.

Upon their entrance he emerged from beneath a deep drift of foreign papers that had accumulated upon his desk, and held out his hand. His hearty greeting put Peter immediately at his ease.

"I am delighted to meet you, Mr. Ashley," he said. "Your uncle and I are old friends, although I am sure I cannot explain why, since I was born a Yankee and am now an ardent Secessionist, while he is a native Carolinian and is suspected of Unionist tendencies."

Without waiting for comment from his visitors, he hurried on to details which had been arranged in conference with Chardon, and Peter gathered that he was to start in to work at once, under the direction of a Mr. Tattenham, an assistant editor. His new chief was summoned and introduced; Chardon departed, and presently Peter found himself being shown over the plant under the enthusiastic guidance of Tattenham.

His conductor, Peter decided, was a man of about fifty, the possessor of an impressive mustache, linen that could have been cleaner, an untidy black string cravat, a suit of black broadcloth well shined at shoulder blades and elbows, and a hobby. This last asset became immediately evident on their tour of inspection. Mr. Tattenham proclaimed that the contention that the South was dependent upon outside sources for its manufactured supplies was all rubbish, and he proceeded to demonstrate his point. Passing lightly over the big new type racks upon which Peter was indiscreet enough to notice the name "L. John-

son & Co., Philadelphia, Pa.," Mr. Tattenham directed
his charge's attention to the great rolls of print paper.
"Manufactured in South Carolina, my boy, and at Green-
ville, the thriving metropolis of our own Piedmont."
And later, when they arrived before the steam engine
that drove the presses, he led Peter cunningly with the
question, "I suppose you think that we are indebted to
the Yankee manufacturers for our power?"

Peter obligingly admitted that he would have thought
so.

"Not at all, young man, not at all. If you are going to
succeed as a newspaper man you must know your own
community." He dropped an affectionate hand on the
machine. "From the foundry of William Lebby, no
farther away than Hayne Street. You have much to
learn, young fellow, much to learn."

Peter meekly conceded the point and followed his chief
back to the offices for his first assignment.

CHAPTER V

ETER turned into Chalmers Street and directed his steps toward the slave mart. The city lay under a bleak rain that slanted out of the northeast. It was, he thought, like London at its worst. It had blown up during the night, and so pervasive had been its dispiriting presence that he had been aware of it even before he had quite awakened that morning.

He did not particularly relish his assignment for the day. Mr. Tattenham had evolved a theory which it was his humble reportorial duty to put into practice. While others were watching the markets on state and municipal bonds for indications of public confidence in the independent state of South Carolina, Mr. Tattenham had decided that the slave markets were logically the most accurate barometers of public confidence. If the prices of slaves held up in the face of a threatening and abolitionist North, it would amount to a popular vote of confidence in the future of the State. It was, therefore, Peter's duty to attend all sales and keep accurate records.

But he hated the work. England had been very upsetting to his theories. He had heard John Bright inveigh against the institution. The air was thick with abolitionist propaganda. And most galling of all had been the attitude of his college mates, who, conscious of England's superior position on the question, invariably pointed to slavery as a confirmation of their contention that the States continued to exist in a state of barbarism. When he returned home, it was with the conviction that the system was, to say the least, outmoded; that while it continued to work in fact, it was wrong in theory, and that sooner or later it was doomed.

But now, on the other hand, here it was under his eyes. And it worked. Even the term "slave" was seldom used among his associates; the occupants of the quarters at Wakefields were always referred to as "our people," and the domestics as "the servants." Personified, the institution presented itself to him in the form of Cæsar and the fourteen members of his household who occupied the brick range in the kitchen yard of the Chardon residence, and who were reprimanded by the big house only when their noise transgressed all bounds and disturbed the peace of the neighborhood.

And as for the plantation: It had been generations since a slave had been sold from Wakefields, the natural procreation which took place in the negro yard having been accompanied by an equal increase in the successive families in the big house. Land was cheap. It had been the custom in the plantation country, as the boys attained manhood and returned from college, to extend the domain and present a certain number of families to each son. So that as time passed and the process was repeated, the negroes became as indigenous to the locality as the masters themselves.

Of course Peter knew that the negroes were whipped. That in the country, when this was necessary, it was attended to out of earshot of the big house by the overseer. And that in town they would be sent to the jailhouse on Magazine Street with a written order for the

number of lashes to be delivered by the jailer. It was
not uncommon in the vicinity of the jail to see a negro
proceeding alone with a paper clutched in his hand, while
behind him stalked the invisible terror of a still greater
evil if he failed, that propelled his dragging feet toward
the high iron gates. As the negroes approached, they
would sometimes burst into loud, anticipatory wailing.
Then the gatekeeper would open the gate and let them
in. Later they would emerge, bent under the burden of
pain, and still clutching the paper, which had been certi-
fied by the jailer. It was all admirably arranged for the
protection of refined sensibilities. The servant returned
chastened, was given a day to recuperate, and life proceeded upon the even tenor of its way.

Chardon had never sent a servant to the jail, as Cæsar
was a sufficiently strict disciplinarian for his own household. In fact, during his periods of intensive training of
some black boy, the unrestrained howls that emanated
from the yard were so disturbing that the master had
been forced to intercede, for fear the neighbors would
think that he kept a "driver" on the premises.

That the slaves of the planters in the Carolina Low
Country were well treated, he knew. He had seen his
own negroes at Wakefields. He knew the reputation of
Gilmore Simms and others of his friends for pampering
their negro yards. And on the other hand, he had heard
of the horrors of the cane fields in the deeper South.
The threat of selling a negro into that servitude was more
efficacious than a dozen whippings.

What standard, he had often wondered, could be so
elastic in its application? Property value: to a certain
extent, yes. But it was warmer, more human, than that.

A moral code, perhaps; but within his own class there was a wide range of personal morality. Then one day he had hit upon a possible explanation. Good form. About the treatment of the negroes in his locality there had grown up as intricate a code of good form as that which surrounded the institution of dueling, or behavior upon a ballroom floor. In the interrelationship that had developed between master and slave during their generations together, there were certain decencies to be observed. A gentleman, confronted by a certain situation, would conduct himself in accordance with the unwritten code. If he failed—well, there were deflections in every social order; it was unfortunate, but the transgressor was no longer quite a gentleman. That the conventions of his particular locality and class had crystallized from the attitude of individuals of high moral character was a matter for gratitude, Peter thought. It made it easier in the present crisis to reconcile conscience and necessity. It buttressed the threatened edifice with certain Christian virtues and endowed the impending conflict with the indispensable elements of a crusade.

This theory, once accepted, explained much to Peter that had been obscure. The historic case of old Dr. Montague, for instance. The doctor had sent his houseboy to the jail for a whipping. The negro had commenced to blubber when he neared the place of punishment, and, blind with grief and terror, had collided with the choleric and overbearing person of Major Radleigh. The moment was that unfortunate one which lay between the major's apéritif at his club and the dinner to which he was hastening. His morning had been fatiguing. The August sun dogged his footsteps down the mournful and naked street that led past the jail, and bathed his body in tepid perspiration. He was writhing under this last gratuitous indignity when the doctor's boy walked blindly into his stomach and well nigh carried him from his feet. The major had promptly anticipated the action of the jailer by giving the boy a thorough caning on the public street.

The doctor had demanded an apology. The major would be damned if he would. There was a significant meeting at the Washington Race Course at the hour of sunrise. Thereafter the negro boy continued to polish a now meaningless brass plate beside the doctor's front door. The major continued upon his choleric way. Dr. Montague, with half an ounce of lead in his brain, retired to the long quiet of a cemetery on the banks of the Cooper. But he had been a great gentleman. There was no doubt of that. And his martyrdom to the code had been a shining example to the succeeding generation.

Now Peter saw all of this in its true perspective. The hasty cane that had brought about the trouble had fallen most grievously, not upon the skin of the boy, but upon the prerogatives of his master. Major Radleigh, an old man now, and still under a cloud, had laid his hands upon another man's negro, and between gentlemen it wasn't done.

And here, in the slave mart, good form was the criterion, covering the bald fact with the garment of an almost too assertive and self-conscious respectability. The days of the trade, when naked negroes were knocked down to the lowest bidder at the ship's side, were a conveniently forgotten page out of a long past. The mart had much the aspect of an employment agency. An open

fire blazed on a hearth at one side of the long, low, bare
room. Near the fireplace, ten or a dozen gentlemen were
sitting. They all stopped their talk and looked around
as he entered, regarding him with what he felt was not
hostility, but a speculative and intense curiosity that was
almost as painful to endure. It was the attitude that he
encountered everywhere and in every gathering, or even
a casual meeting with one of his relatives or boyhood
friends.

His highly sensitive perceptions were immediately and
painfully conscious of it. These men were so extraordi-
narily alike, he reflected, that any variation from type in
one of their own people upset all the customary standards
of evaluation. They did not know exactly how to take
him, and their attitude of tolerant, often even indulgent,
watchfulness afflicted him with the feeling of embarrassment and frustration that had tortured him as a boy on
the plantation. In spite of his height and his Oxford
rowing record, it made him feel in some oblique way
physically inept and inadequate.

The moment of embarrassed silence was broken by one
of the group, who rose and thrust his chair back noisily
as he stepped forward with hand extended.

"Why, it's Peter Ashley!" he exclaimed. "You won't
remember me, but I'm Bert Lawrence of Oak Hall. You
were usually buried in the library while I was hunting
with your brother Wake, but I remember you distinctly."

His manner was charming, gracious; but there was the
old difference again—a difference that implied the infe-
riority of one who sat by the fire while the men were
afield. It left Peter for the moment without anything
to say.

Lawrence sensed it and blurted enthusiastically: "But you were a great rider. My father always said that you had a better seat than any of us."

He led Peter to the fire and introduced him to the others. "You should remember Charles Gilbraith," he concluded, indicating a man of his own age with an expression of boyish gravity upon his face. "He is from our parish, and we're down together to fight it out for that boy over there. He belongs to Archie Holcombe, and Archie's in a chronic state of bankruptcy. At present he's selling out, lock, stock and barrel, and outfitting his own company. He's had to let his negroes go, of course. And as he's from our neighborhood he asked us to come down and see that his stableman didn't get into bad hands. He's a prime hand, too, so I suppose we can make use of him."

They were a thoroughbred lot, Peter thought, as he surveyed his new acquaintances. But he had to control a fastidious distaste for the volleys of tobacco juice that were being continuously directed towards the fire. While he had been in England, he had forgotten that gentlemen chewed.

A desk stood at the farther end of the room, and beside it, upon a bench set against the wall, were ranged the negroes who were presently to be offered for sale. With but one exception, they were evidently house servants. A man of about thirty, a strong finely made woman a few years younger, and a boy of about eight sat close together and were obviously a family. Next on the bench sat a man, tall and intelligent looking, who, Peter speculated, must be about sixty-five, and beyond him, two young women completed the group. At the end of the settee sat the negro to whom Lawrence had referred. He was magnificently proportioned and in the full prime of manhood. His clean jeans and broad, free movements indicated the yard or field hand rather than the house servant. The negroes sat composed but alert, studying with deep and speculative interest each new arrival at the fire.

The door opened and a man of middle age bustled in, accompanied by a clerk who placed several papers on the desk. The official was well dressed and had a manner which, while it took cognizance of the dignity of his own position, conveyed just the proper shade of deference when he addressed the group of gentlemen who had risen upon his entrance and were standing with their backs to the blaze.

"Good morning, gentlemen," he said in a hearty voice. "An unpleasant morning outside, but I hope that our transactions here may prove to be agreeable. At any rate," he added, as he recognized several faces, "I feel that our business will be brief and to the point."

The agent wasted no time over his preliminaries. The house servants were assets of an estate. The order for sale was read. "I am instructed," the agent supplemented, "to offer the first lot as a family. It is the earnest hope of the administrator that purchasers will coöperate with this humane desire, and offer a satisfactory bid for the lot. I presume that all of you were acquainted with the late Mr. Barstow, and so when I say that they were trained in his yard, I can offer no higher recommendation. The man, Adam, is a competent butler and personal servant; the woman, Rachel, is skilled in chamber work and is an excellent seamstress; and the boy, I am informed, is of good character and quick to learn."

He turned toward the bench. "Stand up," he directed.

The three negroes rose to their feet. Their faces were dark curtains behind which their emotions beat invisibly, but they drew together as though the command had shot a magnetic current through their bodies. The agent cleared his throat and transferred his gaze to the group of gentlemen.

"My clients vouch for the fact that these people are of sound health, but if anyone wishes to make an examination it may be done before we proceed with the bidding."

An elderly man with a myopic squint advanced, and leaning on his cane, ordered the man briefly to open his mouth. A shudder ran through the three negroes. The child's eyes grew huge in their sooty black setting. The face of the woman quivered. She raised her eyes and, across the width of the room, her gaze went clear and sharp as a cry to a young man standing before the fireplace. He turned deliberately and spat into the fire. The sudden hiss was the only sound in the room. Then he turned back and smiled, suddenly, warmly, and nodded his head encouragingly.

The tension at the bench went slack again. The examination consisted merely of looking at teeth, eyes and feet. It was soon over. But the other bidders were plainly impatient at the delay.

The young man who had smiled said, "Let us get ahead, sir, if you please. We are all acquainted with the negroes and are anxious to have it over with."

The auction was a tame affair, Peter thought. With the exception of the man who had made the examination, and who soon became irritated at the concerted action of the others and departed, all seemed to be relatives or friends of the deceased and their bidding was not highly competitive.

First the family went at fourteen hundred dollars, then the two women at five hundred fifty and five hundred. The older man, who proved to be a coachman, on account of his age fetched only two hundred fifty dollars. Prices which, Peter concluded as he made his notes, indicated a normal condition of the market.

When the farm hand was put up, something happened that disturbed the harmony of the occasion. During the sale of the house servants a man had been waiting at the door. From time to time he had looked in, but at the inhospitable glances that he received from the bidders, he had withdrawn. Now he entered with an air of bravado, shouldered his way to the fire and spat noisily. Then he walked over to where the negro was standing and measured him with appraising eyes.

Bert Lawrence and his friend drew together in a hasty conference. The man was a trader named Magrew, they told Peter, who bought up gangs of prime negroes and shipped them to the cane fields. He was also what was known as a "nigger splitter," buying up families at a reduced price upon the understanding that they were to be kept together, then splitting them and selling at high prices singly. He was always willing to bid high as he made huge profits on his shipments. There was an understanding among the planters that wherever possible they would keep the local negroes out of his hands. A sale to the cane plantations was considered only as a last resort in the case of an incorrigible.

"The devil take the damned vulture," Lawrence grumbled. "He's going to cost us a pretty penny."

To the inquiry as to whether anyone wished to make an examination, the trader replied succinctly, "Strip him."

The agent's clerk conducted the negro to the far end of the room where a screen was placed for the purpose, and instructed him to undress.

The two planters regarded this performance in silence, but when Magrew went toward the screen they exchanged quick glances and followed him. Several of the bystanders, sensing possible excitement, joined them, and Peter, repelled yet under the influence of a strong and morbid attraction, brought up the rear. It was an experience that was destined still further to confuse him upon the issues with which he was grappling. But it was a memorable moment, big with a certain dark and tortured beauty.

Against the clean blank whitewash of the wall, the negro stood erect and naked. Above him a large high window showed a square of bleak sky from which the light fell neutral and indecisive, assuming character only when it limned the hard clean arc of a breast or shoulder muscle, or brought out planes in the flat straight back, and the cheek, taut from jaw to cheek bone. Between the fullness of the lips, the man's mouth was a hard straight line. The lids were lowered slightly over eyes that were focused upon a point remote in space. Peter had never seen such a physique on any human being. Over six feet in height and perfectly proportioned, it possessed that indefinable added beauty that transcends perfection of form, and springs from that inner harmony which, when repose gives way to movement, becomes suddenly lyric.

Magrew stood before the man, his short heavy legs wide apart, his massive shoulders hunched forward. His face was covered with a beard grizzled at the sides, foul and brown from tobacco under the mouth. Under bristling brows, his eyes were cold, absorbed, impersonal like those of a chess player.

He first made the man turn around, and examined his back for scars. When his blunt fingers touched the skin it moved under them in a swift involuntary shudder of repulsion, then lay still over taut muscle. The unblemished back was Washington's certificate of good conduct. Magrew gave a grunt of satisfaction and said, "Turn around."

The man obeyed.

The inert bulk of Magrew's body surged forward on its short heavy legs. A fist shot out, and delivered a terrific blow to the man's groin. There had been no warning. The muscles of the stomach were slack and unprepared. A spasm drew the negro almost double, but he made no sound. In a moment he was again erect. His gaze was still remote, but under the lowered lids it had the sullen luminousness of molten ore. The line of the jaw leapt out hard as iron.

Peter looked at Magrew's face. The eyes were the same as before—cool, calculating, preoccupied. There was no personal animus. He had nothing against the negro. He was doing his job. That was all. "Good!" he exclaimed. "No hernia." He turned to the small group of gentlemen. He had forgotten that they despised him. He said, with an air of pride in his professional acumen,

"You'd be surprised how many of these bucks are rup-
tured."

The emotions of the several individuals who stood
there congealed into an atmosphere of frigid and menacing hatred. Magrew was a more dangerous enemy than
an abolitionist, for he held their peace of mind in deadly
jeopardy. His existence in the flesh before them im-
periled the beliefs by which they lived, in the support of
which they were prepared to die. They would have torn
him to pieces with pleasure. But they were gentlemen.
All that they could give him was a silence that seemed
to thud in the room like the blows of a club.

But Magrew for the moment was oblivious. He was
engrossed in the technique of his atrocious trade. He
had never yet been guilty of buying an unsound negro.
He had a reputation to sustain. He chuckled in his beard
with a loathsome self-appreciation, and turned back to
his examination. Eyes, teeth, feet. The rest of it was
soon over. The negro was allowed to dress and resume
his seat on the bench.

Back in the auction room, the trader seemed to become
aware of the hostility of the others. They were waiting,
massed solidly before the fire. They looked remarkably
alike, bearing as they did the marks of their class. Clean
cut, high bred, erect. Movements free, easy, assured.
Eyes direct and candid. Not the eyes of analysts, but of
a people with an enormous capacity for faith in its accepted beliefs. Faces singularly free from the marks of
mental conflict, hale and ruddy from good whisky, offset
by hard riding under a semi-tropical sun.

Magrew, standing across the room, lowered his head

and looked out at them through his heavy brows like a charging bull.

The agent put the question.

Instantly Magrew hurled his attack. "One thousand dollars."

As an opening bid it was preposterous. Bidders, especially in times of political disquiet, started at a few hundred at most and worked slowly, eliminating rivals as they advanced. One thousand dollars would not have been an unreasonable final figure. No, this was not a bid. It was a challenge. A challenge from all that Magrew stood for. If the precious gentry with their fine ideals wanted this negro, they were going to have to pay for him.

But this action was a tactical blunder, for it immediately eliminated all competitive bidding among the planters and consolidated his opposition. All except Bert Lawrence and Charles Gilbraith withdrew, leaving the field to them. The two young men consulted together, then Lawrence took the floor. He was evidently a shrewd trader, and was not going to be stampeded into extravagant bidding that would imply a determination to get the man at any price. He mentioned the sum of a thousand and twenty-five.

Magrew promptly lifted it a hundred.

After a conference, Lawrence added another twenty-five.

It was not until the price of fifteen hundred had been reached that Magrew hesitated. At that figure there would be no possible profit in the transaction, and he was beginning to wonder how much more the gentlemen would be willing to pay for their scruples.

Peter joined Lawrence and Gilbraith in their next conference. He found that they had joined forces and were actually bidding together, each planning to use the negro for six months of the year. Suddenly to his own surprise he found himself saying, "Look here, if Father or Wake were here, they'd be in on this. There is no reason why you two should have to carry the parish. I'll answer for Wakefields and take a third interest, if you say so."

They looked at him in surprise. Then Lawrence smiled. "I thought you were a Unionist," he said, "and it's rumored you are even for emancipation. But I am glad to see that you are still one of us."

And Gilbraith warned him, "Your father already has more negroes than he knows what to do with. Of course, you know that."

Peter looked across the room at the negro. He was sitting passively, his huge frame relaxed, his eyes lowered. By his very attitude of withdrawal, in his failure to plead by word or sign, he implied a confidence in their class that could not be violated. "I know," Peter answered, "we're all in the same boat. But if you want to count Wakefields in, go ahead."

A moment later, when Magrew's tentative sixteen hundred was topped by Lawrence's sixteen twenty-five, the trader turned abruptly on his heel and strode out of the mart.

If Peter had expected a melodramatic scene of gratitude, he was destined to be disappointed. The negro got to his feet and looked in their direction with the same cryptic impassivity that he had exhibited during the gruelling twenty minutes of the auction. Peter had the somewhat let-down feeling that he had taken the whole thing as a matter of course, that he had thrown the burden of responsibility upon them and had not for a moment doubted the result. The negro said simply, "T'ank yo', Mas' Bert. Whar yo' want me tuh go now?"

Lawrence looked at him a moment, then he laughed ruefully. "You damned worthless rascal," he said, "I don't know what the hell we'll find for you to do, but you can go down to Adger's wharf and wait at the boat for me. We'll go up the river after dinner."

The negro grinned under the familiar and reassuring words of abuse. For a moment the massive shoulders filled the doorway. A gust of raw air cut through the close room, then the door slammed and a snatch of song came back to them, muffled by the heavy brick walls.

To his dismay Peter found that it was already noon and he would be late for his second assignment. He hastily completed his transaction by giving the agent a draft on his father, and Lawrence promised to call at Wakefields immediately upon his return and explain the situation. The two young planters regarded him quizzically. Peter felt that they were amused at his expense. They stood looking at each other for a moment, then quite spontaneously they all laughed aloud.

"You've been pretty reckless with Mr. Ashley's money," Lawrence said, "but I wager when he hears the story he'll think it well spent, eh, Charles?"

Gilbraith nodded an amused affirmative and held out his hand. "Ride over and look me up the next time you're at Wakefields. I've heard you like horses. I have a two-year-old I am thinking of running in the meet next month that I'd like you to try."

"And don't delay," advised Lawrence. "We'll all be in the army in a week or two and we must make the most of our time."

In the street again, with his ulster buttoned about his throat and the raw salty wind in his face, Peter was conscious of a pleasant inward glow. His action had been unpremeditated. It had been prompted by some imperative impulse and he had been swept forward by it into action before his fatal habit of reasoning it out had arrested him. The sensation of having been understood, approved, even liked was exhilarating.

Continuing on his way, Peter traversed a small park, crossed Meeting Street and elbowed his way through a scattered crowd that waited in the cold before the court-house steps. He was shockingly late and the sale was practically over. It was, however, an unimportant event, and he could get the figures from the office of the sheriff when the crowd had dispersed.

The character of the crowd with whom he was now rubbing elbows differed greatly from that from which he had just come. They were for the most part idlers who were there to enjoy themselves at the expense of a group of free negroes who were being sold into slavery. Everybody distrusted a free negro. They were the tools of the abolitionists. They were dangerous to have on a planta-tion associating with obedient and contented negroes. Ever since the insurrection of eighteen-twenty-two, in which many of them were implicated, every man's hand was against them. This sale consisted of a group who had failed to leave the state under an order of expulsion from the court, and their persons had been promptly seized and placed upon the auction block.

As Peter arrived the auctioneer called for a bid on the last negro of the lot. It was evidently an occasion for mirth. The auctioneer wore a manner of mock gravity. "Come, my good people," he cried, "what am I offered for this likely girl?"

The crowd laughed.

From where he stood Peter could see no one on the step but the stout red-faced auctioneer. He pressed forward, and as he did so the crowd milled and opened, and he saw seated on the step at the feet of the man, the form of a woman, incredibly aged and bent. He noticed first that she was not a full black; probably half white, he thought. And then that she was immaculately clean. Someone had evidently helped her prepare for the occasion, so that, where words were not permitted, her appearance might offer a mute plea to some tender-hearted passer-by. In the cold wind her knees shook under the clean faded calico of her frock. She wore a "headkerchief" of black and white plaid. And under it her gaze was fixed unseeing upon the crowd, somber and remote. From time to time her lips moved inaudibly. Peter wondered whether the words of the auctioneer and the laughter of the crowd had any meaning for her, or whether her thoughts had retreated to that frontier which lies between the known and the unknown and that offers sanctuary to the very old.

The auctioneer was at it again. A fresh witticism reached Peter's ears, and a burst of coarse laughter. A wave of anger swept over him. His muscles tensed and he started forward. Then almost instantly his hatred of the spectacular, his diffidence in the face of crowds, arrested him. He cursed himself for a coward. Something must be done to stop it—but what?

Someone was poking him rudely in the back. It added to his anger, his feeling of impotence. He moved his position. Then he was tapped smartly on the shoulder. He swung around angrily and his confusion became overwhelming. It had been bad enough to find himself in this position, but to have his plight witnessed was infinitely worse. A carriage was drawn up at the curb, and in it sat a young woman. Peter was conscious only of indignant eyes that flashed at him from under a secession bonnet. And the sudden abrupt interrogation,

"Aren't you Mr. Peter Ashley?"

"Why, yes," he stammered.

"Then," she demanded, "are you going to stand there all morning and allow those rowdies to bait her like that? Oh, it's shameful!"

Over the heads of the rabble came the voice of the auctioneer, distinct for a moment, then drowned in a fresh burst of laughter.

The young woman tapped her foot angrily. "Well," she said, "aren't you going to do anything about it?"

Peter's embarrassment became so acute that it affected him with a sort of physical paralysis. His fingers opened and dropped his hat, which he had been clutching, to the pavement. He stooped automatically to retrieve it, but when he straightened up, what he saw frightened him into desperate action.

The young lady had laid hold upon her hoops and was gathering together her voluminous ruffles, preparatory to quitting her carriage. She flashed upon him a look of mingled contempt and anger. "Men are absolutely hope-less," she announced.

Peter extended a restraining hand. "Please, please stay there," he begged. "Tell me what to do."

The agitation in the carriage ceased abruptly. And the eyes under the bonnet met his with a distinct propulsive impact.

"You'll have to buy her. You can't possibly leave her to their tender mercies."

"Buy her!" ejaculated Peter, aghast. "Do you mean acquire her—possess her—for my own?"

Under the bonnet the lines of the face suddenly wavered. There was a bewildering flash of laughter and a full lip caught under white teeth. Then her head dropped and the bonnet fell like a curtain between them.

Peter stood looking foolishly at the black and white cotton ruffles, the coquettish streamers, flaunting their little palmetto trees. Then he blurted desperately, "You'll wait here—you'll tell me what to do when I get back?"

The top of the bonnet nodded an affirmation, and he turned blindly into the crowd. In his pocket his fingers closed upon a paper bill. He drew it out and saw that it was ten dollars. He elbowed his way toward the steps. The auctioneer paused in his travesty and looked up. Immediately his manner changed. His attitude became obsequious. "Are you interested in this woman, sir?" he asked.

Peter said, "I bid ten dollars for her." In the sudden curious silence that had fallen, his words boomed ridiculously in his own ears.

"The gentleman has bid ten dollars. Are there any further bids?"

There was a moment of silence—then, "Going, going, gone to the gentleman for the sum of ten dollars."

The sharp finality of the hammer. The crowd thinning and drifting off in silence. St. Michael's bell across the way rolling out its quarter hours interminably, then capping them with a single deep note. And the auctioneer asking Peter to whom the deed should be executed.

That brought him to his senses. He looked desperately toward the carriage. Yes, she was still there. More than that, she was laughing into her handkerchief. From the box, her coachman was regarding him with a wide grin that he swallowed hastily when he saw that he was observed. A sudden idea flashed across the confusion of Peter's thoughts. He turned from the auctioneer and the woman who was still sitting on the step, and presented himself at the carriage. The humor of the situation came home to him, and with it his complete self-possession.

He bowed formally. "You have an unfair advantage," he said. "You know my name and I am still in complete ignorance of yours."

She controlled her laughter and held out her hand. "I am Damaris Gordon," she told him. "I believe that you and your uncle are having tea with us tomorrow evening, and——"

But Peter excused himself and left her sentence unfinished. She saw him speak to the auctioneer, who gathered his papers and entered the courthouse. Then he spoke to the old negress. She had some trouble getting to her feet, and he assisted her to the pavement's edge.

"Permit me, Mistress Damaris," he said, with deep gravity, "to present you with this memento of our first meeting. Her name, I am informed, is Virginia, and like her humble donor, she is already eager to be of service to so charming a mistress."

Damaris emitted a stifled scream. "But I can't possibly. We live in town, and our quarters are already overflowing."

But Peter paid no attention to her protests. "Virginia," he said, turning to the woman, "this is Miss Damaris Gordon, your new mistress."

The old woman looked hazily from one to the other, then dropped a curtsey to the carriage.

"And now," Peter went on, taking command of the situation, "if your coachman will make room on the box, I will give her a hand up."

The driver shifted the reins nervously and rolled his eyes toward his mistress.

"Move over and lend me a hand," Peter commanded. And at the note of authority the bewildered negro at once complied. Virginia was hoisted to a precarious seat.

Peter turned to the speechless girl. His eyes were mocking, triumphant, but his voice was deferential. "Until tomorrow," he said, "at tea," and with a low bow, turned and walked briskly away.

CHAPTER VI

CHARDON and Peter stepped out of their front door into the still, sharp beauty of the winter evening. The supper hour was at hand, a fact which probably explained the unwonted quiet of White Point Gardens and the absence of sightseers along the sea wall. Out beyond the Atlantic a moon that was nearly at the full hung just clear of the horizon, and had caught the harbor in an undulant silver net. Chardon noticed it, and remembered that there would be a moonlight drill of the Dragoons on the Citadel Green within the hour. Probably that also accounted for the absence of the usual crowds. Well, he would enjoy the brief respite while he could.

The two men turned west, walking side by side in an intimate silence. Chardon suspected that the same subject engrossed the thoughts of both. It was well that it should be kept as long as possible behind the barriers of speech. Once put it into words, and the perfect sympathy that existed between them, and that he could make felt in his silences, might be shattered.

Now that he thought of Damaris Gordon, he wondered that he had not realized her dangerous potentialities from the beginning. He regarded her with disillusioned eyes, he told himself. He was old enough to be her father. And yet in spite of these safeguards he knew perfectly well that when she came and looked up into his face in a certain individual way she had, she could turn him around her finger.

There was a certain type of woman, he thought, who had the power to awaken a spirit of resistance in men, so that their intercourse became a game in which her skill was subtly employed against his will. But Damaris belonged to the far rarer and more dangerous type which breaks down resistance, disarms at a glance, and endows the process of surrender with a strange sensual delight.

But his feeling for Damaris had not prevented him from subjecting her to an amused and impersonal appraisal when he was removed from the sphere of her direct appeal. It was her eyes, he had decided, that did the mischief. To begin with, they were cadet gray. Then they were set under blue-black lashes of such extraordinary thickness and length that when she lowered her face, a watcher caught an effect that was like moonlit water lost suddenly beneath wind-blown fern. But the most extraordinary quality that Damaris' eyes possessed was that of reflecting the emotions that played upon the face into which they gazed. That was their touch of genius and it had proved the undoing of more men than Chardon liked to remember. It also made the real Damaris something of an enigma, and he had often speculated as to whether her own emotions were so facile that, like her eyes, they reflected the sadness, gaiety, or love of the moment; or whether behind that bright mirroring surface she lived her own life separate and apart. It was inconceivable that she should be consciously untrue and at the same time carry such a conviction of candor and sincerity; and yet the celerity with which she transferred her favor from one admirer to another was already a subject for laughing comment among her friends.

Then there was her name, Chardon reflected. It was definitely out of character. You spoke the beautiful word, and instantly all the sterling qualities—constancy, truth, purity—seemed to cluster about it. She would have been less dangerous if she had been named, say, Polly or Betty, and carried at least the suggestion of the ubiquitous innocent flirt of her period.

In another age and setting, Chardon thought, her temperament would have made of her a great courtesan. For she could have given more than mere physical satisfaction. She could have fostered some great ego, by continually presenting its own glorified reflection. But her spirit was as completely armored in the Southern gentlewoman tradition of chastity as was her body in its stays and hoops. Her expression of fresh and serene innocence, her instinctive withdrawal from the obviously and crudely physical, was fundamentally sincere, Chardon concluded.

That Damaris was an uncharted and deadly peril on the difficult course that Peter Ashley had to navigate had become evident the evening before, when Peter had told him of his experience at the slave auction. The boy's alternate bursts of excited narration and abstracted silence had told him that much. It had been on the tip of Chardon's tongue to give Peter a word of warning, but a new element had suddenly come into their relationship —something in the boy that he could best define as a sort of spiritual reticence, and he had, somewhat to his own surprise, held his tongue.

Chardon was on a footing of close intimacy at Proctor

Gordon's, and so upon their arrival the butler relieved the two men of their coats, hats and sticks, and allowed them to find their way, without the formality of an announcement, toward the drawing room. A fresh, untrained soprano voice came to them from the room, accompanied by the soft notes of a piano. Chardon lifted the portières and Peter entered.

The large room, paneled in the severely simple style that marked the earliest colonial period, was filled with warm half-lights and shadows. A bright open fire blazed on the hearth, and the soft hiss of the burning lightwood made a friendly undertone to the music. Two candelabra, set upon a square piano near the fire, flung the face of a girl into high relief as she sat at the keys and played with her head turned toward a man who leaned forward above her. The man showed only in silhouette, tall and well proportioned, with powerful shoulders. But from where the two visitors stood the girl's face was distinctly visible. As she sang, her eyes were fixed upon the face of the man. Her lip trembled, and Chardon could have sworn that there were tears in her eyes. Borne on the soft, flexible soprano voice, the words of the song filled the room with an atmosphere of heavy and delicious melancholy:

> "Will you place a wreath, love,
> Upon my little mound,
> At evening's holy hour, love,
> When shadows hover 'round?"

Peter uttered an involuntary ejaculation. Chardon gave him a single penetrating glance. Then he disrupted the tableau at the piano by stumbling against a chair, and replacing it with meticulous care while the atmosphere resumed its normal temperature.

By the time the furniture was in order, Damaris was halfway across the apartment, her hand extended charmingly in greeting. The funereal sadness had vanished. There was not a trace of self-consciousness or embarrassment. She welcomed Chardon affectionately, and turned to Peter. He felt the soft resilient bump of her hoops against his ankles, then from very close she was looking up into his face. Peter looked into her eyes, and a sudden inexplicable pang of jealousy that had assailed him upon his entrance passed. Chardon, the stranger, the room blurred from his consciousness while her eyes held his. They gave him the impression that they were standing together in a walled and private space, and what happened beyond it was of no consequence. Her soft laugh broke the spell.

"It was nice of your uncle to bring you tonight," she said. "Does he know that I have a score to settle with you?"

Peter smiled and nodded. He felt singularly at ease. He knew little of women, but Damaris, he felt, made him flatteringly aware that she liked him.

"I hope that you are not going to punish me too cruelly," he begged.

"I certainly shall," she told him, laughing. "It's many a day since I have been taken in so neatly. But remember, he who laughs last——"

"Mightn't we compromise by laughing together and calling it quits?" he suggested.

"Indeed, no. You shall never escape so easily."

"Then it's a challenge?" Peter asked.

"A challenge and a fair warning. But I am forgetting my manners." She swung back toward the fire. "Perhaps you are already acquainted with Captain Holcombe. He's from Lower St. John's and must have been an old neighbor of yours. His company has been ordered into service at Morris Island, and I was singing him a song of parting when you came."

The presence of the stranger returned to his consciousness with a distinct shock. The name, too, awakened unpleasant associations. But it was not likely that the Archie Holcombe whom he had always disliked as a small boy, and who had forfeited his right to the society of his class by his excesses, could be here on terms of such intimacy.

But the moment the figure by the piano turned, he recognized him, not so much by his personal appearance, for he was now quite gray and the close lines of the uniform that he wore made his form seem more spare and fit than he remembered, but by the immediate recurrence of an old dislike so acute that it left no possible doubt in his mind. He advanced, however, and extended his hand.

Holcombe said in a rich lazy voice, "Yes, I know Ashley. Used to see him occasionally when he was a boy at Wakefields."

They shook hands briefly, and Holcombe continued, addressing him directly,

"Your brother Wakefield is a splendid fellow. I hear he's recruiting his own company in Middle St. John's. I suppose you've come home to join him?"

Peter was beginning to have a morbid feeling that

everyone knew that he was not enlisting. He was certain that Holcombe knew it, and that the thrust had been deliberate. He met Holcombe's insolent gaze squarely.

"No," he answered firmly, "I haven't joined up. As a matter of fact I'm writing for the *Courier.*"

Holcombe's only comment was, "Oh?" spoken on a rising inflection. He turned his back just casually enough to miss being a deliberate insult and sauntered over to the fire.

The situation was saved by the entrance of Proctor and Mrs. Gordon, who, happily oblivious of any discord, immediately established their mood of easy and gracious hospitality. It seemed to Peter that their attitude towards Chardon and himself was one of peculiar solicitude, much as though he and his uncle were suffering from some obscure and painful malady that time would heal, but that in the meantime called for sympathy rather than censure from old friends.

Presently supper was announced, and then, facing each other around the circular table, the lack of harmony became so apparent that it was almost impossible to ignore it. The party fell into two parts; the three younger members, tense under the opposing currents of positive and negative magnetism that played between them, were too excited for the flat level of table talk.

Damaris sat silent for the most part. This in itself was not unusual, for she was of the type which takes little part in general conversation. She wore her hair in a braided coronet that completely encircled her small beautifully modeled head. Under the lustrous blue-black crown the pure oval of her face showed with the warm pallor of ivory. The dark accent was repeated in brows and lashes, which framed the extraordinary eyes. Her mouth was small, and her rather full red lips were usually parted slightly, giving her face, as she watched that of some speaker, an eager, breathless and virginal look. This look of eager attention was on her face now; but as she turned it from one speaker to another, Chardon, watching with dark apprehension, decided that the trick was purely mechanical and had nothing to do with what was taking place behind the luminous shallow eyes.

Holcombe contributed practically nothing to the evening. He sat gazing at Damaris. His eyes were fixed in a slight characteristic stare, and had little lambent flames in them. From time to time she allowed her eyes to meet his, answer their fire, then fall demurely. Again she would turn to Peter and give him a flash of the peculiarly intimate and isolating look that she had given him during the brief moment of his arrival.

With consummate tact the host and hostess kept the conversation from touching upon politics and the war. They led Peter to tell of England, the rowing at Oxford, the grand tour. Unlike Holcombe, he was anxious to put himself out, to carry his part of the burden. But inclined to be distrait at all times, he was now mentally incapable of sustained attention. His answers to their questions were rambling, prosy, and rather pointless.

Eventually the gift of the decrepit slave was mentioned, and the incident was the subject for much chaffing. Proctor Gordon declared that the joke had really been on him, as he would now have to pension her for the remainder of her days. But the subject, which was clung to until it reached the repetitious stage, had eventually to be abandoned. One by one they quit it, like sailors leaving a sinking ship, and finally left it to founder in an embarrassed silence.

It was now equally obvious to everyone that beneath the surface of their intercourse, under the technical perfection of the Gordons' hospitality, the evening had been anything but a success. Chardon brought it to an early close soon after the return to the drawing room, by making the move for departure. There were the inevitable expressions of surprise and disappointment from the hosts, of regret that such a charming evening could end from the guests, and they were saying good-bye.

Holcombe did not come forward. He was standing with his back to the fire in an attitude that impressed Chardon as definitely truculent, and he bade them good night from that vantage ground, bowing with stiff formality from the waist.

Damaris engineered her farewell of Peter cleverly. She was, of course, too much of a lady to leave the drawing room with a departing guest, and besides her mother was observing her. She allowed her father to precede them through the door and escort Chardon down the hall. Then as Peter crossed the threshold she stopped on her side of it, took each side of the portière in one of her hands and held it spread fanwise behind her, shutting them from view. The curtain was of a deep wine color and she gleamed against it like a jewel flung upon a velvet cloth. For a second she said nothing, standing, looking up, isolating Peter from the rest of the world.

Then she whispered, "It has been perfectly terrible, hasn't it? But there's no doing a thing with Captain Holcombe. His manners are shocking—and at times I think he's quite mad. But you'll come back some time soon when he's not here, won't you?"

At the front door Chardon was already in his cloak. He looked back toward them. Time was passing. Peter couldn't go like that, with everything at loose ends. He must see her soon. He was excited. He could not manage a subtle approach. He blurted out, "Tomorrow night, then. May I come?"

Her glance softened suddenly as she looked up into his face. He felt the fleeting pressure of her fingers on his hand. Then he was blundering over a final good-bye to Mr. Gordon at the door, and a moment later joined Chardon in the street.

They walked in silence for a few moments, both apparently reluctant to open the only subject that was occupying their minds. Finally Peter came at it obliquely:

"What I can't understand, Uncle Pierre, is the Gordons permitting that rotter to pay open court to Miss Damaris. Why, when I last heard of him he was practically ostracized from respectable society!"

" 'C'est la guerre,' my boy. Holcombe is a typical soldier of fortune. It has been his great opportunity. Two years ago he appeared at the races with a long-legged roan filly. Nobody knew where he had got it. The odds were tremendous. He hired Major Cantey's boy, Bedo, to ride him—he's probably as good a jockey as there is on the American turf. They swept the track clean. That summer they wiped up the Pineville races, and in the autumn the filly ended in a blaze of glory on the Virginia tracks. She cleaned up all of the lesser events and was actually about to run against the great

Planet when she tore some ligaments and had to be shot.

"Holcombe bought back his plantation, collected his negroes—who all adore him, by the way—from various purchasers, and was just settling down to plant when secession came along. He has sold out, lock, stock and barrel, and is putting the money into his own company. His outfit's the best in the service. Uniforms by Yglesias, the best tailor in town. The new Enfield rifle, gotten at thirty dollars each, God knows how, from England. Every private with his personal negro to shine his boots. Everyone's gone wild over him. And why not?—he's a perfect barbarian, and although we may all not realize it, our civilization has ended. This is his world—not ours."

"But," Peter continued, "that does not change Holcombe's fundamental attitude toward the opposite sex. He is obviously of a type that cannot appreciate the difference between a lady and a—well, a woman. He scarcely took his eyes off her tonight. And what they said plainly was insulting. She is, of course, too innocent to read a look like that, but she should be protected."

The older man's hand fell affectionately on Peter's shoulder. "My dear fellow," he said, "please don't think me an old satyr, but believe me when I tell you that the purest ladies in the world are invariably the most attracted by that attitude in a man that you find so detestable. The body, the mind and the spirit may be chaste, but under these the instincts are those of Eve in the Garden of Eden. If such a man is careful not to offend by word or gesture, he may say what he will with his eyes—and Eve will see and respond. A man of Holcombe's type possesses a fatal attraction. How else can you explain the fact that the notorious rake invariably captures the most desirable woman of his set when he is ready to marry and be reformed?"

Chardon felt Peter draw suddenly from under his hand. Then he stopped and faced him. In a thick and unfamiliar voice he said, "If you mean to intimate, sir, that Miss Gordon deliberately invites that sort of attention, that she is so common as to enjoy——"

"Don't be a fool," Chardon snapped. "I wasn't criticizing the lady. I was stating a general rule. But since we are on the subject, suppose I were to tell you that while Miss Damaris Gordon is probably the most irresistible young lady in town, she is also the most dangerous flirt in the city of Charleston, what would you have to say then?"

"I would say, sir, that you are too much of a gentleman to tell a lie, and that I can, therefore, only conclude that you are grossly misinformed."

They had reached home now, and were standing on the top step before the front door. Chardon paused in the act of inserting the key in the lock and, turning, regarded his nephew with an expression of deep solicitude not unmixed with irritation.

"God help you, then," he said. "I see it's too late for me to do anything about it."

CHAPTER VII

ALWAYS as a prelude to war there comes a time when the rhythm of the life of a people changes. A man sensitive to such influences can almost mark the hour that saw the passing of the old, the arrival of the new. Before this moment isolated events possess the power to disturb the forward measured swing of time, but the dominant beat persists. Destiny, while it is not subject to the will of the people, is at least influenced by it. Then suddenly the rhythm quickens. The human equation disappears. It is the event that determines destiny.

Events having their genesis in causes so remote as to have lost all identity with the immediate issue pile one on top of another. The rhythm changes, becomes faster, its pull upon individual destinies becomes more and more irresistible. Each day accelerates the process. The clatter of printing presses, the ranting of propagandists, snatch the rhythm forward into higher and higher speed. Excitement mounts. Individual opinions, aspirations, hopes, dreams capitulate, each surrender adding weight to the mass that drives forward with dizzy speed toward the abyss. A thousand petty but insoluble Gordian knots in as many homes are instantaneously severed by the bright blade of war. A thousand domestic prison doors swing at the imperious, liberating command. In a headlong atavism mankind sweeps back to its simple, uncomplicated beginnings, and suddenly freed from the satiety that has been bred of soft living, it turns with a new zest to the delights and satisfactions that centuries of civilization have created.

It is at this moment that the civilization which has grown slowly through centuries of patient cultivation pours its life into a last incomparable flowering. For those who have tended it, and watched it spread and bud, it is all too often the moment of delirium that precedes the oblivion of death.

Now for the individual the final moment of decision has arrived. There is no turning back. There is no standing still. He must conform or he must be destroyed.

In the face of these simple alternatives, why should he hesitate? He has but to march into camp and lay down his arms. He is acclaimed a hero. He at once surrenders his will to that of the mass. He has thrown from his shoulders the intolerable burden of deciding for himself which act is right, and which act wrong. He is of that number which, having delivered themselves over to the new, frantic rhythm of life, are possessed by it—are given in this brief interval which precedes the crash over the brink, their priceless hour of romance, their illusion of great and imperishable splendor.

And for the nonconformist—what? Only the approval of a small, stubborn, inner voice that will not be silenced. And for food, the bread of that utter loneliness that is possible only in the press of a crowd.

It was during the months of January and February of eighteen-sixty-one that Charleston entered definitely into this phase of existence. The democratic defeat at the polls, secession, the occupation of Sumter, even the *Star of the West* episode—these were the preliminary jars that started the movement. But it was not until after the turn of the fateful year that each day delivered its separate impetus to the forward drive. Not that these events were of great significance, taken singly; but they flowed in an ever-hastening stream until the pace became irresistible.

And yet, with the new accelerated rhythm pulling at his foothold like some deep undertow, Peter Ashley continued to experience the frustrating sensation of being apart from it—of being unable to let go and drift with the tide. There would be times when some experience would seize upon his imagination and drive him forward. But inevitably there would come the moment of sickening reality that left him disillusioned and cold.

It was strange that from the swarming canvas that unfolded before him how few individuals detached themselves from the picture and impinged definitely upon his perceptions. His uncle, his mother, Damaris, Holcombe. For the rest, they were little more than a background that shifted into new groupings behind the principals in the drama of his days. He would go about his work, recognizing faces and saluting acquaintances with some part of his mind that functioned automatically.

At times, plowing ahead on his routine tasks, the result would be so puerile that even Mr. Tattenham, whose literary standards were certainly not exalted, would tear the work up and write it over in his own peculiarly grandiose vein. Once he said: "Look here, Ashley, this won't do. It reads like a college thesis. No one to read this would know where the paper stands on the question."

Peter had replied that he supposed it was his duty to report facts. He pointed out politely that this was a news item and not an editorial.

"News item or not," his superior had snapped, "you are working for a Secessionist paper. You are expected to be partisan. Why is the *Mercury* forging ahead of us in popularity? Because they are on fire with indignation, because they're fighting mad."

He snatched up Peter's copy and attacked it vindictively with a blue pencil. The word "soldiers" which appeared three times flowered gloriously into "our gallant defenders," "the flower of chivalry," "predestined heroes of many a hard fought field." A senator became "that doughty defender of our honor."

Then there were other times when Peter's pen would get out of hand, spilling color, sound, rhythm into his story, discarding unimportant details, fixing essentials where they belonged, until the result would bring Mr. Willington himself to his desk with a word of approval.

Chardon's theory that, in placing his charge with the paper, he was giving him an opportunity to observe and decide his own course, failed to take one thing into account. This was Peter's inability to think effectively in the midst of excitement. Of solitary and studious habits, the constant interruptions within and the general turmoil without destroyed his powers of concentration and increased rather than diminished the confusion of his mind. His desk in the large general room was by a window that was directly above the bulletin board, where hourly bulletins that arrived by the Morse Line were exhibited.   And there by day and often well into the night, a noisy crowd waited, and responded with cheers or groans as the items were posted.   At a short distance down the street, "Old Secession," the cannon that had sounded South Carolina's withdrawal from the Union, had been stationed in a vacant lot beside the Exchange. Scarcely had he entered upon his duties when it crashed out the news of Mississippi's secession, followed two days later by a double salute to Florida and Alabama.

Less noisy, but of equally vital importance, was the flood of news items that poured through the offices of the *Courier*, and appeared for a brief life upon the bulletin board, then vanished beneath others before the ink had fairly dried.   No sooner had South Carolina become an independent republic than the revenue cutter *Aiken*, "captained by a gallant Southerner," surrendered to Governor Pickens.   The *Harriet Lane* was ordered South to take her place.   The governor dispatched word that she would be allowed to enter the harbor only under a flag of truce.   "Down with the Tariff."   "Three cheers for Free Trade."   And a serenade for the governor by the regimental band.

January fifteenth Colonel Isaac W. Hayne, special envoy from the governor of South Carolina, arrives in Washington for the purpose of negotiating for the peaceable purchase of forts and other government property. President Buchanan receives him for twenty minutes of personal talk, but refuses to have any negotiations with him as the representative of an independent republic, for, as such, South Carolina does not exist.   "Civis," "Civitas" and "Secessionist" all write letters to the daily papers proving conclusively that secession is constitutional. Street corner orators affirm it. But on the seventeenth Colonel Hayne leaves Washington for home. The status of the forts will be maintained.

On the streets smoldering suspicion bursts into flaming anger. "Civitas" and "Secessionist" speak again: "Military despotism." "Yankee avarice unmasked."

But sustained anger requires concentration. It must remain fixed upon its object. And over at the Arsenal the Sumter Guards have taken possession. The Palmetto Flag is soaring up the flag pole. The band is blaring. Crowds surge to the Arsenal grounds and cheers can be heard half across the city.

News from Washington: "An affidavit has been taken before Judge Taney charging treason against senators and representatives of the seceding states." What effrontery! "Well, at any rate the mask is off. We know what we have to expect from the Black Republicans!"

There was a story going around started, surprisingly enough, by a paragraph in the Washington *Star*. Christmas Eve night, while Major Anderson was the honored guest of certain distinguished Secessionists of Charleston, he had pretended to become so intoxicated that he had to be carried by friends to his boat, while under cover of the ruse his men were spiking the guns of Fort Moultrie and slipping across the bay to occupy Fort Sumter.

Peter was assigned the task of ferreting out the truth. He talked with a number of gentlemen who had been present. The consensus of opinion seemed to be that if the Yankees chose to think such a violation of hospitality clever they were welcome, but "By God, sir, Major

Anderson was too much of a gentleman to pretend to be drunk when sober."

As a matter of fact Major Anderson seemed to enjoy a surprising degree of personal popularity among the gentlemen who had entertained him in Charleston. But for some reason Captain Doubleday, his second in command, was everywhere damned as a "Black Republican." And there were those who hinted that it would be unwise for him to venture about the city, so potent was the effect of that label upon the minds of the populace.

It was a time for labels. President Buchanan, confronted by a situation infinitely beyond the scope of his capabilities, and determined to do nothing that would commit the country to either war or peace, became "The Property Man of the United States."

When Anderson had occupied Sumter, the fateful migration across the bay had included a number of women and children, families of the officers. With the failure of Colonel Hayne's mission to Washington came a brief ominous tension. It was evident that the garrison was to remain. If it remained long enough there would be war. It was as simple as that. A man could stand upon the ramparts of Sumter and sweep the horizon with his gaze. Within the compass of his vision lay the stage upon which presently Destiny would make manifest the success or failure of the world's greatest democratic experiment.

It was decided that the women and children must leave the fort at once. A dispatch boat conveyed them across the harbor to the *Marion,* which lay in readiness to transport them North. Scarcely a month ago, these ladies had been intimates in Charleston homes. They had been received with that peculiarly warm and possessive hospitality that the old city, with its military past, always reserved for the service. Now they were bidding their soldier husbands and fathers farewell, and leaving them to their fate.

The ladies of Charleston were tremendously touched. In the spectacle each saw for the first time a prophecy of her own heartbreak. They were extravagantly kind to the voyagers. Negroes with great baskets of waxen petaled camellias followed their mistresses up the gangplank. Proctor Gordon, ruddy and genial, moved about among the ladies, a black boy at his elbow carrying a basket from which protruded the necks of half a dozen of the master's vintage Moët and Chandon.

"Excellent for the mal de mer, Mrs. Adams, and to keep our memory green at least until you reach New York."

"Oh, thank you, major. You'll promise to keep our boys well blockaded, won't you? We aren't afraid of you, you know. But we are terrified at the prospect of leaving them exposed to the fire of Miss Damaris' eyes."

Laughter everywhere. Laughter too bright, too determined, that kept lips from trembling, but died before it reached the eyes.

And at the last, bright-cheeked Northern faces and magnolia-pale faces of Charleston belles, alike dabbed with infinitesimal lace handkerchiefs. "It will soon be over, dear. You must plan to visit us in Newport next summer. We shall never forget." Voices still warm, human, calling across the chasm that was opening before them.

A final blast from the steam whistle. The visitors

troop ashore.   A band of muddy water widens between the feet of the voyagers and the soil of South Carolina. Under a crystal sky a north wind gallops seaward, striking cold white fire from the bay, neighing in the rigging, enveloping the steamer in smoke from her belching funnels, and driving her out towards the blind horizon.

"Good-bye."

"Godspeed."

"Until next summer, then."

CHAPTER VIII

WESTWARD the tide of secession rolled. It had already swept South Carolina, Florida, Georgia, Alabama, Mississippi, and now out in Baton Rouge, the Governor of Louisiana accompanied by his staff in full dress entered the convention hall where the ordinance had just been passed and presented the president with the Pelican Flag of the state. Down to New Orleans then with the booming of a two hundred gun salute, the blaring of bands, and the state rising and following the triumphal procession.

Two thousand miles from home, Pierre Gustave Toutant Beauregard, the pride of New Orleans, major in command of the United States Military Academy at West Point, heard the call of his mother state, resigned his commission, and turned his face South.

In Charleston the hot wire of the Morse Line stuttered out its exciting dots and dashes, and Old Secession caught up the news and smashed it against the eardrums of the populace. A day of celebration. Six states out now! Discipline would be relaxed on the harbor defenses. Visiting would be permitted, and at night most certainly someone would be accorded a serenade by the regimental band.

When the announcement came from Baton Rouge, Peter was starting on a tour of the harbor defenses. It was the sort of routine that he liked. The little steamer would puff from pier to pier, and he would note down such small items of news as the officers in command cared to give him. "Packages for the Palmetto Guard should be left in care of the Wharfinger at Adger's Wharf." "Mail for the Zouave Company should in future be addressed to Headquarters." His function was purely mechanical, and his thoughts were free. He could think of Damaris. He could recreate in his own mind that sense of being utterly alone with her that she could make him feel whenever she looked into his eyes. He could remember the way her braided hair crowned her small bright head.

The *Antelope* had already cast off, and with a huge splashing and snorting had commenced to back her way out of the deep slip, when the salute set the air rocking. Peter guessed its purport and congratulated himself upon his escape from the excited confusion of the streets. There would be talk and cheering at the landings, but there would be quiet intervals while the boat steamed about on her rounds. But the *Antelope* had gone scarcely a hundred yards when a carriage drove furiously to the pierhead and an officer leaped out and signaled for her to return.

Peter was dismayed. He had avoided his old friends and relatives as much as possible since his return. That day at the pier when he had landed they had all been so cordial and affectionate. But their reception of him had been based upon a false premise. He could not speak then. He had been too confused, too disturbed by conflicting emotions. And besides he could not have arrested Cousin Bull-Smith in full career and shouted above the noise, "Oh, but I am not at all sure that I am going to fight." And now, with the passage of weeks, explanations had become more and more difficult.

The little steamer docked and the party trooped aboard. Peter had stayed seated unobtrusively in the stern, hoping that he would remain undiscovered in the shelter of the afterhouse. But in a bright flurry of uniforms, blowing scarfs, ballooning hoops and small talk, they were upon him. There were five in the party. Damaris, Alicia Pringle, René Berrenger and Holcombe, who was escorting them upon a visit to his battery, under the chaperonage of Mrs. Gordon.

"Why, it's Cousin Peter Ashley," exclaimed Alicia. "You don't deserve to be spoken to, sir, after the way you have avoided us since your return. But I suppose we must forgive you if you will promise to mend your ways." She smiled up into his face. Her glance was as clear and bracing as a windy sky. She was not like Damaris. About her there was no ambiguity—mystery, Peter thought, was a better word. Her eyes had depth. You looked straight through them, and when your glance touched bottom you found nobody there but Alicia Pringle herself. An Alicia who was telling you quite candidly exactly what she thought of you.

Damaris gave him her hand and her long isolating scrutiny. He responded to it as he always did with a hot wave that started at his feet and suffused his neck and face with color. She was "Cousin Damaris" now. It had been easy to exhume from a welter of family records a remote mutual ancestor. It was the fashion to "Cousin" anyone you liked, upon the most tenuous grounds. And in this case it lent a touch of protective intimacy to Peter's feeling for the girl.

René greeted Peter in his characteristic drawl. He was frankly glad to see him. He was "acting as a military courier to Governor Pickens." It would do well enough for the present. But when the fighting commenced, no headquarters job for him. And had Peter heard the news from Louisiana?

"Of course he has," Damaris replied for him. "That's the great thing about being on the paper. He hears everything and we get only what he chooses to tell us. It is terribly important work—and so thrilling."

Peter voiced a modest disclaimer. But he was grateful to Damaris. He liked Alicia, too, and René, and Mrs. Gordon was always more than kind. Then he realized for the first time that Holcombe had left the party, and had left it without exchanging greetings with him.

Damaris spoke of it at once, and with a proprietary note towards the man that was vaguely disquieting to Peter. "You mustn't mind Captain Holcombe today," she told him. "He's having one of his moods."

But when they had landed and the captain joined them in his capacity as host, he greeted Peter with an exaggerated and ceremonious politeness. They were honored to receive a representative of the press. The boat would remain half an hour. There would be a champagne punch in honor of Louisiana. He had promised that the ladies should see how a cannon was loaded and fired. Perhaps Mr. Ashley would be interested in the demonstration. The faint mockery of his smile tinged his hospitality with ridicule.

Damaris practically turned her back on Holcombe, and slipping a hand lightly through Peter's arm, said, "I don't think that any of us are interested in that at the

moment, and Cousin Peter will be here such a short time
—we had better just visit the camp so that we can enjoy
his company before he has to leave us."

Holcombe flushed. His slight cynical smile tightened.
"Today Miss Damaris is the officer in command. I am
only her obedient lieutenant." He bowed with exaggerated deference to Peter. "You should feel deeply honored, sir."

"I am more than honored, Captain," Peter replied. "I
am exalted."

The immediate burst of laughter, in which all joined,
showed that everyone had been sensible of the tension
that lay beneath the light interchange. Mrs. Gordon
slipped her hand through the captain's arm. "Come,
Captain," she urged, "we are wasting time. And we are
eager to view the hardships of camp life, that we have
had only in vivid description."

They had reached the first row of tents that sheltered
Holcombe's company, and now paused before the large
one that housed the officers' mess. Against the outer
wall were piled a number of packing cases which contained imported French pâtés, English biscuit, and vintage
wines. Several negroes were busy opening the boxes
and carrying the contents inside. Holcombe lifted the
flap and the party entered.

Around a long table were seated a dozen men, officers
and privates alike. A large punch bowl occupied the
center of the table at which two of the company were
busy with bottles and ladle. Air heavy with warmth
from a glowing stove, tobacco smoke, and the heady
bouquet of rum greeted the guests. Instantly the sol-

diers sprang to attention. Holcombe saluted. Then everyone commenced to laugh and talk at once. A lad in a private's uniform called, "Late again, Archie. We've been waiting for you an hour." Someone else suggested a court-martial.

There was a glitter about them. Holcombe's battery was composed of the faster element among the young gentry. He had drunk and gambled and raced with them. They were his kind. The old life with its petty wagers was already a stale taste in the mouth. Youth, Life, and all of their tomorrows were on the table now. They were all on tiptoe waiting for the word that would launch the ultimate throw of the dice.

Glasses were filled and lifted "to the ladies." The news of Louisiana's secession was announced and cheered. Outside, the word leapt from tent to tent like wind-blown fire. You could hear the cheering sweep eastward along the island—leap the narrow waterway to the next and dwindle away until it met the Atlantic.

Louisiana! Six states now! A Southern Confederacy assured!

Alone again on the *Antelope* and with a moment for retrospection, Peter lost the sense of elation that had come from his hour with Damaris. He could not get the picture of the camp out of his mind. Boys with beautiful bodies and bright gambler's eyes, waiting for the throw of the dice. And there, on his right now, and almost within a stone's throw, Sumter holding the word until all of the stakes were laid. Waiting until the moment when Destiny would call and the game would begin.

CHAPTER IX

RACE WEEK. The words sang like the notes of a hunting horn. The echoes rode the waters of the Ashley and Cooper up into the rice and cotton parishes. They reverberated along the Wando and Stono to the great baronies of the sea islands. On a hundred plantations excited grooms oiled leather, polished brass, greased axles, and burnished sorrel and chestnut flanks. Small black jockeys became infuriatingly self-important. Negro trainers developed into autocrats, and respectfully but firmly told their masters what they could and could not do in the domain of the stables. In the big houses pianos were tinkling "Camptown Races." And in the quarters the negroes turned from the inadequacies of native work songs and spirituals to echo: "Gwine to run all night. Gwine to run all day. I'll bet my money on de bob-tailed nag. Somebody bet on de bay."

Down to Charleston, then, for the great social and sporting week of the year. Roads burdened with a procession of carriages groaning on their leather hangers, and waking to the fast clip-clap of saddle horses, wagons with luggage and racing equipment, the delicate self-conscious stepping of thoroughbreds under gay blankets. Among the sea islands, owners' barges being refitted, and the ten best oarsmen among the negroes triumphantly taking their places for the row to town. The life of the

Low Country running again in its familiar channel. Flinging off a brief, gay valedictory before it submitted to the inevitable interruption of war.

For Race Week was a permanent institution. What if civil conflict was inevitable? War, after all, was only an interlude. Certain definite aspects of life would survive, would be transmitted to sons and daughters as they had been received from fathers and mothers. Last year Exchequer had showed her heels to Congaree. This year Crinoline was in perfect form. Those Doswells of Virginia would have to look well to their laurels. And there was Major Ferguson's Albine to try conclusions with Virginia's famous Planet. It should be an epoch-making year on Carolina turf.

Harmonicas along the road. A band in the distance: "Gwine to run all night. Gwine to run all day." February contributing a week of perfect weather dropped right out of the middle of winter. Sun so warm that jessamine was showing faint yellow tips in the tangles along the way. Cardinals were flickering among the scrub oaks. Greetings and laughter flashed from carriage to carriage. And on the rivers, impromptu races, as the barge of one plantation would overhaul that of some neighbor, and between the rhythmic grunts of the oarsmen taunts and challenges would ring back and forth.

Only occasionally some older squire loping along the sandy road, or some matron in the shadows of a carriage, looking at it all with the faint wistful nostalgia of those who know that all life is mutation. There would be other Race Weeks, of course. But times change. And wars have a way of dislocating old traditions. Their children would doubtless be wealthier after the war, with the incubus of the North flung from their shoulders. There would be finer strains in their stables, and the old records would go down before new and faster mounts. But the old life was the best. And the youngsters would never know it.

The Wakefields carriage swung from the plantation byway into the old state road and headed south toward the city. Someone in the neighborhood was burning brush, and the atmosphere was tinctured with the deliciously pungent smoke. It made the shadows in the pine woods royal purple, and turned the sunlight a warm copper where it fell through the open window upon the folded hands of Emily Ashley.

They were interesting hands—frail, long fingered, and showing not even that first telltale slackening of the skin that one might look for in a woman who had passed her fiftieth year. They lay with fingers interlocked on the blue ladies' cloth of her dress. But in spite of their conventional attitude of idleness, they gave the impression not of repose, but of briefly arrested action. And this note was repeated in the face that lay back upon the cushions under its bonnet of blue quilted silk. The look of bright serenity that she turned upon the life that she shared with Thomas Ashley was gone. Devoid of all expression, and with eyes closed, the face lay with its defenses down, like that of one wrapped in heavy slumber. But here again, as with her hands, the impression that it threw off was one of arrested motion rather than repose. Her maid, Phœbe, was the only living being who had seen her like this, and even now the woman, who sat among bandboxes and valises on the front seat, was staring out of the window, her eyes bright in anticipation of the four days in town. For Emily Ashley it was a moment for retrospection, for counting over the gifts of the gods and estimating the usury that had been exacted of her in return.

She decided that, everything considered, she had triumphed. It had been all so strange and hard at first. But Mr. Ashley had been gentle and kind, and had given her time. She remembered poor Rose Brailsford and the spectacle she had made of herself on her wedding night, running with screams in the dead of night to her mother's room, while the whole house party had rushed upon them thinking the house was on fire. She smiled at the thought and felt very tenderly toward Mr. Ashley. And in the fullness of time she had given him two sons, and had survived to care for them in a community where many of Mr. Ashley's contemporaries were living with their second or third wives.

And Mr. Ashley was always considerate of her wishes. He had never chewed tobacco because she thought the habit revolting. And it was at her solicitation that he had remained clean-shaven. As long as the good God gave her strength to meet the emergency, she would never complain at the magnitude and unexpectedness of his hospitality. If she was called upon to provide for a hunting party of twenty on a half-hour notice, it was as little as she could give in return for such consideration.

She had gone to Wakefields a green city-raised girl, and all of the St. John's belles had laughed at her husband for getting a wife who had never kept a house and knew nothing of plantation management. But within a year, and despite the fact that Wakefields was one of the least well-to-do plantations in the parish, she had learned to hold up her end as well as any of them. Now Mr. Ashley was going to town in a riding suit that she had, with only the help of the plantation seamstress, made from breeches to the embroidered linen shirt. And the fit of the coat over his broad straight back had occasioned favorable comment even among the dandies in town.

That coat had marked the apex of her career. It had proved that Mr. Ashley had been a man of sound judgment as well as one of an impressionable heart. She had justified him. She was content. But then the war had come. Mr. Ashley and Wake working upon each other until they both emerged in a perfect lather of patriotic zeal, and filled with inordinate pride in her accomplishments, had volunteered to organize and uniform a company. It had been one of those magnificent gestures that had survived in the family when the means for their fulfillment had expired with the preceding generation. Mr. Ashley was always making them, and she had to see them through. But the magnitude of this commission staggered her imagination. It was this that she would have to meet when she returned from the excitements and extravagancies of Race Week.

But she was glad of the brief respite. In the round of balls, races, the opera, she would close her mind to the thought of war that was hovering over her days like some bird of prey. And she would see Peter. It was odd how he had shunned Wakefields since his return. And there were tales going about that he was openly Unionist. Strangely, the idea did not fill her with horror. That she should with her own hands fit a uniform upon one of her boys was quite enough to endure for the present. Let Peter wait. There would be time enough later for her youngest.

A short distance behind the carriage rode Thomas Ashley. He was mounted on Starling, a night-black filly with a white star between her eyes. She was swinging along in the slow suave canter that was the favorite gait of the Low Country gentry, a gait that, alternated occasionally with a running walk, could carry a rider on the plantation rounds all day long without exhaustion to either man or mount. Starling had run Two Bitts off her feet last year, and he had fully intended entering her again this season, but for once in his life Thomas Ashley was going to the races dominated by a motive other than that of pride in the performance of the Wakefields stable.

It was imperative that Ashley win a certain sum of money at the meet. Just what that sum would be, he would not know until after his conference with his factor. According to custom, this very practical business was disposed of on the day preceding the opening of the meet. It was the moment of the year most dreaded by the planters, for it opened the door suddenly upon a world of harsh realities. It had a way of taking life which expressed itself in terms of sport, hospitality, industry inspired by the joy of bringing crops to fruition, into terms of marketable produce, cash, credit, and, all too often, summing up the interview with the hideous and blighting word retrenchment.

Against the soft blue distance of the landscape he got a sharp visualization of his factor, Mr. Travers. He had not seen him since he and Wake had called on Governor Pickens and offered to outfit the Berkeley Mounted

Rifles. But he was sure that he knew what they had done. The man knew everything, and besides, the papers had published their application for a charter. Thomas had a vague feeling that his shipments of cotton would not quite meet the advances on the past season. Travers would, of course, be prepared to finance the new crop. He always complained, but he invariably ended with the necessary credits. But cash was a different matter. And Ashley needed cash—an alarming amount of it. Travers would demand assurances that anything that he let him have would go into the land and not into military equipment. Thomas said out loud, "The narrow-minded penny-pincher. He'd skin a flea for its tallow." He knew that this was unjust, but saying it made him feel better.

He chirruped to Starling, and passed the carriage at a smart lope, bowing with formal gallantry to Mrs. Ashley as he came abreast. Well, if luck and his good horse-judgment were with him, he would not have to cut his patriotism to Mr. Travers' measure. He had seen Major Ferguson's mare Albine perform on the Camden track that fall, and he was going to back her with every penny that he had been able to get his hands on. If the mare won the four-mile heat race against Planet, he could equip the company without difficulty and he could laugh at Mr. Travers. If Albine lost—well, he wouldn't dwell upon that. If he did it would lead him to the last alternative of a Low Country gentleman. He would have to sell some of the Wakefields negroes and that was unthinkable. As a matter of fact, while they belonged to him legally, they were actually his only in trust for Wake and Peter.

Peter. He was feeling easier about the boy today. He had broken his strange silence and had written to his mother the day before. He hadn't said a word about enlisting, but he had told them that he had been assigned to report the races. That, at least, was something that a gentleman might do with credit. And Peter should be able to do it well. If he had taught the boy anything at all, it was to know a horse when he saw one. It was this news that had decided him to ride Starling to town for Peter's use. The boy would cut a good figure on the thoroughbred, and even in the crowds he could be depended upon to handle her.

In the anteroom of Mr. Travers' office on East Bay Street sat four gentlemen. The room was bare and none too clean. A large pot-bellied stove maintained an uncomfortably high temperature. The faces of the gentlemen grew red. They slipped fingers inside their collars drawing them away from moist necks. They fidgeted and looked uncommonly like small boys waiting outside the office of the headmaster with a caning in imminent prospect.

Mr. Gilbraith of Normandy Plantation, who sat next to the perspiring form of Thomas Ashley, said in the tense conversational whisper that one employs while a mourner in a house of death, "I suppose you have heard about Colonel VanderHorst?"

Ashley moved his head in negative reply.

"He's given up Travers and gone over to Broughton."

"No!"

"Yes. He says it was a matter of principle with him. He had always refused to meet Travers. Said that it was impossible for two gentlemen to combine a social with a business intercourse. He never came down, you know. Always transacted business by letter. Well, during the Christmas holidays a friend introduced them at a meeting of St. Andrew's. The colonel expressed his pleasure at the meeting and immediately invited Travers to visit and hunt at Green Acres. Travers accepted with alacrity, feeling that he was getting along famously with his client. But immediately, VanderHorst paid up his account, and moved to Broughton."

The three gentlemen listened to the tale with relish.

"Yes," Gilbraith concluded, "VanderHorst now pursues Travers with invitations. Says he is a capital fellow and that one friend is worth a dozen factors."

"An opinion, I take it," Mr. Ashley remarked, "in which Mr. Travers does not agree."

The door of the inner office opened, and the laughter died from four perspiring faces. A shabby elderly clerk approached, pulled his spectacles to the tip of his nose, and over them identified Thomas Ashley.

"Good morning, Mr. Ashley," he said. "Mr. Travers will see you at once."

The planter rose, passed his tongue over his lips and entered the private office.

A half-hour later he returned. As he paused for his hat he cupped his hand over Gilbraith's ear and whispered, "A paltry thousand in cash."

Gilbraith's depressed shake of the head accepted the news as virtual defeat.

"I will see you at the track tomorrow," Ashley said. "Now I am going to look up Colonel VanderHorst and shake him by the hand."

CHAPTER X

PETER awoke Wednesday morning with an unwonted sense of elation. For a moment he lay unquestioning, experiencing the new and sudden freedom from his habitual mood of depression and doubt. Then from the street sounded the rattle of a cart and the rich baritone of the driver: "Gwine to run all night. Gwine to run all day." Then he knew. It was Race Day. It was going to be the day when Peter Ashley would show old Tattenham what could be done with the story of a race. Something definite to do at last. Something that he could put his heart into.

He lay for a moment gloating over the incident that had so changed his fortunes. A week ago Mr. Willington had called him into his sanctum and had told him that their regular racing reporter had enlisted, and that as Tattenham didn't know a trot from a single-foot the assignment was his if he thought he could cover it. Then had followed a glorious week of preparation, memorizing the records of the various entries, looking over the horses as they arrived at the track, talking horse with the trainers and jockeys.

He bounced out of bed, threw on his robe, and called to Cæsar for coffee and the morning paper. There it was. His own words. Yesterday, carefully selected and strung one after another in his penned copy, they had seemed of little significance. Now, thrown back to him with all of the authority of the press, they became somehow credible, important: "The Equine Carnival." The preliminary news. The racing card for the day. Planet, Albine, in the headlines. Then Exchequer, Rosa Bonheur, Ninette, Two Bitts, Repartee, Miss Tobacco-fly. Names to conjure with on the Carolina turf. Outside across the harbor the sun was rising. The water, the lucent air, drenched with warm lemon-colored light. God, what a day for a race!

His glance swept the page again. He couldn't believe that it was the same paper that yesterday, and numberless days before that, had thundered nothing but politics and war at its readers. Life was back in its old channel with a vengeance. "Telegraphic News" held its columns, but in the face of the races, society, entertainments, even that was definitely on the defensive. "Grand opera at the theater." "Messrs. Du Prez and Green's original New Orleans and Metropolitan and Double Minstrel Troupe at Institute Hall. Lovers of Ethiopian minstrelsy have a great treat in store for them. Presented for the first time upon any stage in South Carolina the new songs: Our Flag and Dixie Land." "Stewards of Jockey Club and St. Cecilia Society summoned to attend important meetings."

From below came Chardon's voice urging him to make haste with his dressing, and reminding him that he was to start the day by accompanying his uncle on his round of the hotels. Into his breeches, then. The new ones with the proper Piccadilly flair. Into stock, and smart London boots. Then down the steps two at a time to begin the day that should end with the breaking of a lance on the soiled linen of Mr. Tattenham's superior bosom.

Into the press of the Mills House lobby Peter followed his uncle. He was struck by something odd in the deportment of the older man. Then it came to him that this was the day when Chardon proved to the satisfaction of all—himself included—that, in spite of sundry aristocratic trappings, he had the heart of a democrat. As steward in charge of the public stands, he stood in the capacity of official host to the populace. And, as it is the first obligation of hospitality to infuse a guest with a sense of equality—if not actual superiority—to his host, Chardon was expending his most gracious manner to right and left.

In the midst of the excited crowd he encountered an individual who was obviously a stranger. The man was tall and angular, and stood looking about him in utter bewilderment. Chardon said,

"Permit me to present myself, sir. Pierre Chardon. I take it you are a stranger in our city."

The man looked down his nose at Chardon. He was frankly suspicious of such unexpected civility. When he spoke the reason for his suspicions became evident. His nasal twang marked him at once as a Yankee.

"I only arrived last night," he said. "I calculated to transact a matter of business and leave at once. But I can't get anyone to talk to me. Perhaps you can tell me what the disturbance is about."

Chardon laughed. "Why, my dear sir, of course no one will talk business today. This is Race Week, and all visitors in the city are guests of the Jockey Club."

He drew a ribbon from a bulging side pocket and presented it with a flourish. "I trust you will do us the honor of attending, sir. You will have no difficulty in finding the course. Doubtless by next Monday you will find your friends in their offices and ready to talk business with you." Chardon smiled his bright, annual, democratic smile and passed on to the next prospective guest.

The angular individual stood looking after him. His bewilderment gave place to definite alarm. It was quite evident now that the town had gone mad. But at any rate the inhabitants were apparently harmless and not as dangerous as he had been warned before leaving New York.

Everywhere there was talk, laughter. Wagers were called and taken. In a corner of the lobby a group of young men were gathered about several plantation belles. The St. Cecilia Ball would take place the following night, and there was talk of dances and supper engagements. Two of the men caught sight of Peter—Bert Lawrence and his brother Wake. In a moment they had him in possession, urging him toward the group. They wanted him to meet the others. They wanted to know what he thought of Albine's chances. And would he go to the track with them?

It was a new world for Peter. Or rather, was it not his old world that had been submerged by the alien invasion of war? He was infected by the gaiety, the high spirits of the crowd. But he could not stop with them now. He had to continue in pursuit of his copy. And he was engaged to escort Miss Damaris Gordon to the track. "Ah!" said Wake on a rising, significant note. And Lawrence queried, "Really—unchaperoned?" Then they called him a lucky dog and told him he had better look out for Archie Holcombe, who, rumor had it, was her affianced, and not a man to be trifled with. Then they ended by slapping him warmly between the shoulder blades.

In the court behind the hotel all was confusion. Chardon had preceded him, and Peter repressed a smile as he heard him addressing his tailor as My Dear Sir, instead of My Good Man. Peter finally caught sight of Starling with one of the Wakefields' grooms at her head. From a second story window above the court Thomas and Emily Ashley watched him mount. There was a moment of exhilarating buoyancy as his body rose feather-light on his left stirrup—the soft slap of the Whitman saddle—his right boot finding security on the off stirrup and his knees gripping. Then a spring was released beneath him, lifting his body and flinging it sideways. "Steady, girl. Quiet, now." Then he was waving to the approving faces at the window, and he knew that his seat had not given an inch on the smooth pigskin of the Whitman.

Through the tangle of horses, grooms and riders, Starling picked her way delicately out into the comparative freedom of Queen Street, and Peter headed her south to keep his appointment with Damaris.

At the city limits, Peter and Damaris had no alternative but to leave the quieter streets by which they had traveled and plunge into the tide of vehicles, riders and pedestrians on upper Rutledge Avenue. Progress became slow. There was no attempt to regulate the traffic. It flowed north in a broad established stream, each in-

dividual maintaining his relative position until the flood
finally opened out and washed in a colorful tide over the
broad expanse of the Washington course.

Peter had ample time to study Damaris. To note each
detail of her daring costume. To thrill to a purely
æsthetic delight at the picture she made—a delight that
was impersonal and detached from the vertiginous surge
of emotion that swept him every time the press of the
crowd brought their mounts together and there was a
fleeting contact of knee or shoulder.

She was not wearing the conventional riding habit.
Trust Damaris for that. She was flaunting the first
garibaldi blouse that had appeared in Charleston. Its
daring scarlet note above the severe black of her skirt
and topped by a jockey's hat trimmed with cock feathers
made a costume that few other ladies would have ven-
tured. But it so completely matched her air of irrepres-
sible gaiety that it became somehow an inevitable expression of her personality. The whole effect was one that
challenged and at the same time disarmed criticism.

But when Peter's glance took in her mount, his thoughts
suddenly darkened. That was something about which
he had puzzled and his puzzling had always led to a
doubt. The animal was, he had to concede, the most
beautiful ladies' mount that he had ever seen. Fifteen
hands high, snow white, with one black stocking and a
black star, she was almost a copy of Starling with the
colors reversed. Peter knew that she had been a gift
from Holcombe. Lately Damaris had been so open in
her favor of Peter that, especially when they were together, he was convinced that she had given him her
love. But here was the mare. Damaris, he told him-

self rather proudly, was above the ordinary meaningless conventions that bound the other girls of her set. But this was not a case so much of convention as it was of personal dignity. She may possibly have accepted such a valuable gift from a man to whom she was not betrothed. But that she should continue to keep it, if she was definitely out of love with Holcombe, was something that, Peter assured himself, a nature as fine as hers could not be guilty of. What, then, was the answer? It would be unwelcome in either case. He'd rather just close his mind, forget the horse, and sink back into happy contemplation of the rider.

At the gate of the course the press became terrific. On a vacant lot across the way, a cock fight was in progress. A banner stretched before a tent announced:

> "A Great Main of Cocks.
> South Carolina against Georgia.
> 21 Cocks on a Side.
> $10.00 on each and every fight."

The lot was black with negroes in high excitement at the prospect of enjoying their favorite sport. Most of the house servants would be at the races in the capacity of either maid or groom. But there were the others, the laborers, the great substratum of the city life. They swarmed about refreshment booths. Here and there one would pass with a treasured cock held carefully in the curve of his arm. The air was loud with unrestrained African laughter. Colors seethed, shifting from harmony to discord and back to harmony, as cobalt,

magenta, purple, flamingo, orange touched and parted
with the movement of the crowd.

There was a moment of intense compression as the
crowd surged between the gate posts. Then Peter and
Damaris were free of the jam and cantering over toward the stand. They were a couple to cause comment
among the gentry that had already assembled. The
black mare and the white, the distinguished young
writer about whom there was so much discussion, Damaris Gordon with a new man in tow. And, "Yes, my
dear. It positively is one of those outrageous garibaldi
blouses. Well, I never thought that a Charleston lady—"
"Of course, I'm going right over to speak to her. I can't
wait to have a good look at it." And, "Do you suppose
that Madame La Vargne could make a convincing copy
of it? Not that I, of course——"

Cæsar, with one of his satellites, was waiting to take
their horses. They dismounted and went in search of
the Gordons' party. The grandstand was an imposing
structure. Behind the tiers of seats which formed the
front of the building from basement to roof ran the
grand saloon. This was a sort of foyer, with high slender windows, showing the open country and the silver
band of the Ashley River in the distance. The floor was
richly carpeted, and chairs and settees were arranged in
semicircles before several great fireplaces.

From both ends of the saloon, doors let into the drawing and refreshment rooms. In one of the latter the
Gordons were discovered. Besides the older couple there
were Alicia Pringle and René Berrenger. They were
seated at a small table upon which servants were setting
a luncheon brought on hot plates from the kitchen in

town. A ham, a pair of wild ducks, and a bottle of Proctor's favorite Madeira were already in place. Besides themselves there would be Pierre Chardon, who would join them as soon as he could escape from his duties in the citizens' stand that stood on the other side of the track.

About them everywhere families were settling to their luncheons. And servants, almost as numerous as guests, were thronging the aisles with steaming platters. The races were scheduled to commence at one o'clock, and it was customary for many of the Jockey Club members to lunch on the grounds before going up into the stands or descending to the paddock. At a distance of several feet from the Gordons' table, Peter paused for a final word with Damaris. He touched her arm and she waited, smiling up into his face.

"I hate to leave you," he whispered. "I was wild to do the race, but now it is going to take me away from you. That's different. I wish I could stay—be near you."

"But you'll come back after the race and we'll ride home together. It won't be long," she reminded him.

"It will be an eternity."

She patted his arm lightly. "I like you today, Cousin Peter. You aren't so afraid of being—nice."

The Gordons saw them then, and commenced to beckon and wave. Peter felt a surge of self-confidence. He said: "Remember, no matter whom you see until I return, you still belong to me for the afternoon. You'll promise me that, won't you?"

Her smile deliberately tantalized him. "Yes, for the afternoon."

The parting could be deferred no longer. Peter delivered Damaris into the care of her parents, and pleading duty as his excuse for missing a good luncheon and better company, turned to find his way to the basement.

He paused for a moment at the Ashleys' table. It was typical of his father, he thought, that three of the smaller tables had to be placed end to end to accommodate his party. For a moment it gave him the old boyish feeling of resentment. There had always been this crowd between his parents and himself. It had always stood there, a barrier of sound and movement, barring the way to a real intimacy, a silent communion of spirit, such as he had with his Uncle Pierre. But now as he paused beside his mother's chair and looked down the double row of faces, he experienced a sudden change of feeling.

They were all St. John's Parish folk, neighbors of Wakefields. Seeing them together in the midst of this cosmopolitan assemblage, he realized what a tight little clan they were. Generation succeeding generation in the same surroundings, facing the same problems, old faces fading away at the hunting club dinners, the race meets, their places filled by young faces varying little from the hereditary mold. Cousins marrying each other with shocking regularity, intensifying neighborhood loyalties, welding the whole into something more than merely a neighborhood, endowing it with a common personality that dominated its individual egos, and that looked upon its own with a certain possessive pride that somehow could not be ignored. This was the thing that he felt most strongly as he stood answering their greetings. This solidarity. This possessive interest in him that had remained unaffected by his long absence and even by his failure to visit the plantation since his return.

They greeted him with eager questions about the race. They were to a man, he discovered, backing Albine in the big event. The reason was summed up in Bert Lawrence's explanation: "She belongs to Major Ferguson, you know. And the major is from Lower St. John's." But apparently clan loyalty was reinforced by judgment, as several of them had seen her run in the recent Camden races and were enthusiastic over her performance.

Peter left his kinsmen, promising to meet them later in the lobby, and descended to the basement. He was out of the world of society now, and stepping over the threshold into the strong male atmosphere of sport. The long, low room smelled of leather, spirits from the bar that ran its glittering length along one end, and the faint, not unpleasant, tang of the stable. Groups of gentlemen stood about in animated discussion. From one of these Mr. Lowndes, the president of the Association, looked up, caught Peter's eye and came forward cordially.

"Delighted to welcome you, Ashley," he said. "We are proud to think that the story of the meet is going to be in the hands of one of our own boys, born and bred in the traditions of the Washington track. I suppose you know that it bids fair to be the most distinguished occasion in Jockey Club history? You must come and meet the Doswells, and their delegation of Virginians."

Peter found himself in a group of some twenty gentlemen. The two Doswells formed the center of the group. As the owners of Planet, the undisputed champion of the American turf, their position in the sporting world was preëminent. They welcomed Peter warmly, and wanted to know if he had entered Starling in the two-mile heat. They had seen her run the year before. She would end by making a record.

Then they were at the bar. There was a glass to Planet, and one to Albine. Virginia and South Carolina. Virginia, Peter remembered, had been anathema to the hot-heads no longer ago than the day before yesterday. Next Monday, when the race had become history and the fellowship of the track and paddock broken, she would again be the target for jibes at her tardiness in casting her destinies with the Confederacy. But for this week—no politics, no war. Two score gentlemen from the two great commonwealths, speaking the same language, swearing by the same gods, feet on the same rail, and glasses touching. Eyes that met and seemed to say over the glasses:

"These are the verities. These gestures that express the life that we have brought to full flower; these moments of clean sport, of chivalry out of the past, and by God's help, on down beyond us into the future. Next year—the year after, maybe—Planet, Albine. Today's loser will have the loser's chance to recapture lost laurels. Glasses will go around again. And the horses back in the paddock, pawing furrows in the frosty ground, fit, clean-limbed, and wild to run. Next year perhaps, but oh, certainly, at all events the year after——"

It wanted only ten minutes to one o'clock. In a moment, now, Brown the barber would have his great moment. Dressed in a sort of uniform which he had designed for his official duties, he would sound a long roll on his drum as the signal for saddling.

Peter had respectfully declined the invitation of the officers of the club to occupy a position in their stand. He did not want to view the race from an Olympian height. He wanted to be down where he could feel, touch, breathe it. He had lost his feeling of being watched, of being exterior to the life about him. He had for the moment even forgotten that Damaris was above him in the stands. He was living only in the event.

The power of fusing all his faculties into a single intense receptive sense came to him now in the midst of the crowd. Nothing escaped it. Sunlight in a ripple of gold on a sorrel flank. Brown's red, self-important face. His drum with the sticks caught under one of its thongs. His Excellency Governor Pickens with his staff in full military dress, and the British consuls from Savannah and Charleston as his guests, entering—the stand raising a flurry of cheers as they took their seats. The crash of the band into "Camptown Races."

Peter's mind switched back to the race. Swiftly, logically, he weighed the chances of the contenders. Planet: four years old, by Revenue; dam, Nina. A clean sweep of the country behind him, starting with the New Orleans track and ending in a blaze of glory at the Fashion Course in New York, where he had run away from Congaree and captured the great sweepstakes prize of twenty thousand dollars. The Virginians considered him invincible, and were offering odds. Never had there been so much money on a Washington course race. Tobacco against King Cotton. The stables of the Old Dominion versus those of the Palmetto State.

And Albine: enough of a mystery to draw suspense to the breaking point. The best racing blood of South Carolina. Sired by Jeff Davis of the Medway stables, and for dam, a mare of Colonel Wade Hampton's, by Imp Monarch out of Imp Eliza. Albine had started her career as a stable Cinderella. No one had understood the long-legged chestnut colt. No one had wanted her. Colonel Ferguson, her owner, looked her over, then had her turned out in the pasture. There Samuel G. Stoney, who owned her sire, found her with her tail full of sheep-burrs and offered to give her a try. She had been entered in an event for two-year-olds in 'fifty-nine, and had been so badly beaten that she had been returned to Colonel Ferguson, who in turn presented her to his son, Major Du Gue Ferguson. Major Ferguson laughingly passed the filly along to Major Jack Cantey, who was attempting to revive racing in Camden. Cantey was the first man who took Albine seriously. He borrowed Hercules, a famous negro trainer, from Charles Sinkler of Belvidere Plantation, to get her in condition, and prepared to run her on the Camden track. The ungrateful filly requited him by taking a beating in every event in which she had been entered.

Determined to give her one more trial, she was taken to the Pineville meet, where she repeated her performance. For a month she stood facing oblivion. But Hercules begged for another chance. She was taken to Charleston in 'sixty. And what she would do for no white man she did for old Hercules. At the roll of the drum she lifted her nose out of his horny, gentling palm, gave a soft, confident whinny and romped away with one of the biggest events of the meet. The following

December, just two months before the present race, she had on the Camden track defeated Exchequer, full brother to Planet and probably second only to the champion in speed and reputation.

But now a new element of chance was introduced. Albine had never essayed anything longer than three-mile heats. This race would consist of two successive four-mile heats. The Washington course was notoriously heavy. Planet's forte was distance running. He had never lost a four-mile race. Could the mare stand up under the terrific eight-mile grind and win? Virginia said no, and said it emphatically with fat tobacco bankrolls. South Carolina said yes, closed its eyes to the future, and pledged next season's cotton.

The roll of the drum sounded across the high excited chatter of the stands. The whole area of the course went silent. Voices of the men busy at the saddling sounded out suddenly loud. The weighing had been done under one end of the stand. The jockeys stood ready. Hercules was saddling Albine. His hands were deft, steady. He talked to the mare in an incessant monotone of which no words were distinguishable. Peter saw the Carolina horse now, standing quiet under the voice. He noted the broad hips, the powerful thighs, the strong loin for speed, the deep heavily muscled chest for endurance. She was not built for beauty, except in the sense that a perfectly articulated, highly sensitized, and tremendously powerful living creature is always beautiful. Her rump sloped sharply. She still had the look of a rangy colt about her, in spite of her fifteen hands three inches of height. She was rather short coupled and her legs seemed disproportionately long. Peter thought that she looked rather like Fisherman, the English champion.

She was saddled now, and Bedo, the little negro jockey who had ridden her in every race, was settling himself in the saddle. Hercules handed him the reins. Then he took the soft muzzle in both of his hands, pressed it, then threw it sharply away in the direction of the post. The mare turned and moved into the open. The bright chestnut of her coat caught the sun; a white streak on her face became sharply apparent. Bedo, with his high stirrups, and clad in his red and white silk, looked like a small tenacious monkey squatting on her withers.

Planet was already at the post. Like Albine, he wore a rich chestnut coat. But unlike the mare he was possessed of extraordinary beauty. And he was feeling high in his masculine superiority and his consciousness of racing supremacy. The Doswell colors were orange and orange, and like the Carolina sportsmen they rode their horse with a negro jockey, a small very black boy called Jessie.

Up to this point Albine had exhibited no signs of nervousness. She had gone to the starting post under an easy rein. Her wide, intelligent eyes had taken a survey of the field, then had remained fixed upon the judges' stand. Suddenly she looked at Planet, and commenced to tremble. The starter was preparing to give the signal. In a minute or two they would be off. The trembling increased. The mare did not move her feet. She stood in a tense agony of expectation while spasm after spasm shook her. It was as though suddenly confronted by the champion the realization of her tremendous responsibility had come home to her.

Immediately behind Peter, Tom Doswell and Major Cantey were standing together. They were old friends, and the fact that their stables were in constant rivalry had strengthened rather than diminished the bond between them. They looked at Albine's distress.

Doswell spoke impulsively: "Too bad, Jack. We shouldn't have let you enter her. Planet doesn't need this race. We could have given you a chance with one of the other horses."

"Thanks, Tom," Cantey replied, dryly. "We're not asking quarter yet." Then after a moment, "By the way, what are your jockey's orders?"

"A killing pace from the start. Planet can hold it. He'll run Albine off her feet in the third mile."

"That's interesting, at any rate. Bedo's instructions are for a waiting race until the third."

Peter was so intent upon this conversation that his gaze had wandered from the starting post. Now a sudden cheer from the stands jerked him sharply to attention. The horses were off, and were almost immediately abreast of where he stood. Planet had already settled into his long invincible stride. He crossed Peter's vision in a blur of orange and chestnut. Then the impression sharpened to details. The jockey was virtually letting the horse run his own race. It was sport reduced to mathematics. Planet, even on that heavy track, would better eight minutes for the heat. And eight minutes, according to the calculations of the Virginians, would provide an ample margin.

Peter's gaze dropped from the horse and picked up the mare. She was still nervous. Her rhythm was interrupted. She had not yet found herself. According to instructions, Bedo was riding her under a strong pull. She was already a length behind Planet, and clods from her rival's spurning hooves were worrying her. One caught the little jockey in the face. He wiped it on his sleeve and his teeth flashed out a short white accent as he passed.

Tom Doswell's voice said, "Tch, tch. Too bad."

And Cantey replied laconically, "She'll steady."

Then the increasing distance absorbed details. All that one could see was chestnut and orange trailed by chestnut and red, the distance remaining a length. They passed the citizens' stand across the course. Massed humanity rose automatically—cheered—subsided.

Now they were in the stretch, pounding down upon the stand on their first complete circuit of the course. If Albine had got herself in hand now, there would be a chance for South Carolina. Then they were passing Peter, and the sight was reassuring. One could not tell whether Planet was giving his best. Of course, all depended on that. But Albine was holding her spot behind him, not varying the distance by an inch, and doing it under a strong pull. And now she was performing beautifully. Her nervousness had disappeared. Her stride was long, free, perfectly coördinated.

The race had entered upon its second phase. In a four-mile heat it was impossible for either watchers or participants to maintain the agonizing tension of a short event. This was no tour de force. It was a protracted engagement. Tactics played a part as well as speed. The race would be run at this level for a number of circuits of the track, then as the finish loomed ahead the final test of speed and even more of endurance would determine the winner.

Peter was glad now that he had followed his impulse to remain beside the track instead of joining the officers in their stand, even though the elevation would have given him a better view of the distance running. He turned now and joined the small group of which Cantey, the two Doswells, and Major Ferguson were the center. Hercules was there beside Major Cantey. He seemed the least excited member of the party. He was cleaning the stem of a blackened clay pipe with a bit of straw.

Tom Doswell said: "Well, Herc, you don't seem much worried about the race."

The trainer looked up from his task. "I ain't gots no 'casion tuh be, boss."

"You think she'll win, eh?"

"I knows it, boss. Albine done tol' me so."

Everybody laughed except Hercules. He gave them a surprised look and then returned seriously to his pipe. He was counting off the laps on his fingers, and as they closed one by one into a fist his work became difficult. Finally he gave it up and placed the pipe between strong white teeth from which the lips were drawn in a tight muscular grin.

Peter felt a hand on his shoulder and turned to look into the face of Thomas Ashley. He was instantly struck by the older man's pallor, and by the slight unsteadiness of his voice as he asked: "What do you think of her chances, son?"

"There won't be even a guess, sir, until the third mile; but we're almost there." Then after a moment, tentatively, "In deep, sir?"

"To the hilt, boy."

Major Cantey turned to the trainer. "Where are we now, Herc?"

"Beginnin' on the third, suh. Now's de time." He left the group and leaned forward, elbows on the rail.

Down the course, the horses swung the curve and swept up toward the stand. A wave of cheering met them. The monotonous grind of the first and second miles was over. The crowd surged to its feet. At the rail the group of rival sportsmen stood with blank, noncommittal gamesters' faces, but with bodies fixed in a revealing tension, hands gripping, knuckles showing white.

But on the track the tempo remained unchanged. Planet passed, holding his position without apparent effort. Albine trailed him by a length, still under a strong pull.

Behind Peter a voice said loudly, "God damn a four-mile heat. Give me a short race with an end to it." The watchers at the rail barked out a short answering laugh, one voice keeping it up to the edge of hysteria after the others had closed.

Cantey's voice cut the silence sharply. "Herc."

"Yas, boss."

"Last quarter of the third."

The horses were around again. Peter was standing beside the trainer. He got a sudden electric impression that the man was actually in communication with Bedo and the mare. That he had projected from himself some obscure directing force that assumed command of the hurtling nerve and sinew of horse and rider. Albine seemed to draw out. Her short-coupled ungainly height gave the impression of flowing down, assuming the horizontal. Her reach became enormous. Bedo gave her the reins and swung forward to her withers. In a flash she was running nose and nose with Planet. The Virginia jockey applied spur and whip. Red and white merged with orange, and the two racers thundered abreast down the course. For the last quarter of the third they held their places, then at the lap that signified the beginning of the fourth, Bedo suddenly pulled the mare back to her old position a length behind the horse.

Someone said, "There! I told you she couldn't hold it."

"Nonsense! The boy was just testing her. He'll save her now for the finish."

The horses were passing the stand. A cheer lifted— hung fire—changed to a sort of composite groan. The group at the rail leaned far into the track. Both horses were coming. Then they saw Albine was switching her tail up and down in the unmistakable signal of distress.

Tom Doswell said impulsively, "By God, Jack, I'm sorry. She put up such a magnificent fight."

Major Cantey smiled a secret smile. "You needn't send flowers yet, Tom."

One of the Virginians who happened to be near Thomas Ashley turned to him and challenged: "A thousand dollars to a hundred on the horse for this heat."

Ashley's pallor gave place to a heavy flush. He repeated the odds, and the Virginian nodded.

Then in the moment of acceptance Thomas Ashley hesitated. The Virginian stood looking at him with a slight sardonic smile, as though questioning the Carolinian's sportsmanship.

Ashley said: "I can't take your money, sir, without

acquainting you with the facts. I have seen Albine switch her tail before, and finish strong."

The sardonic smile deepened, and the pleasant voice drawled: "That's very generous of you, sir, but my offer stands. However, if you're not backing the mare——"

Ashley cut him short with, "Taken."

The horses were in the stretch again. Albine was still holding her spot a length behind Planet. They were entering the third quarter of the fourth mile. But the monotony of their relative positions had now given place to intense drama. Albine continued to switch her tail, and she was sweating freely, while Planet exhibited not the slightest sign of fatigue. His magnificently muscled body continued its perfectly disciplined performance. His long, springy stride kept hurling the track behind him. Neither he, his rider, nor the Doswells standing beside the rail, seemed concerned at Albine's short burst of speed that had carried her abreast in the third. It was obvious to them that the mare was breaking down in the fourth mile, according to predictions.

A lad in uniform broke through the group. Peter recognized him. His name was Colfelt and he was a lieutenant in Holcombe's company. He seized Major Cantey by the arm and cried in a hysterical voice, "For God's sake, major, make your boy turn her loose. Can't you see if she's got any run in her she's got to give it now or it will be too late?"

Cantey turned and smiled understandingly into the boy's face. He detached the tense fingers from his arm. "Hold your horses, Harry," he cautioned gently, then he turned the boy around and gave him a slight shove.

Holcombe strode through the crowd and took charge

of the lad. "You'll have to forgive him, major," he said. "He'll apologize later."

Cantey went and stood beside Hercules, who had remained leaning without motion upon the rail. The horses were in the stretch. It was the beginning of the last quarter of the fourth. Hercules leaned far out over the rail. Peter saw Planet hurtle past. Then he got again the odd impression that Hercules was in communication with Bedo and the mare. He saw the reins go slack, and the little negro swing forward to the withers.

And then he saw what can be done by sheer nervous energy that has been compressed to the verge of an explosion then suddenly released. The mare shot toward the inner rail, securing her position in a single bound. She flattened to the track. The red and white of Bedo's silk jerked past the Doswell orange, and working like a pump to the pounding rhythm of Albine's stride, dwindled down the perspective of the track.

Planet's surprised start was caught abruptly by spur and whip, and he burst out of his routine into hot pursuit.

On the next lap it looked for a brief moment as though he might close in, but Albine was running now like a creature possessed. Gradually Planet dropped back. As they turned into the final stretch it was evident that the race was won. The stands were a bedlam of demented humanity. Albine was leading by five lengths with the finish a split second away. As Albine crossed the line, Planet stopped with a suddenness that nearly unseated his jockey. And the mare thundered in alone for a record of seven minutes thirty-six and a half seconds.

The mare was instantly surrounded by a shouting crowd. Hercules fought them savagely back, and led his charge away for a brief rest before she would have to go into the final heat.

But Planet was a sight to remember. Having scorned to finish second, he came up the stretch to his owners, stepping high under a slack rein. He passed the whooping, cheering stand, the blaring band—the embodiment of regal arrogance. His manner patronized the judges. He deigned a condescending toss of his magnificent head to Governor Pickens and his staff. Then he stepped to the rail where his masters stood and thrust his muzzle over the barrier between them.

Tom Doswell stood looking at him a moment, then in a voice that shook a little under rueful laughter, he said: "Well, old man, you carried it off like a gentleman, anyway, didn't you?"

CHAPTER XI

DURING the brief rest, the crowds flocked into the lobby beneath the stand. Much of the independent betting had been on the first half of the event, each heat being considered as a separate race. And now with money in their pockets and flushed with victory, the Carolinians would have been willing to offer odds on the second heat. But so sure were the visitors that Albine had blown herself out in her spectacular finish, that they were free in offering even money.

Peter went at once in search of his father. With the excitement of the race over, there came into his mind the memory of Ashley's face as he had seen it last. His father had never been a gambler, always backing even his own horses conservatively. Winning had meant a gay season at Wakefields; losing, less entertainment at home, and more under the roofs of luckier neighbors.

He found his father surrounded by a group of jubilant kinsmen. Local loyalty, it seemed, had paid handsome dividends. Now that the ordeal was over, Ashley had told the younger men how much had been at stake. Funds for the company were in hand. There would be Enfield rifles like those in Holcombe's organization, and cloth for uniforms from the stores in town. Nothing short of champagne would do justice to the occasion.

As Peter approached, Wake, Bert Lawrence, Charles Gilbraith and half a dozen others of his own age spied him, dragged him into the circle, thrust a glass into his hand, and told him the news in an incoherent chorus.

"Damn it all, Pete," Wake exclaimed with his face shining, "you've got to quit this damn Yankee business and come with us." The others laughed delightedly.

Peter could not help joining in. Their refusal to take his scruples seriously made them in that atmosphere of infectious high spirits seem a little ridiculous. But the imminence of the second heat brought their attention back to the race.

Peter was amused to see how entirely they considered the business of one of their group a communal affair. Ashley made a hasty calculation.

"Pocket half of it," Wake suggested, "and bet the rest. If Virginia isn't going to fight, she might as well give us tents and blankets as well as uniforms and rifles."

The suggestion met with unanimous agreement. And Ashley went in search of the visiting sportsmen.

Peter Brown appeared before the official box. He stood looking as though he were inflating himself. The buttons of his coat seemed to strain across his chest. He tightened the head of his drum. Then he sounded a long roll with a flourish on the end of it.

The crowds flowed out of the lobby and paddock, back to the track-side. Presently the horses appeared. Albine looked fit after her rub-down. If she was blown she showed no evidence of it. Planet led the way to the post. He still had the air of a conquering hero, and the stand gave him a generous round of applause as he passed. But it rocked the building for Albine.

The mare's victory in the first heat had given her confidence. She showed no evidence of nervousness at the

start. The behavior of the two while waiting for the
signal was typically masculine and feminine. Planet was
superbly arrogant, and regarded his rival with a super-
cilious air. Albine exhibited a deceptive submissiveness,
and once she extended her nose toward the horse and
whickered in a soft ingratiating manner.

They got away to a perfect start. And the stand rose
in a bright pattern of color as they passed. Peter saw
Damaris, a jewel in the matrix of the crowd. She was
standing beside Holcombe and was waving a crop that
flaunted the Carolina colors. Peter was so engrossed with
the race that for a moment he was conscious of her only
through his emotions. She penetrated his excited preoccupation like the thrust of a bright blade. It turned in
his mind sharply. Then he became cognizant of Holcombe and knew why the sight had pained him. Almost
instantly he was drawn back to the race. His father had
come up and was saying, "Major Cantey has been asking
for you. He and Mr. Doswell. They'll have some interesting news for you."

Damaris and Holcombe left his consciousness then. It
was like the slow withdrawal of a knife from a wound,
leaving him free but with a rankling hurt. He joined
the gentlemen who were standing at the rail. Major
Cantey told him that they were running the second heat
as they had the first, with Planet as pacemaker and Albine saving herself for the finish. The Virginians were
confident that the mare could not stand the terrific pace
for eight miles. That she would go under before the
finish of the second heat. Peter thought that the confidence of the Carolinians rang a little hollow as they
asserted their faith in the staying power of the mare.

But when the last quarter of the third arrived, Albine managed to pull abreast of Planet, and to hold her position for a lap. Then Bedo pulled her down, and the crowd waited in tense excitement for the final quarter of the fourth. At last the moment arrived. Albine was lathered, and it seemed to Peter that as she approached, the jockey no longer had her under a tight pull; that she was still her length behind Planet, and was spending herself freely.

Hercules was standing near him, leaning far over the rail. He saw the negro's face as the mare came up. The jaw was a hard line, the lips compressed, the eyes narrow slits under lowered lids. When the mare took the bit and shot forward he had a recurrence of the odd impression that the propulsive force had emanated from the man at his side.

The crowds leapt to their feet. The shouting was a curtain of sound dropped between Peter and the racing horses. Their hooves were feathers brushing a padded track.

Major Cantey stood with a stop watch in his hand. Under the roar of voices Peter heard him ejaculate: "Great God, the last mile in less than two minutes!"

They came home like hurled lances with flapping pennants of orange, and red and white. Both entries finished strong, with Albine five lengths in the lead. Time for the second heat: seven minutes forty-two and a half seconds.

A basket of champagne in Albine's stable! Hercules had ordered it. He had won enough money to pay the bill. But Hercules could pay for nothing under the sun that day. He went among the gentlemen who were standing about the mare, touching his cap and handing them glasses of wine. He told everybody that God could have his soul any time now. He had lived to see Albine beat old John Planet.

The race had taken complete possession of Peter's imagination. It kept repeating itself in his mind in vivid flashes. His fingers twitched with eagerness to get at his story. Behind it, like a cloud along the horizon of his mind, there was a sense of something important left undone. He made a conscious effort to think clearly, to rid himself of the feeling. The drum rolling out the signal to saddle for the second race brought a moment of almost complete demoralization. With a tremendous effort he collected his faculties and brought them to bear on the impending event. Mechanically he jotted down the entries, weights, colors.

The Hutchinson stakes for three-year-olds was always a popular feature. But now, under the shadow of the great Albine triumph, it was a predestined anticlimax. Then, too, the favorite was an "up country" horse, Rosa Bonheur, belonging to the stable of Tom Puryear of Columbia. However, the race was soon over, the favorite proving an easy winner in both of the one-mile heats. Peter jotted down the time, closed his notebook and slipped it in his pocket.

Instantly his thoughts turned to the major event. He was seized by an overwhelming urge to write. Sentences commenced to form themselves in his mind. He was in a state akin to intoxication. His thoughts were possessed by a fixed idea upon which they kept building and elaborating. His body without conscious guidance proceeded toward the stables. He found Cæsar, and called for Starling. While a boy was saddling, the negro stood looking at Peter uneasily, and when he handed him the reins he asked: "Yo' sho' yo' is all right, Mas' Peter?"

That brought him up for a moment. His smile was vague, preoccupied. "I'm not drunk, if that's what you mean, Cæsar." Then he turned Starling toward the gate and lifted her into a smart canter.

He had proceeded a dozen lengths when an idea struck Cæsar. He called loudly, "Mas' Peter—oh, Mas' Peter!" There was no response. The distance widened. Cæsar turned to the stable boy who was standing near him with his mouth hanging open.

"Great Gawd, boy," he ejaculated, "Mas' Peter done gone off an' forgot he lady."

CHAPTER XII

THE crowds had not yet commenced to disperse and the road to town was open. Starling had been tied up for hours, tantalized by the sights and sounds of the track, listening to the flying hoofbeats of more favored horses. Now, with a clear road before her, it took a steady hand to hold her. It kept Peter's faculties on the alert, but beneath their constant play, his mind hung tenaciously to his story.

He knew now how he would attack it. He had studied previous accounts. Through annual repetitions the paper had fallen into certain stock phrases, the continued use of which had established what was virtually a convention. "The Equine Carnival."—Rot! It was a horse race. It had been handled as an adjunct to a week of society, instead of being accorded its proper place as one of the great sporting events of the country. "Elegant," "recherché," "Haute Société"—all very well for a St. Cecilia Ball, an opening night of grand opera; but they were petticoat words; they could not express the strong male life of the paddock, the trampling of hooves in the stalls, the small black jockeys. And Hercules. The bond that united the negro trainer and the victorious Albine. What had "Haute Société" to do with the racing history that had been made on the Washington track that afternoon? If he expected to make people see the race, feel it as he had done, he'd have to step out of all of

156

that into a vocabulary that had the smell of the paddock and not the perfume of the boudoir.

Starling's hooves had ceased to thud in the unpaved road. They dropped into a single-foot, and rolled like the music of a kettledrum on the cobbles of upper East Bay. Then they were slowing down before the marble front of the *Courier*.

Peter hitched the filly in the small untidy yard, and left her pawing disdainfully in a litter of soiled print paper. With the exception of a biscuit or two at the bar, Peter had eaten nothing all day. But he had consumed rather more than enough champagne. His body felt ridiculously buoyant as he bounded up the steps, down the corridor, and to his desk. The office was empty. It would be several hours before Mr. Tattenham would return, and Peter thanked God devoutly. He seated himself, filled his pipe and lighted it. The habitual gesture brought him back to reality for a moment. He was assailed by the annoying presentiment that there was a loose end somewhere in his day. That there was something that he had left undone. He felt it weakening his hold on the race, and resolutely closed his mind to it. Before him lay a sheaf of clean white foolscap. Like a man lost and starving who at last finds himself at home before a laden table, he reached greedily for it, and picked up his pen.

Tattenham was leaning back in his chair, his feet on the desk. He folded his mustache back from his upper lip with the tips of his fourth and middle fingers. Then he smote the bull's-eye of a large brass spittoon with an expert discharge. Peter had noticed that he always got an odious satisfaction from his marksmanship, each bull's-eye being the occasion for a minor triumph. Now he looked up and said: "Where are you going with that, Ashley?"

"I was carrying it to the printer, sir. It's late, and I thought I'd better get it in."

His senior brought his chair down to its four feet, and extended a soiled hand across the desk. "I'll take charge of it," he said, then added fretfully, "I've been waiting an hour for you to finish." He took the sheaf of papers from Peter's hand. "You needn't wait," he told him. "I'll look this over and put it through."

Peter felt light-headed, dizzy. He couldn't think. Inside of him there was only a great vacuum that hummed, and made it hard to hear and understand. He stood without moving, regarding Tattenham with fascinated horror. The older man's left hand took one of his drooping mustaches between thumb and forefinger and commenced to twirl it slowly, absent-mindedly. His right hand pursued its familiar route to the blue pencil that lay beside the inkwell. Under the mustache a slow, amused smile flickered. Then he drew a bold blue line through the opening words of Peter's story.

Peter leaned forward, his hands gripping his side of the desk. His face was white, and his eyes blazing. To the older man he looked very big, and, perhaps because of a slight uncontrollable tremor of the lip, very young— and yet somehow old. As old as all of the Ashleys—all of the Chardons. It was this feeling that added a peculiar relish to Mr. Tattenham's task. This realization that in humbling Peter he was demonstrating the intellectual superiority of his class to that of the aristocracy.

Peter said, "If you put your damned hands on that story, Mr. Tattenham, sir, you can go to Mr. Willington and tell him that I have resigned, and you can tell him why."

Tattenham did not raise his glance. The fingers that caressed his mustache paused a moment, then slid on to complete the slow sensuous twirl at the end. The pencil point descended, moved across the paper, left an obliterating trail. Peter turned on his heel and strode out of the office.

In the street he was oblivious of the beauty of the cool, far stars, the harbor lying quiescent under the midnight sky. He stormed furiously along until he was nearly home, then he remembered Starling. He retraced his steps and got the filly. Then, as the kitchen wing was shrouded in darkness, he unsaddled and fed her himself rather than call Cæsar.

In the house, he realized that he was famished. It was while he was sitting in the pantry with a turkey leg in one hand and a shortbread in the other that the presentiment that had been dogging the steps of his thoughts all afternoon overtook him. He paled suddenly.

"Great God," he said aloud, "Damaris! Will she ever let me speak to her again!"

Peter slept little that night. What would Damaris think? That he had been drunk, of course. Perhaps, after all, that would be best. It would certainly be more forgivable, more understandable, than—the truth. That he could have forgotten her, and have calmly ridden away without so much as an apology was something that he could never explain. He could not plead his work as an excuse. That had been taken into account when they had planned the day. It had been arranged that he should join her party after the races and escort her home. This would have left ample time for him to go to the office and get his copy in before midnight. The fact that his last impression of her was that fleeting glimpse in the stand with Holcombe in attendance added appreciably to his alarm.

Toward morning he sank into a troubled sleep, and dreamed that Tattenham was taking Damaris to wife. Hercules was performing an interminable marriage ceremony in which the words "Equine Carnival," "elegant" and "recherché" were constantly reiterated. When he attempted to interrupt, Holcombe with his company in full parade dress appeared before the church door and charged him with fixed bayonets. He awoke with his body drenched in sweat and his heart thudding.

It was several minutes before his life resumed its continuity. He was aware of the exact moment when it lifted him from inertia and commenced to carry him forward. It was inevitable that he should rise, cross the room in the early chill and call to Cæsar for the morning paper.

When he had it he stood with it gripped in both hands behind his back, staring out of the window until Cæsar had kindled his fire, placed his hip-tub before it, and retired. Then he turned, spread it out with deliberation and read. He had known instinctively what he would find. The opening paragraph confirmed this. It was not his story at all. The thing that he had created, in travail of body and spirit, lay before him now a corpse grotesque in its mutilation.

He read it half through, then crushed the paper in his two hands and flung it into the fire. The flame howled in the chimney's throat. A black, lacy fragment whirled in the draft and settled on the hearth. Against the charred background the print showed ash gray. The word "equine" stared up at Peter. He ground it under his heel. That was over—done with. Mr. Tattenham could report today's race himself. It was an unimportant event. Given a pair of shears, a glue pot, a last year's paper and the new names and time, and the job would be simplicity itself. Eventually, Peter reflected, he'd have to call on Mr. Willington and thank him for his past kindness, but not today. The amenities would have to wait until he could explain calmly, unemotionally, just what the violation of his story had meant to him. And besides, now he must face the situation that had arisen through his desertion of Damaris. He must see her at the earliest possible moment and beg her forgiveness.

She had given him the supper engagement for the St. Cecilia Ball that would take place at the St. Andrew's Hall tonight. Peter knew that Holcombe had asked her too, as well as several others. He knew the significance of her choice. This was the final ball of the season, and it was a tradition that supper should be given to the most favored suitor. In fact, it was a rare final ball that did not see the announcement of at least one engagement among the younger set. Yesterday the knowledge of his good fortune had been one of the factors that had contributed to the self-confidence that had made him equal to the opportunities of his assignment. Now his story was gone, and he was tortured by the fear that he was losing Damaris as well.

But he was daunted by the prospect of venturing on the street and meeting friends and acquaintances. They would have read the papers. They knew that he had been assigned to write the race. You could not say: "My story was done to death. I am not responsible for what you have read." You could only hold your tongue, and take it standing up. Finally, however, he managed to overcome his morbid dread of an encounter, and repaired without misadventure to the Gordon residence, only when he arrived to be told by the butler that Miss Damaris was not at home. She had gone early to the Washington course and would not return until evening.

For a moment Peter seriously debated the question of saddling Starling, riding to the track, and having an end of the suspense. But, back at home, the prospect of meeting his father, Major Cantey, the Doswells, again was too overwhelming. Chardon had gone, punctilious as ever in his attentions to his public stands. Peter had the house to himself. The day was a long agony of frustration and suspense.

When evening came, Peter dressed with elaborate care, and thanking Providence for the early dark, returned to the Gordons'. The house was dark, he noticed, only the fanlight over the door showing a faint half-moon of illumination. The butler responded to his knock with a promptness suggesting that he had been waiting to discharge this single duty before taking his evening off. In answer to Peter's hesitant inquiry he imparted the information that the Gordons were at supper with the Pringles, with whom they would later go to the ball. Miss Damaris had left word that as she presumed that

Mr. Ashley was indisposed, she had given her supper engagement to Captain Holcombe.

Peter did not return home at once. For an indeterminate time he tramped the crushed shell walks of White Point Gardens, trying to convince himself that Damaris had meant only what her message had said, and not the note of finality that a reading between the lines implied. That this difficulty should have arisen at this particular and crucial moment in their relationship struck him as a deliberate blow of fate.

The preceding day, in their brief intimate interchange just before he had delivered her to her parents, he had, he felt, come as close to an avowal as was proper without having declared his intentions to Mr. Gordon. After the ball tonight, he would have asked that gentleman's permission to address his daughter, and tomorrow perhaps, if all had gone well, his future would have been settled. He would have held Damaris in his arms. He would have known her kisses. With her, proving her belief in him, sharing his aspirations, he could have endured anything, even the pitying, tactful cozening of his relatives and friends, that reminded him at times of the treatment accorded the mildly insane, and that he would willingly have exchanged for a forthright attack that could be met and answered.

Now he wondered miserably if she would ever let him see her again; if, after all, she might not be in love with Holcombe.

CHAPTER XIII

WHEN he reached home he found that Chardon had dressed and gone to the ball. He poured himself a pony of brandy, and tried to settle down in the library with a book, but a fever of unrest seized him. He changed his clothes and went out again. He reached Broad Street. From the direction of St. Andrew's Hall came the high, sweet crying of fiddles. He flinched from the sound as from a blow, and took his way up Meeting Street.

Secession Hall was a blaze of light. He could hear a voice talking inside. Laughter. Then the "Oompah, oompah," of a minstrel band. He remembered then that the New Orleans troupe was playing a week's engagement. Driven by a desperate need of escape from his thoughts, Peter crossed the street, purchased a ticket and entered.

Inside the great hall that had so recently seen the signing of the Ordinance, that essentially American institution—the Minstrel Show, was in full blast. Behind their burnt cork, Bones and Tambo were lampooning President Buchanan, the "Property Man." Their broad obvious humor kept the crowd in a roar of laughter.

The scene changed to a conventional plantation set. Behind a fringe of rigid cotton bushes, and against a distant background of lofty porticos and cupolas, an ancient negro tottered forward and sang Foster's latest

slave ballad, "Old Black Joe." From the wings the
"gentle voices" called him in a close harmony that
seemed to move the audience as profoundly as it did the
decrepit black.

As the song neared its conclusion and the invisible
chorus became more insistent in its invitation, Peter saw
tears in the eyes of many who were seated near him. It
drew him out of himself. His own despondency seemed
to lessen in the general and pervading sadness. He began
to feel a sense of kinship with the audience. From where
he sat there was not a familiar face in sight. Then he
remembered that all of his acquaintances would be at
the ball. This audience was composed of the great middle class, the people who, in the final analysis, would
determine by their attitude the success or failure of the
impending conflict.

He was glad that there was no one to recognize him,
and he found himself wondering if, in the crowd, there
were not others like himself who still hesitated, still wondered about it all. It was easy to see why his own people
were bitterly partisan. They had everything at stake.
But these citizens, the shopkeepers, artisans, small
farmers. He supposed that scarcely any of them owned
slaves beyond, perhaps, a domestic servant here and there.
Their lives in a victorious South would differ very little
from an existence under the Stars and Stripes. What
then, he asked himself, had they to go out and die for?
Certainly not a democratic ideal. With the plantation
gentry in the saddle and determined to out-England the
mother country in class exclusiveness, not even the most
deluded could cling to that motive. And yet already
there were the Irish Volunteers, the German Fusiliers,

in uniform. And other companies had been granted
charters by the state.

Through an hour of boisterous humor and heart-
rending balladry he followed the moods of the crowd;
and then, as the grand finale approached, he began to
feel a growing excitement in the air. It was something
quite different from the facile emotionalism that had prevailed. Beside him a large blond woman was sitting.
She turned to Peter and said in a strong German accent,
"Now they vill sing it—that song." Her man, sitting in
the seat beyond, leaned forward. His large, florid face
glowed with good fellowship. "You vait," he whispered.
"Ve haf already heard it vonce. It make you feel—"
He raised both hands, palms up, in an eloquent gesture.

On the stage the last gag had been sprung. The two
blackface comedians withdrew to right and left. The
curtains parted and lifted. The gas footlights, augmented
by calcium burners in the wings, flooded the stage with
intense light. High against the rear wall the gorgeously
uniformed band sat beneath the emblazoned shields of
the seven seceded states. Below the band the chorus was
massed, and, sitting cross-legged on the floor before the
singers, six banjoists in black-face were ranged with their
instruments ready. From the wings stepped a large man
in black make-up. He advanced to the center of the
stage, bowed formally, and in a magnificent baritone
voice began:

>   "I wish I was in de land ob cotton,
>   Old times dar am not forgotten,"

Then, with the banjos joining in:

"Look away, look away, look away, Dixie Land."

"In Dixie Land whar I was born in,
   Early on one frosty mornin'——"

And again the banjos:

"Look away, look away, look away, Dixie Land."

Then the chorus with the singers only joining in:

"And I wish I was in Dixie, Hoorah! Hoorah!
   In Dixie Land, I'll take my stand
   To lib and die in Dixie,
   Away, away, away down South in Dixie,
   Away, away, away down South in Dixie."

Then the second verse, in the deep swelling baritone:

"Old Missis marry Will de Weaber,
   Willium was a gay deceiber—
   Look away, look away, look away, Dixie Land."

Peter, listening intently, and not yet swept out of himself by the music, was conscious of a remarkable phenom-
enon. The ridiculous words of the song, written as they
were in the broad burlesque of the minstrel tradition,
were not getting a laugh. On the contrary, the audience
sat in a tense portentous silence, leaning forward in their
seats, their eyes riveted on the singer. When the second
chorus came, this time by both the singers and the band,

they commenced to sway in unison. The German couple next to Peter were humming the refrain. Feet were commencing to tap in time to the music.

> "But when he put his arm around 'er
> He smiled as fierce as a forty pounder,
> Look away, look away, look away, Dixie Land."

The chorus this time was given once with the performers all seated, and some of the bolder voices in the audience singing with them. Then the full troupe rose and reprised the refrain.

Lifted by a common impulse the audience leaped to its feet. A cheer was raised, but was instantly drowned by the stirring music in which three thousand throats in the auditorium vied with the performers for supremacy:

> "In Dixie Land I'll take my stand
> To lib and die in Dixie,
> Away, away, away down South in Dixie."

The show was over, but the audience would not allow it to stop. They kept the curtain up for fifteen minutes longer while the band blared and the people shouted "Dixie." Then, carrying the song with them like a torch to sweep the city with its flame, they surged out into the street.

About the exit the crowd was packed densely. Rubbing shoulders with Peter, as the mass moved forward, was a man of about his own size in a private's uniform. Peter thought that there was something vaguely familiar about him. But the stiff flat visor of his cap threw his face into shadow, and his mouth was puckered to whistle the already familiar refrain. The man turned and looked into his face. It was Dennis Callaghan. He was something or other in the printing department of the paper. Peter remembered having handed him copy occasionally when he was leaving for the night.

The man stopped whistling and regarded him with surprise. "Why, hello," he exclaimed, "Whatever are you doing here, Mr. Ashley?"

"Just what you are, I suppose; enjoying a good show."

"But the ball—I'd have thought you'd be there along with the rest of 'em. Or else down at the office."

"I'm through with the paper." Peter was glad, at last, to put it into words. He made it more emphatic: "I'm out for good. Thank God!"

Under the visor Callaghan's eyes twinkled. "Got your bellyfull of old Tatters, eh?"

Peter laughed. "How'd you know?" he asked.

"I'm in the same boat. Been gettin' sicker and sicker. Last night he brought in that race story. It was so messed up I couldn't read it. I told him so, with lots of trimmin's. Then we had it nip and tuck. Him to tell me to get my hat, an' me to grab it before he could speak the words."

"You haven't wasted any time joining up," Peter said.

"I was quittin' Saturday anyway. They had my things ready at the armory. All I had to do this mornin' was to go an' get dressed up."

"You're lucky."

"Sure I'm lucky. I'm free, white and twenty-one."

They had reached the street. Callaghan said: "What

d'ye say to a glass o' beer at the Garden? We ought to have one to old Tatters."

Peter did not want to be alone again. He accepted gladly, and presently they entered the big noisy room with its homely reek of tobacco and spirits. Callaghan was signaled from a table.

"Come on," he said. "Meet my friends." There were half a dozen of them, all in the uniform of the Irish Volunteers. Callaghan said, "Meet Mr. Ashley, boys. He's just quit the paper, too. He's goin' to join the Dragoons."

Strong hands gripped his fingers. A German waiter slammed a foaming mug down before him. Peter's breath had been taken away by the unexpected announcement. Before he could think of anything to say they had forgotten him and were all talking at once about a rumor that they were to go to an island battery within a day or two. Then a group of men from the minstrel show came in. The house set them up, and a crowd gathered about their table. They got them singing "Dixie," with the crowd joining in and banging time with their mugs.

When Peter left at two o'clock, his new friend accompanied him a part of the way home. They were both warmed with good German beer, and they talked together freely and without self-consciousness like old friends. It was only when their ways were parting and they paused for a moment beneath St. Michael's portico, that the thought came suddenly to Peter that their comradeship was built upon the assumption that he was a comrade in arms. He touched Callaghan on the arm as he turned to leave, and asked: "I say, in there tonight, what made you say I was joining the Dragoons?"

The printer looked at him in wide-eyed surprise. "You're a great one for horseback riding. I thought sure it would be the cavalry. But maybe I was wrong. Is it the Sumter Guards or the Washington Light Infantry?"

Peter said, "Well, you see, I hadn't decided yet."

"Ye're a funny one. The racket about to start, an' ye don't know which organization ye're joinin'. Well, I'll tell ye one thing—ye'd better get a move on, or the show'll be over before ye're in."

Callaghan's footsteps died away in the distance. For a moment there was silence, then from St. Andrew's Hall two blocks away came the sound of a slamming carriage door, followed by the ring of shod hooves upon the cobbles. Then the call of the doorman. And another carriage.

The ball was breaking up. It brought Peter back sharply to his present situation. To the mess that he had made of things since he had come home a short month ago. He had been confident then that he could order his own destiny, that he could fight it through alone. Now each barrier that he had raised was down. His job on the paper. His brief illusion of success with the race. His feeling that Damaris approved him, and that with her approval others no longer mattered.

Now he would have to start all over again, and at what? The thought of Callaghan's words came back to him, invested now with a sort of oracular authority. For the first time in his life he felt that his will was being bent by outside forces. For the first time he wondered whether after all we are free agents, or whether willingly or unwillingly we all eventually conform to an unknown and preordained pattern.

The thought came to him that perhaps for some natures, of which his was one, there was no joyous giving over of oneself such as was being done by his friends. That at the last there must come merely a forced, ungracious and disillusioned surrender to an enemy who met you with irresistible force. Well, he wasn't giving in yet. Tomorrow he'd see Damaris. If she could be won back, he'd still have the courage to hew his own way.

CHAPTER XIV

RACE WEEK was over. The Virginians boarded their steamer for Norfolk, and the regimental band stationed on the pier-head blared a hearty godspeed as the sportsmen put to sea. The Hamptons, the Puryears, the Canteys, the Boykins, and the other guests from Columbia, Camden and the Piedmont, packed the coaches of a North Eastern Railroad train that, with bell clanging and funnel belching clouds of wood smoke, rattled and clanked its way northward. Again the sandy roads of the Low Country took up their burden of traffic. Home-bound carriages swayed and groaned, and the pine barrens waked to the songs and laughter of returning retinues of servants and stablemen. On the rivers, the plantation barges turned prows toward the islands, and chanting oarsmen bent their backs to the long homeward pull. In the drawing rooms, the hotel lobbies, the clubs, it was the consensus of opinion that the meet had touched high-water mark in racing history.

Standing before an open fire in the club room of the South Carolina Society, Mr. Lowndes, the president of the Jockey Club, was saying: "I tell you, gentlemen, there's nothing on the American turf that can touch Albine. Next year we must enter her at Saratoga, and——"

A jarring detonation crashed across the sentence, breaking it off short. In the room the silence was absolute. Then came a second report, and a third. The door burst open and a lad in the uniform of the Citadel cadets flung into the room; then, seeing the circle of gentlemen, he backed against the wall, breathing hard. One of the men before the fire said, "Come here, son, and tell us what's the news?"

The boy said, "I have been looking everywhere for you, father. The delegates have met in Montgomery, and Mr. Davis has been elected President of the Confederacy."

Down the street Old Secession continued to boom out its salute. The gentlemen rose, and looked at each other guiltily. They had the look of boys who have been detected at some illicit game. Racing was over—well, for this season at any rate. During these few days, while they had been loitering by the wayside, the world, it seemed, had gone thundering on its way. They must make haste or they would be left behind in the mad procession. One by one they shook themselves awake. One by one the sportsmen of an hour ago became again the Secessionists of the previous week. A Southern Confederacy. By God! They hadn't wasted any time in Montgomery. They'd show the Yankees now. A bottle of brandy. Yes, certainly, the eighteen-forty. Heat, vehemence, passion. And South Carolina in step again.

And now, as though to make up for lost time, the pace quickens. The curtain that was so recently rung down upon a scene of carnival rises upon a city that has become an armed camp. South Carolina has ceased to be an independent organism, battling single-handed for a place in the sun. It is now a member of a great and powerful body. Its arteries take their rhythm from the heart that beats night and day in Montgomery. Behind the Doric columns of Hibernian Hall, the two houses of the state legislature drop the reins of national government from their unaccustomed hands. Great matters—Interstate Commerce, the Postal Service, the Army—slip from their minds like shoes from tired feet. There is, without doubt, a drink all around in the club room of the building, then the august bodies reassemble and pass: "An act to amend an act affecting the status of certain itinerant peddlers."

And now the Morse Line has changed its character. It has assumed a new significance. Instead of its daily Washington message telling of rebuffs to the Southern commissioners, vacillations and hesitations of the National Government, attacks by rabid abolitionists, it has become a motor nerve of the Confederacy, animating the various members in response to the central will, lifting excitement to fever heat as the new Southern Congress settles into its stride.

The flag. The various states have been requested to submit designs. In a dozen Charleston drawing rooms committees of ladies are busy with needles and thread, shears, and bright silks. Ash Wednesday comes and goes, yet scarcely do the ladies realize that the social season is over, so immersed are they in the thrilling competition. The favored design is forwarded to the capital. It is called the Southern Cross, and consists of a blue cross on a red ground. Stars representing the states are ranged along the arms of the cross. But Montgomery has a theory of its own. The new flag should follow as nearly as possible the familiar pattern of the Stars and Stripes. And so the telegraph raps out the choice, "Blue union in upper left hand corner, containing seven stars, and three bars, the center of white, the top and bottom of red."

February twelfth. The Southern Confederacy is formed. The new flag is adopted amid scenes of wild excitement.

February eighteenth. The inauguration of President Davis and the members of his cabinet.

February twenty-second. Old Secession fires the familiar salute of thirteen guns to the original states, then tops it off with seven guns for the "Redeemed States."

On the twenty-third, Henry Timrod, afire with the new patriotism, attains stature as a war poet and salutes the flag:

> "Hath not the morning dawned with added light,
>   And will not evening call another star
>   Out of the infinite regions of the night
>   To mark this day in Heaven? At last we are
>   A nation among nations: And the world
>   Shall soon behold in many a distant port
>   Another flag unfurled——"

It is a long poem, but by evening it is on every tongue. An enthusiastic committee of citizens proposes Timrod as the poet laureate of the Southern Confederacy. The matter is urged upon the Charleston delegates to the Provisional Congress. But Montgomerty has no time now for poets. The mills of government labor night and day under their forced load. Laws prohibiting the slave trade, regulating Interstate Commerce, inaugurating a Postal Service. An act creating an Army and a Navy. Another authorizing the President to borrow fifteen million dollars. An act placing an export duty on cotton to retire the loan. And then, amid wild acclamation, the passage of the Military Bill authorizing the President to call for a hundred thousand volunteers for a term of twelve months, to terminate once and for all the presumptuous and despotic tyranny of the Yankee.

And now, with Lincoln's inauguration at hand, all eyes are turned toward Charleston, where each morning Fort Sumter shoulders the night mists from her battlements and runs the Stars and Stripes up against the dawn. The circle of island batteries nears completion. Under the brave new colors, the encompassing guns crouch and wait.

A strange siege. A situation presenting almost fantastic contradictions. For the guns are not trained on Major Anderson and his handful of soldiers, but on a vast abstraction that looms against the northern sky and jeopardizes the realization of that immemorial and unattainable chimera, in pursuit of which, from the beginning, man has labored under successive masters, and which we define as human liberty. But to one endowed with a sufficient understanding, this situation furnishes a key to the character of the gay, fierce, hospitable, truculent, lovable and intemperate city, and brings her apparent inconsistencies into harmony.

The *Star of the West,* bearing supplies for the beleaguered fortress, is met by a burst of gun fire. And immediately the military authorities in Charleston invite the garrison to purchase daily in the city markets supplies of meats and fresh vegetables. In the course of time, Major Anderson decides that it is unseemly to be beholden to the seceded State of South Carolina for assistance, and his market boat remains at the fort.

A plantation barge approaches the fort. It is laden with vegetables and fruit. There is bronze of a turkey's wing; the sun strikes fire from the plumage of a string of ducks. A wide-eyed negro is shown into the presence of the commanding officer. "With Colonel Broughton's compliments, suh, and he hopes Major Anderson is enjoyin' good healt'." Ah, this is a different matter. This is a private affair between gentlemen. "My compliments to Colonel Broughton, and I hope that I may some day be so situated that I may return his kindness."

And now a new menace faces the city. It is the talk of the clubs, the street corners. It is obvious that with the support of the South withdrawn, the North will fall into industrial chaos. Without cotton the mills will close. Without Southern markets commerce will collapse. It is, therefore, logical to assume that thousands of penniless laborers will pour into the South to fatten at the expense of those to whom the fair land belongs. Mayor McBeth meets the issue with characteristic resourcefulness. The steamship owners are all notified that they will not be allowed to land a passenger unless he shows evidence that he expects to return, or has a hundred good dollars in his pocket. Another catastrophe has been met and averted.

From up-state comes a story. A Yankee abolitionist has been caught at a secret meeting of negroes, his pockets full of inflammatory pamphlets. "He must have been tired after so long a trip," the papers observe, and applaud the action of a number of citizens who allowed him to "fall asleep with his toes six inches from terra firma."

But over on Beaufain Street the new Girls' High School is closing. The teachers, almost without exception from the North, await transportation. They are honored guests in private homes. They dine at tables where the discussion touches upon *Great Expectations,* that is running serially in a magazine, on Mr. Darwin's strange theory of evolution, the paintings of Rosa Bonheur. Finally they leave, but they will return at the opening of the fall term when—vaguely—"this" is all an incident of the past.

It is the hour of morning service at old St. Michael's. And it is an occasion, for the historic ritual has by the unanimous action of the vestry been changed to conform to the spirit of the day. The voice of the clergyman drones through the service. The moment arrives: "Most heartily we beseech Thee, with Thy favor to behold and bless Thy servant The President of the *Confederate States,* and all others in authority." There is an indignant shuffling of feet. Over the bowed heads of the worshipers the form of James Petigru lifts itself to its full height. He stands for a moment. The latch of his pew door clicks. Then thud, thud, on the deeply-carpeted aisle. The utterly incredible is happening. Mr. Petigru is walking out on God and Mr. Davis! The voice of the minister hesitates. The congregation waits in a paralysis of horror. The old Unionist reaches the door, opens and closes it deliberately, and turns his steps unconcernedly toward his private sanctum around the corner on St. Michael's alley.

And so, damning the Union, complimenting Major Anderson, winning a horse race, equipping an army, hanging an abolitionist and smiling indulgently upon the eccentricities of its own Mr. Petigru, the Confederate State of South Carolina casts behind it one by one the twenty-eight days of that altogether mad month of February, eighteen-sixty-one.

CHAPTER XV

DAMARIS allowed the week following the big race to pass before she permitted Peter to speak to her. During that week Holcombe's unit had been relieved from duty on Morris Island, and when Peter had met her on the street she was invariably accompanied by the dashing captain. Several times Peter had sent Cæsar with a note entreating an opportunity to explain and offer his apologies. Always she had been regretfully, yet coolly and definitely, engaged. At last, on a vicious night that came roaring down from the north, nipping the jessamine buds and stamping the early violets under an icy heel, she allowed him to call.

In nothing so much as estimating the exact psychological moment for an apology is the wisdom of a woman in dealing with a man revealed. Three days ago, after his second rebuff, Peter's mood was one of humble contrition. But now that moment had passed. His pride was up in arms. Out of the complete collapse of all his plans had come a sort of desperate fatalism. He had come with the apology for the broken engagement to which she was entitled. But he had no intention of apologizing for himself. His reasoning was now distinctly masculine. If in the great moment of a man's career love became of secondary importance, it did not imply a continued neglect. He must try to make her see that if he was going to succeed there would always be times when, under the tyranny of a single thought, he would be smitten with a momentary blindness; that where he had failed once he might fail again. But that it was unimportant. It did not mean that he could ever really forget her existence, but that only by giving himself utterly when his work demanded it could he ever be worthy of himself, worthy of her respect.

That it would be a new point of view to her he realized. But the time had come for honesty. He wondered how she would take it. And then he realized how little he really knew her. She presented such baffling inconsistencies. There was the Damaris who was bent upon maintaining her position as the undisputed belle of her set. There had been moments when, with his inconvenient faculty for subjecting emotion to analysis, he had, in spite of his love for her, seen her as a callous coquette, feeding her vanity upon the jealousies and disappointments of her admirers. Then there was the other Damaris, the one who had insisted upon his rescue of the old negress. This Damaris, he knew, was impulsive, tender, sympathetic, capable of breaking some long anticipated engagement to spend an hour with an ailing and aged relative, extravagant of herself in the care of some sick dog or cat that she had acquired and brought to the Gordons' overcrowded town yard.

Suddenly he wondered bitterly whether, as a person, he really mattered to her at all. Whether any of them did. Perhaps his claim upon her interest was merely that of a new and unknown admirer. Perhaps, because he was out of it all, he was merely another lost dog to be fed, patted, and later forgotten. He was possessed by a sudden resolution to find out where he stood. Tonight, he told himself, she would have to give him something definite to go on.

She entered the drawing room and crossed at once to where he was waiting before the fire, her hand extended in formal greeting. Her look was cool, remote, impersonal. Peter had changed subtly since their last meeting. The boyish look of confidence that he had worn at the track was gone. In the brief time he had matured astonishingly. There were evidences of recent suffering in a tightening about the mouth. In the shaken firelight his face seemed dominated by the broad, high brow and the strong uncompromising line of the nose.

For a moment of silence she studied him speculatively, a slight frown between her brows. Then she said simply: "Won't you sit down?"

Peter noted that she had not addressed him either as Cousin Peter or Mr. Ashley. It put him on notice that for this meeting he was on trial—neither reinstated nor dismissed until he had made amends. He acknowledged her invitation with a formal bow, but remained standing with his back to the fire. She seated herself on the piano stool, her hands folded loosely in her lap.

"Miss Damaris," Peter began. "I have come to offer my humble apologies for my outrageous neglect of you at the track. I hope that you were not seriously embarrassed, and that you will forgive me."

She regarded him calmly, her eyes noncommittal. "I refused three escorts for the ride home. I waited for you until the track was nearly deserted. Then after I had started alone, Captain Holcombe took pity on me and saved me from being a laughing-stock." She let that statement have a moment of significant silence, then added, "—but of course you have some good excuse."

Now the moment had arrived. The social lie would make it so easy. An imperative summons from the office. A message sent by a trusted servant, but never delivered. Something that she would probably not believe, but would accept because it was the correct social gesture. The sort of explanation that would have been given by a man who had been overtaken in his cups, and the veracity of which it would have been unsportsmanlike to question. He had a feeling that by her manner she was signaling him in the code that implied a gentleman's right to a private life, and a lady's right to her romantic illusions. And that in granting the one she would demand the other.

For a moment Peter almost yielded. She had never been so desirable. That quality in her that always disarmed opposition and invited surrender was almost too much for his resolution. But a stubborn devil of honesty had taken possession of him and drove him on. And with it came the wild hope that he might break through this maddening surface that Damaris was presenting to him, and touch the woman who lay beneath.

"You see," he began, "it started with my story of the race."

Damaris did not look up. She said in her best drawing-room manner: "I saw your account in the paper. I thought it very prettily written."

The remark staggered him. He stopped in full career and regarded her curiously. He suspected her for a moment of being deliberately cruel. In his morbid sensitiveness he had been sure that the whole town had heard of his break with the *Courier,* and its cause. He said incredulously: "You read the story of the race, and you liked it?"

She gave him a brief, surprised glance. "Why, yes. It was quite as good as the account of the races last year. I thought you'd be pleased."

She had, it seemed, heard nothing about his quarrel. It made him feel suddenly of no importance. It invalidated the premise upon which rested the justification for his neglect. "That wasn't my story," he said at last. "It was a travesty of what I wrote."

Her brief glance was merely puzzled.

He realized then, with a sort of premonitory hopelessness, that if he would explain his behavior, he would first have to explain himself. That he must try to present concretely in words things that had existed only in his spirit.

He started at the beginning. Damaris sat, her gaze resting pensively on the fire, her hands folded in unnatural stillness in her lap. Peter told her first how he had always been different from the other boys. How things that had meaning for him had meant nothing to Wake, his father, the neighborhood boys. That he had always been lonely until Uncle Pierre had given him his chance.

He told her how the years that had passed since then had been devoted to the single act of preparing him for his work. That when you wrote it was different. He tried to be specific about this. "You can plant. Like Wake, you know. And you can think of other things. They're all outside of you. Things that you can touch, shape with your hands. But this—you see—this is different. If it's any use at all, it comes from down inside of you. And once you've started, it shuts you off from outside things."

Then he told her of his break with the *Courier*. He had talked to no one about it, not even Chardon, and now his pent emotion threatened his self-control. But he managed to keep himself in hand. He selected his words carefully so that she would understand. She must see that his story was not merely a daily stint on the paper, but an expression of himself that would justify everything that he was—that would explain his shortcomings. And that Tattenham's destruction of it was an affront to his spirit that could not be forgiven.

While he talked, he experienced the frustrating realization that his words were carrying no conviction. The very restraint that he was forced to exercise made them sound cold, dull, lifeless. His voice ceased, and his eyes plead for understanding.

Damaris continued to sit, staring into the fire. To Peter there was something shocking in her utter immobility, in the way she let the silence draw out in the room. At last she said, "I see. When all is said and done, you simply rode away and forgot my existence."

Instantly Peter saw that she had overplayed her hand. That she was not being either deliberately heartless or deliberately stupid. Her attitude was not negative, but one of positive resistance. She was resisting him with her most powerful weapon, an assumed indifference. Behind that indifference Peter knew that the real Damaris was hiding. If he could break through now—in this very moment—he would have his answer.

He took a short quick step, and stood over her. She

sprang to her feet and put the piano stool between them. Peter seized both of her hands in his, and bore down upon her with his gaze. He said tensely: "Look at me, Damaris." She raised her eyes. They neither reflected his passion nor gave any clue to her own emotions. Her mystery maddened him. He swore that he would break through her deliberate barriers and learn the truth before he quit the house. He had reached the limit of his endurance. His voice was harsh, peremptory. He said:

"Now listen to me! It's foolish for me to be telling you that I love you. You've known that from the first. But you don't know this—you are the first woman that I have ever loved—and you will be the last. I have wanted to give you time. I should have seen your father first, I know, but I need you now, desperately. You have made yourself a part of me. I can't go on without you."

He felt her hands struggling in his grasp. Something told him that if he let her go, he would lose her irrevocably. He must hold her until she had heard him out. So much depended on it. He must make her realize that before he let her go free.

His grasp tightened, and the hands gave up their struggle. He hurried on breathlessly. "Life, life is so terribly short. Something tells me that if we don't take it now, and live it, we'll find ourselves suddenly at the end of the world. It will be over. And we won't have had it at all."

He stopped, stifled by his emotion, and under his grasp the hands recommenced their struggle. He went on with desperate insistence. "Let me go to your father now.

He's been kind to me. I don't think he'll be unreasonable. He'll give me the right to address you."

She interrupted him, her cool syllables cutting across his impassioned utterance. "Let go of my hands, please. You are hurting me."

He released her, and she turned her back upon him. The toe of one small slipper rested upon the low fender, her gaze upon the coals. She said, without looking around: "Now go, please."

Peter stood looking at her. Without leaving the room she had managed to remove herself to some utterly inaccessible height, leaving an impassable chasm between them. Peter strove to bridge it, knowing in advance that he would fail. "Do you mean," he asked, "that I am never to return?"

After a moment the small head with its dark coronal of hair shook in negation. "No," she answered, "not quite that, but you must wait until I send for you. Now I want to be alone, please."

There were his hat and cloak to be got, his stick to be fumbled for and found. Then he was out in the savage night, with the lash of rain against his face.

Striding obliviously along, he realized with a stab of angry pain that he had left Damaris exactly where he had found her. Whether behind her bright, superficial responsiveness or the maddeningly remote mood of to-night, she had kept her secret self a complete enigma. Thinking over the past half-hour, he experienced the shame of a genuinely reticent soul that has bared itself, and has been given nothing in return. He had poured out his dreams and aspirations, and she had listened in polite silence, and then had asked him to go home.

With his fatal habit of analysis, he estimated her known characteristics one by one. From the first, she had given that flattering responsiveness that promised so much for the future. It seemed to him now like an anteroom to her intimacy, where one was kept waiting hour on hour until at last the lights were extinguished, and one was out in the street again wondering vaguely how it had happened.

She had beauty. There was no denying that she delighted the senses; but that, he told himself impatiently, was not enough. He had known beautiful women before, and he had ridden away and forgotten them. She was not intellectual. Not even very clever. He tried to think of a single memorable phrase that she had uttered. There was nothing to lay hold upon. Why did he want her so? Why was Holcombe mad about her—and the others? She had never been without a devoted suitor, he had been told. He went on ruthlessly stripping her of her charms, as one deliberately tears the petals from a flower; and then when he had finished, there in his hand lay the warm golden heart of the blossom: the single indestructible fact—he loved her. But why? he asked himself again in exasperation.

Then, suddenly, his great need for reassurance flung an answer sharply into his consciousness. He stopped in his tracks and said aloud, "By God! I never thought of that." Fixed inescapably in the ultra-social environment to which she had been born, this personality that she presented to the world was the shield behind which she held her innermost self inviolate. Like himself, she was one of those who must go alone, but for her there was no escape. This was her compromise with life.

She was young. Within the limits fixed by the conventions of her class, her youth was swinging its free, bright arc. But beneath the surface she was, like himself, a lone explorer, leaving behind her the trails that others had blazed, keeping her own council, following her own guiding star.

His anger, his sense of defeat, vanished in the face of this revelation. Something very like exultation took their place. Now he was confident that it was not her beauty, her manner of subtle flattery, that had captured him, but this deep bond of spiritual kinship. He was no nearer to the knowledge of whether she loved him or not, but the immediate situation had ceased to be of such vital importance. Given time now, and they would meet on that common ground that lay beyond the radiant horizon of her smile. Given an even chance, and he would win the Damaris of whose very existence Holcombe was unaware.

CHAPTER XVI

MOONLIGHT on White Point Gardens, white and ghostly on the crushed shell walks. Caverns of blackness under the live oaks. February, and yet already a faint premonition of spring in the air, violets breathing in their sleep along the borders, and the steady pressure of the land breeze warm and earthy from the mainland.

Peter had surprised Chardon by suggesting a walk before going to bed. And without even topcoats they had stepped out into the night. The beauty of the setting and the warm seduction of the night moved Peter strangely. He was sensible of the deep intimacy that existed between himself and his companion; an intimacy that grew stronger with the passage of time because it was fed on reticence, and not utilized as a confessional for every trivial or vulgar thought.

He slipped his arm through Chardon's and they walked for a while in silence. At last Peter said: "Suppose the unthinkable should happen, Uncle Pierre, and you were to marry again. What qualities would you most prize in a wife?"

Under cover of the dark Chardon indulged in a brief, secret smile. "Marriage here in our class is a comparatively simple matter. We expect certain virtues of a thoroughly conventional nature. Generations of delicately reared daughters have slowly perfected the pattern. We know in advance exactly what to expect of each other. It could not be more definite if we signed a marriage contract. We differ from the Continental arrangement only in our articles of barter. We deal in intangibles."

"For instance?"

"Well, of course, the domestic arts are taken for granted. Generations ago the Charleston matron was established as the most gracious and accomplished hostess on the globe. But there is something more, something requiring infinite finesse, something that we ourselves have imposed upon them, and that must require an especial and very subtle talent. We demand that they satisfy the hunger of our bodies, and still remain divine; that they conceive our children, and continue immaculate. That, in short, they shall consort with us, and exhibit no signs of contamination. We have created a deity of our womanhood, and we can forgive it anything short of disillusioning us."

"And for many of us," Peter commented bitterly, "the brothel or the negro yard is the preparatory school."

"Ah, there you have us, my boy. And yet of late I have come to wonder whether even that has not its place in the scheme of things. Life is a brutal taskmaster. He drives us forward flesh and spirit manacled together hand and foot. If by being utterly animal we can free the spirit, perhaps our gains exceed our losses. Perhaps if, in our youth, we render to Cæsar the things which are Cæsar's, we may still, when the time for marriage arrives, have something of the spirit left with which to render to God the things which are God's."

There followed a long pause. Then Peter said: "You

haven't spoken of mental congeniality. Don't you think that important?"

"That, I am afraid, my dear Peter, is not in the curriculum. So few of us demand it. It would be there for us, no doubt; but besides a superficial brilliance, we ask nothing."

Peter said hesitantly: "But Aunt Bella—surely you and she——?"

"I was young then. I was in love. I never explored her mind. She was so utterly perfect in meeting all of my other needs. I was like the others, you see—I wouldn't tamper with my illusion. But that didn't matter. We had the same fastidiousness about unexpected things. We both had a gift for a certain sort of sublimated passion." There was a pause. Then, "She looked a little like Damaris. You know that they were cousins. Perhaps that is why the child could always do what she pleased with me. Her eyes were between the two shades of blue and black. They looked like an evening sky showing its first stars. She satisfied my need for beauty."

In their absorption they had wandered without noticing their direction. Now they found themselves at the corner of Orange and Broad streets.

Peter paused involuntarily and let his gaze dwell on the picture before him. To the left, under the soft moonlight, the Cathedral took on an airy quality, its details sketched in a few bright strokes against its soaring shadowy mass. There were several magnolia trees in the churchyard. The night breeze had fallen, and their glossy leaves, reflecting either the moon or the fathomless night, and poised motionless in the still air, gave them the appearance of being clothed in numberless

small plaques of ebony or silver. Then, directly opposite the spot where Peter stood, St. Andrew's Hall completed the composition with its perfect Georgian façade.
Set slightly back from the pavement, behind a wrought
iron fence, and with jonquils blooming in its dooryard,
it seemed more like a gracious residence than a club-
house and a place of public meetings. The large front
door stood hospitably open and snatches of talk and
laughter drifted out into the night.

Chardon suggested going in for a nightcap. "You'll
probably find your old friend Simms there, and possibly
Paul Hayne. And I want you to see the Hall. It's quite
perfect in its way."

To Peter there came in the moment of assent a disconcerting doubt. It was blown across his mind like a cloud
over a sunny landscape, then was gone. He told himself
that it was his diffidence in the face of crowds, his
wretched self-consciousness when the inevitable war talk
was going on.

Chardon, sensitive as ever to his nephew's moods, felt
it. "Of course, if you'd rather not——"

That decided him. Whatever it was, he must face it.
"We'll go, by all means," he said.

A number of men were seated around a table in the
center of the large room. Upon the table rested an as-
sortment of toddy glasses and a snuff mull fashioned
from the skull of a great ram. Several gentlemen were
speaking at once with extraordinary vehemence. There
was an echo somewhere under the lofty ceiling. At a
distance words were indistinguishable. There was only
sound, passionate and reiterative.

Chardon led Peter to the table, and the talk fell into

silence. Peter felt their eyes, not hostile but intensely curious, neither accepting nor rejecting him, still holding him on a sort of probation—giving him rope, and waiting.

Mr. Simms was there and had as usual been doing most of the talking. He greeted Peter warmly, but with a shade of indulgent amusement. Mr. Petigru, from the far end of the table, lifted his glass in greeting. There was a sardonic suggestion in the act and the smile that accompanied it, but Peter drew immediate comfort from his presence. The man was so deliberately and uncompromisingly himself that while the heat and pressure of public opinion molded those about him to the universal pattern, by simply remaining immovable he seemed to grow in stature, to become more uniquely individual.

Greetings and introductions over, Chardon took Peter on a tour of inspection. The portrait of Queen Victoria which Sully had painted from life and presented to the Society, Peter thought as fine a piece of work as the artist had done, and he liked also the portrait of Dr. Alexander Baron, a former president of St. Andrew's, done by that extraordinary fellow, S. F. B. Morse. They paused for a moment before an admirable model of the city of Edinburgh done in copper, then joined the group at the table and accepted the spiced brandy toddies that were passed to them by an attentive manservant.

Then Peter noticed that Holcombe had come in and joined the party. It was odd how his presence seemed to change the rhythm of the room. Peter felt it mentally in an acute awareness that the man's attitude was definitely inimical to him, physically in a defensive muscular tension that would not let him relax. Holcombe sat slouched low in his chair, his powerful shoulders lax against the high back. He had evidently been drinking. Between the iron gray of his thick hair, and the army gray of his jacket, his face, dark and set, was an ominous background for eyes wide in their slight characteristic stare, intensely blue, and unnaturally bright.

Simms was holding the floor, and this time without competition from the others. Peter could see that he had worked his accustomed spell upon his hearers. It switched his memory back to the old days around the fire in the rear of Russell's Book Store. It had been Byron then, or perhaps some of his own poetry, momentarily lifted from the level of the commonplace to the plane of art by the compelling personality, the enormous and convincing gusto that he could summon at will and pour into the rendition.

Peter set this vivid picture beside that of the man who now sat opposite him, and he realized with a start the ruin that the years had brought. The fragments of news that had reached him abroad, and that had seemed remote and isolated, fell into place now and presented the tragic story. His two favorite sons had died on the same day in the yellow fever epidemic of 'fifty-eight; his home with his treasured library had been destroyed by fire. Then followed plantation losses, rebuffs from his literary friends in the North as the political tension grew, and finally, his latest novel, the *Cassique of Kiawah,* on which he had staked his failing faith in himself, utterly ignored in the babel of politics and war.

Peter had not sought Simms out since his return. He had felt that in the thundering war propagandist he would find little of the poet whom he had worshiped as a boy. But now as he listened he commenced to experience a deep compassion, and with it an enormous admiration for his old friend. The essential Simms was still there. He could still wrap his cloak about him in his old impressive manner, and with his blue-gray eyes flashing, rise above personal disaster and spend himself with the old reckless extravagance upon a town that, in spite of his literary eminence, had never accepted him into its inner social life, and that he had once in a moment of bitterness designated as "a place of tombs."

Peter's moment of retrospection passed. The steady drive of the heavy, vital voice seized his attention. It was plain that past grievances and bitterness were forgotten. With the passage of secession, Simms had plunged into military science with the same energy that had accomplished his daily stint of thirty pages of manuscript. He had evolved a complete system of harbor defense, and had delivered his plans to the authorities. Now he was expounding his theories:

"Palmetto logs did well enough against the British in the Revolution. But we are living in a new century. Sandbags are satisfactory for hastily thrown up defenses. But mark my word, the ironclad battery is the fortification of the future. Our Morris Island batteries, which must eventually be matched with Sumter, should be placed on the highest sand hills. That would offset Sumter's elevation. They should be framed with logs and sheeted with railroad irons laid at an angle. And this is an important point. We should get away from the humbug of point-blank fire. We should in every case place the guns so that the shot would enter Sumter's portholes at an angle. Do you gather the significance of that?" His glance swept the circle of intent faces.

"No? Well, I'll show you: The crews stand to the side of the gun, not directly behind it. A shot striking the side of the embrasure at an angle would damage the masonry, kill the crew on that side, ricochet and probably dismount the gun."

Immediately a discussion was in progress. Several of the officers present plunged in at once. It seemed that the proponents of direct fire held to their own opinions. It was a matter upon which no one was in doubt. It struck Peter how typical this was of all of the discussions that he had heard. No one ever seemed to hesitate. Upon apparently trivial matters definite opinions had been formed and these opinions were expressed and defended with passionate earnestness.

The discussion was finally interrupted by the entrance of Mr. Tattenham. He brandished a copy of the London *Times*. "Listen, fellow South Carolinians," he declaimed. "England has at last seen the light. I have here an editorial upon the subject of slavery in the British West Indies. It tells of the complete lapse into a state of barbarism following emancipation, then closes with these significant words": He paused, produced his spectacles, placed them very deliberately upon his nose while he savored the suspense, then read:

" 'If England has ruined her own colonies, there is no reason why she should seek to check the progress of the whole American Continent.' " He threw the paper dramatically down upon the table. "There!" he said, in triumphant conclusion, "you may read it for yourselves."

There were cries of "Hear, hear!" and a scattering cheer went around the board. A rather beautiful lad in the straps of a lieutenant lifted his glass and proposed a toast to "Our mother across the seas," thought it over a little fuzzily, and amended it to "Britannia, our sister beyond the Atlantic." Upon the wall Victoria's painted smile seemed suddenly to become less patronizingly remote, more intimately indulgent.

The excitement died down, and there followed a coincidental moment of silence. In the midst of it, Petigru's high voice piped unexpectedly:

"As a matter of fact, we are in the happy position of being able to get a first-hand report on England's attitude. Mr. Ashley was living there only a few months ago." He turned toward Peter. "Perhaps you will give us some of your personal impressions. What do they really think of secession, slavery, the prospects of war?"

All eyes were turned upon Peter. Why couldn't they have let him alone? He met the cryptic smile of Mr. Petigru and for a moment suspected him of deliberate mischief. He was acutely uncomfortable and wished himself well out of it. He said rather weakly: "I am afraid, sir, that they are more interested in Mr. Darwin's new theory of evolution, or their unemployment problem, than they are in our affairs."

But Petigru was not going to allow so easy an escape. "Come, come, young man, do you mean to say that with the Prince of Wales so recently returned from his triumphal American tour they have nothing to say of us?"

In the watchful silence that followed, Peter felt again the keen measuring scrutiny of eyes.

"Of course," he said at last. "It was too good an opportunity to miss. The Yankees fêted him day in and day out. They loaded him with Union propaganda, and sent him home cocked and primed."

Simms leaned forward and there was a note of challenge in his voice. "You believe, then, that England favors the Union?"

Another voice cut in: "Perhaps England does not realize that we hold her in our power. That by the simple measure of withholding our cotton from her manufacturers we could shut down her industrial districts, and probably precipitate a sympathetic revolution."

Peter looked into the speaker's face. It was solemn, humorless and complacently triumphant. He thought, "My God, he really believes that." Then, "I must be careful."

"Go ahead, Ashley,—you haven't told us anything yet."

Peter looked up and met Petigru's eyes, bright and sardonic, leading him perhaps to destruction, but somehow inspiring courage and self-confidence.

"It isn't a question that you can dispose of with yes or no," he began. "It's infinitely more complicated. And, of course, it has nothing to do with altruistic motives. Our affairs are interesting only in so far as they react upon their own body politic." He paused and lighted his pipe. The familiar feel of it in his teeth, and his brief introduction, served their purpose. They had got him started. Now he said quietly: "I don't believe that it has occurred to them that the Cotton States are in a position to plunge them into a revolution. But I think on the whole, in spite of the recent hullabaloo over His Royal Highness, the majority of opinion favored secession. The Conservatives are openly gratified. The masses are becoming truculent, and are demanding an extension of the franchise. The bogey of democracy is in every Tory closet. The United States of America represented the world's great, and apparently successful, experiment. Now that experiment has failed. The thing that we created has lacked the necessary cohesive force to survive as a powerful government. They predict complete disintegration—chaos, even—we are invaluable to the Conservative politicians. We have given them a bludgeon to lay upon John Bright and other agitators of his ilk."

Chardon, watching closely, saw his nephew's face change. It was taking on the absorbed, almost blind look that it wore when he was writing, or when intense mental concentration shut out the world of externals. He had the feeling that the boy was advancing obliviously across a mined battlefield and that at any moment he might touch off an explosion that would blow him to pieces. Something must be done to extricate him. He pushed back his chair. The harsh sound waked an echo, but failed dismally as an interruption. He saw Petigru's slight, amused smile, and Holcombe's, dark and malicious.

Peter sat forward, his elbows on the table; in the fingers of his left hand he held his pipe, lightly, fastidiously, his gaze fixed attentively upon the tobacco fuming in the bowl.

"Then, of course, there's the tariff," he went on. "That's another point in our favor. American tariff legislation has always aggravated the commercial interests. And now the passage of this new measure immediately after secession will show them exactly what they will have to expect in future from a manufacturing North. They know that we favor free trade, that our own manufacturing is inconsiderable. Nothing could be more satisfactory to them than a wide open market with the agricultural South."

He paused for a moment, his brows drawn into a heavy frown, then continued. "I wonder if you realize how very kind the Republicans have been to you in passing their iniquitous schedule the moment you walked out and closed the door. They have spoken more convincingly for secession than we have ever done for ourselves. England couldn't puzzle out why we quit. Lincoln had been frank in his statements on slavery. The status quo was not to be disturbed. Why, then, should we bolt? When I left England they had reached the conclusion that we were merely a mob of disgruntled hot-heads whose political party had been defeated. Now the tariff will explain us. It gives us a dignified exit, and one that they can understand. We have seceded in order to terminate a state of unreasonable commercial oppression."

"Then," Simms interjected, "if their interests are ours, we can count on them as allies in the event of a protracted war."

"Ah, war! That's a very different matter. They are a long way off. They see things in perspective. They cannot conceive of America engaging in anything so destructive as civil war."

Mr. Tattenham bristled. "When they learn that the Yankees are the aggressors, that we have had war thrust upon us——!"

Peter's fingers closed tensely about the pipe. Chardon thought he caught a ghost of a sigh. Then Peter spoke:

"England will never ally herself with the South. Never. I said that nations were not sentimentalists.

That is true. Their God is their pocketbook. Behind the friendly gesture is the motive of self-interest. But that is not true of the masses, the people in the street. They possess nothing, so they have nothing to lose. They can afford the Christian virtues. The common people of England have been raised in a tradition of violent hostility to slavery. They believe it to be a survival of the Dark Ages. The abolitionists have had their way with them. They rejoice that we have severed ourselves from the North, because that great territory has been relieved from the stigma of Slavery. Because, with the institution narrowed to the Southern states in a forced isolation from the rest of the civilized world, it must eventually languish and perish. They would not ally themselves to the South because they would believe that by doing so they would be allying themselves with crime."

The silence which followed Peter's words was heavy with impending drama. Peter looked up, and his eyes became aware of the circle of faces. His own words, lingering in the background of his mind, kept repeating themselves like an echo prisoned among cliffs. He was a little frightened at what they said, now that he could hear them for himself.

Simms got very deliberately to his feet. His cloak had fallen back from his shoulders. He threw it about him with a broad impressive gesture.

Peter thought, "Now it's going to be done properly. It is going to be an oration." But the sonorous syllables were slow in coming.

"Son," Simms began at last, "we are sorry, but if you came here tonight expecting to receive an apology for your English friends from your kinsmen for their mode of life, you are destined to be disappointed. You have many friends in London and at the University, no doubt. I suggest that you invite them to compare the condition of their starving laborers, who are at this moment waiting for the gift of a crust to keep them alive until the factories are ready to employ them again, with the lives of the negroes in our fair country.

"But in urging this comparison, do not for a moment imagine that we are attempting to evade the moral questions involved. Once and for all, say that we hold slavery to be an especially and wisely devised institution of heaven; devised for the benefit, the improvement and safety, morally, socially and physically, of a barbarous and inferior race, who would otherwise perish by filth, the sword, disease and waste, and destinies forever gnawing, consuming, and finally destroying."

Simms was fairly off now. His eyes flashed like steel blades. His face, with its full lower lip that in repose often expressed petulance, and its heavy dogmatic jaw, was suddenly lit by a transfiguring zeal. The deep, resonant voice fell into a definite rhythm. He had ceased looking at Peter, and seemed to be addressing a vast invisible audience.

It came suddenly to Peter that this was not merely a discussion for his private edification, but that it was a confession of faith to which he was merely a fortuitous listener.

The voice continued: "If it be admitted that the institution of negro slavery is a wrong done to the negro, the question is at an end. No people can be justified for continuance in error and injustice. Once admit that there is a wrong and a crime, and it must be followed by expiation and atonement. In the South, we think otherwise. We hold the African under moral and just titles, founded upon his characteristics, his nature, his necessities and our own, and our accountability is to the God of both races. We alone are in possession of the facts of the case, and our consciences are in no way troubled in relation to our rights to hold the negro in bondage."

Simms dropped into his chair. His face was wet from the stress of his emotions. He drew out his handkerchief and mopped his brow. In the stillness that followed the passionate avowal of the creed a voice said, "Amen." It seemed even more appropriate to the mood that the speaker had evoked than did the loud burst of commendation that succeeded it.

When the noise died down, Mr. Petigru leaned forward. "I am sure Mr. Ashley will be very glad to set his English friends right. We should appreciate all that he has told us. And it behooves us to remember that what he said was in answer to our questions. He was good enough to tell us what the English thought. His remarks naturally could not be interpreted as an expression of his own personal opinions on the subject."

Peter looked gratefully toward the older man, but his glance was intercepted by a look from Holcombe. Their eyes met and it seemed to Peter that there was an audible metallic ring.

Slouched low in his chair, and with eyes mocking Peter from under heavy brows, Holcombe said loudly and deliberately: "However, I think this a very good time for Mr. Ashley to tell us just what he does think of our prospects in regard to war. It is not a time for reticence upon matters affecting the welfare of our state. And why should he hesitate? He is among friends."

The last word was uttered with peculiar emphasis. The challenge was as definite as though Peter had been struck in the face.

Peter knew that the moment had arrived. With absolute clarity he saw the situation in all its ramifications. If he had a creed at all it was one of intellectual honesty. He had been asked the point-blank question at last. There could be no evasions.

"Very well, gentlemen," he said, and was surprised at the controlled strength of his voice. "I have no reason to conceal my personal opinion of our position. Especially so since what I may think will have nothing to do with our ultimate destiny. But I believe that we are face to face with a situation in which we cannot hold the slightest hope of success. If we fight, we meet a double enemy. We must save ourselves from extinction upon the field of battle. That alone is not impossible. It has been done before and against great odds. But we have a still greater task—that of preserving our illusions—the illusion that in cotton we hold an invincible weapon—the illusion that slavery can continue to survive in a civilized democracy."

Instantly Holcombe was on his feet, his back turned squarely upon Peter. He laid his hand on the shoulder of a young officer.

"Let's get out, Bob," he said in a loud, clear voice. "We didn't come here tonight to listen to a damned abolitionist."

CHAPTER XVII

THE word that Holcombe had spoken seemed to roar in the silence like an exploding shell, then it passed, leaving a sort of vacuum in which the two men stood facing each other, with the others in a fixed circle behind them. On the table the eyesockets of the great ram's skull stared vacantly up at Peter. From the wall Sully's Victoria looked down, scepter poised, placidly awaiting the inevitable.

To Peter there came a moment of extraordinary lucidity. What was the cause of the sensation? The silence that hung in the air like a sustained gasp? If being an abolitionist meant that he was opposed to the principle of slavery, very well, he was one. But it meant more. This had nothing to do with literal definitions. Into the single word was packed the poison of a hundred insults. It meant that he was a traitor to his clan, to his past. That here on his own soil he was being disinherited, flung out, a man without a country.

Behind Holcombe the austere soaring beauty of the great Georgian Hall caught at his gaze, pulling it away from the heavy sneering face of his antagonist. It was a part of the incomparable beauty that was in turn a part of him. His town, his state. And these men about him, waiting, headstrong, blind perhaps, but generous, impulsive, passionate, surrounding him, pressing in upon him with the weight of a single unalterable idea. He felt it seize him. The rhythm of the crowd pounded in his blood. His moment of clarity passed; for a vertiginous second he felt his brain swing. Then he was stepping backward—a single, quick, watchful step, his body at an aching tension. His right hand was tingling—quivers running along the arm to the elbow. His gaze was focused on Holcombe's face, gone ashen on one side and scarlet on the other where the blow had fallen.

The room roared with sound; two, four, a dozen bodies thrust themselves between him and the man who had said the word. They were urging calmness. Someone was patting him persistently on the shoulder. "Good boy." "Nothing else for it!" "Archie's drunk." Hidden in a moving group of friends, Holcombe had been hustled to the end of the room.

There was a babble of talk in the corner. Momentary silence. Then a figure detached itself from the group and came towards the place where Peter was standing. A figure dressed in a new gray uniform with red artillery trimmings. Under sparse blond side whiskers the soft boyish curves of his cheeks were distinctly visible. Peter recognized him at once. He was young Colfelt, a lieutenant in Holcombe's company. He was also the boy who had burst in upon Major Cantey during the race. Over the wide, brightly polished planking of the floor he advanced—very erect, very much of the military, his boot-heels clipping off the fractional parts of the seconds that it took for the traversing of the room.

He paused before Peter, and in a voice that shook from excitement said: "Captain Holcombe has considered the impropriety of meeting as an equal a man who at this time has not seen fit to wear the uniform of his state.

But he has decided to waive the question. If Mr. Ashley will name his second I am authorized to meet him and arrange the details."

Instantly Chardon stepped between Peter and Holcombe's ambassador. His slender form seemed to have lifted itself inside the close-fitting blue frock coat. His voice was cool, his manner urbane, yet touched with the well-bred condescension that he employed unconsciously to people of an inferior social class. "You may tell Captain Holcombe that I, Pierre Chardon, will represent Mr. Ashley as an advising friend, and that any communication preliminary to a meeting may be addressed in my care. You may say to him further that it is a matter of regret to Mr. Ashley that he has not seen fit to secure the offices of some gentleman at least familiar with the first principles of the code. That it is a matter of common knowledge among gentlemen that the cartel must be presented in writing, and that should the challenger be so lacking in common courtesy as to employ insulting or derogatory epithets, the cartel will be returned to him without notice, as to an inferior."

Colfelt's face went a dull red. He started to reply, stopped almost instantly, saluted stiffly, and turned on his heel.

Chardon said, "One moment longer, please."

Colfelt paused, and half turned in the direction of the speaker.

"There are, I believe," the cool voice went on, "several books on the code in the library. I can recommend a recent pamphlet by Colonel Rhett, a brief and excellent handbook for those who have not been raised in the tradition."

The lad started to go, then turned impulsively back. His face cleared under the flicker of an embarrassed smile. He looked Chardon squarely in the eyes, and said steadily: "I reckon I deserved that, sir. I acted hastily. I hope that you will accept my apologies."

Chardon stepped forward and threw an arm across the boy's shoulder, turning him away from the crowd and walking a few slow steps with him. "It's all right, son," he said. "We've all got to learn. I needn't have been so hasty, myself. But this thing hits me right over the heart. It's going to be hard on us all. But we're in for it. Suppose you wait here after the others have withdrawn, and we will talk it over together. And I withdraw what I said about that pamphlet. Let's shake hands, and forget it."

Colfelt's fingers closed over Chardon's with a grateful pressure, then the young officer saluted again and rejoined Holcombe's party.

"And now, gentlemen," Chardon addressed the others, "I hope you will accept our apologies for a violation of the hospitality of this Society. But I think you must agree with me that there was little else that a gentleman could do under the circumstances. We hope for an early adjustment of this unhappy affair. And in the meantime, I am sure that you will agree with me that the less said about the contretemps, the better."

Peter felt an arm slipped through his, and looked down into the face of Mr. Petigru. The eyes were smiling quizzically and with a trace of pity that was too remote, too affectionate, to be offensive. The face was ruddy, but not with the floridity of too good living that characterized many of his contemporaries. Under the lines that age and humor had etched about his eyes, his cheeks wore still the quick fresh color of an inextinguishable vitality.

"I am going in your direction, Ashley," he said in his high, singularly youthful voice. "Suppose we walk together. I imagine Chardon will want to remain awhile." He propelled Peter quietly toward the door, but they had gone only a few steps when his charge turned impulsively back toward the group about the big center table. The buzz of talk that had lifted behind them fell into sudden silence.

Peter said, impetuously, "There's something I want to make you gentlemen understand. It's hard to explain. It hasn't anything to do with my personal quarrel. It's about—what I said here tonight. You were kind. You got me talking and I forgot where I was. I am like that. But I don't want you to think I'm an outsider. That I'm different from you all here." He paused for an instant. Then he conquered his emotion, and plunged on. "This—this is my country. Just give me a little time—and—forgive me."

He turned quickly and found himself out on the pavement with his arm pressed close in the grasp of his friend. Behind them the Hall rose in simple and dignified beauty under the soft stars. A small damp air moved through the garden across the way and flung the perfume of jessamine against their faces. In his heightened emotional state, it struck Peter poignantly. "My God, it's beautiful," he sighed.

But his conductor very practically allowed him no time for rhapsodies, and directed their steps toward a narrow lane that ran between garden walls in the direction of White Point Gardens.

Petigru broke the silence. "I hope you'll forgive me, Ashley, for my wretched mischief-making. I knew that you could give them an impartial point of view, and they need it. But upon my word, I couldn't foresee the behavior of that drunken reprobate."

"Please do not concern yourself," Peter begged. "Why he should want to fight me I cannot imagine. But this was obviously merely an excuse."

They walked for a moment in silence, then the older man said abruptly: "I like your independent spirit, but I suppose you know you're behaving like a young fool?"

"Like many kinds of one, I'm afraid," Peter conceded in a rueful voice, "but specifically just what variety do you mean, sir?"

"By attempting to reason yourself into a state of patriotic fervor; by trying to rationalize a cause. War, my dear boy, is concerned only with the emotions—not the intelligence. It's a fools' holiday. If you don't believe me, open your ears on any street corner tomorrow. But do not attempt to argue. In there tonight I could see plainly what you were after, whether you yourself realized it or not. You're young—you're terribly out of it all —and you have inconvenient convictions. You marshaled your arguments, hoping they'd be refuted. Hoping to be converted. And what did you get? An outwardly courteous silence from a couple of dozen gentlemen, because you were born one of them and consequently, while perhaps personally mistaken, are of a class that can do no real wrong. Then Simms gives you a confession of faith, and a drunken boor insults you."

Peter thought this over for a moment; then: "But you, sir,—everybody knows that you are a Unionist. And you are respected for your honesty. Is that only because you are one of them too?"

"My dear fellow, I am invaluable. I cannot even play the martyr. Like your uncle, I am of the Clan. We are too old to fight, anyway, and so instead of becoming dangerous, we are merely eccentric. We are allowed to say what we please. Our resignations have not been requested by one of our clubs. We fulfill a civic function—we are Charleston's excuse for considering itself broadminded. If anyone accuses them of intolerance, they have merely to say, 'Intolerant? Ridiculous!—why, there's Petigru, there's Chardon.'"

Peter could not help laughing. "And you don't mind being alone?" he queried.

"I rather like it. Old age, my boy, and the crystallization of a naturally cantankerous nature. But it is different for you. Youth must run with the pack, or die of loneliness."

"That's it, sir," Peter said. "All my life I've been lonely. I've wanted to forget myself—to be one of the crowd. When I was a small boy here I knew I was different. But in England, with the rowing, the riding, and the University crowd, I got along well enough. I thought I'd changed. I told myself that when I came home I'd fit in—be one of them. And here I am. And the war. And this damned attitude of everybody's as though I were temporarily out of my head. And everybody watching me with a sort of amused curiosity, as though I'd come from Mars. Even the friends I had counted on: Simms turned military engineer, Hayne a soldier, Henry Timrod, the gentlest fellow in the world, a war poet."

"And Peter Ashley," his friend concluded, "slapping a gentleman's face for calling him an abolitionist."

In his absorption Peter had forgotten the impending duel. Now it brought him up short.

"I'm sorry," Petigru hastened on. "But I wanted to show you that you're not far behind your friends. It comes like that, you see—not through any process of logic, but through instinct, and a capacity for faith. It is like a religious conversion. Some day, like St. Paul, you will see a great light; or even more appropriate to this situation, you will be like Balaam—you will hear an ass speak and you'll believe him. Then your troubles will be over. You can believe miracles, even the one that a Confederacy of Southern States can whip the Union."

Peter could not restrain a laugh at this pungent analysis of his problem. But in a moment he said seriously, "Do you know, you're wonderfully clever. I have had flashes like that, but they don't last, and afterwards I cannot help feeling ashamed of them."

They walked in silence a while, and presently they turned a corner and before them lay the White Point Gardens, misty and beautiful under a westering moon. From the bay came the throb of paddles, and the sleek, dark water was shot with flares from the night patrol.

"Oh, well," Petigru said as they neared the Chardon home, "perhaps it will all clear up without war. Perhaps, after all, the government is not making jackasses of our commissioners, and will sell us Sumter and march Anderson home."

Peter looked him in the eyes. "Do you believe that?"

"Of course not."

"Neither do I."

At the door Peter paused and gave the customary invitation. "Won't you come in for a nightcap, sir?"

Petigru looked at him a moment, then said with decision, "No—go to bed; you need rest."

Peter felt a sudden surprisingly strong grip on his hand. Then the older man was disappearing in the faint moonlight, his figure moving with its slight characteristic roll, like that of a sailor who had somehow got lost on shore. Peter entered the empty house, sat down and waited.

CHAPTER XVIII

B EHIND him a door opened and closed, and instantly Peter sensed his uncle's presence in the room. The air was suddenly astir with enveloping and protecting emotion. He looked up, and instantly both men took refuge behind smiles that were grim, almost impersonal.

Standing by a small table and looking down at Peter, Chardon said, "In spite of my rebuke to young Colfelt, I am afraid that we have both taken decided liberties with the intention, if not the letter, of the law. The purpose of the code is to interpose certain formalities between the challenge and the meeting, so that passions may cool and there may be an opportunity of negotiating a peaceable adjustment. There are advising friends to be consulted, acting friends to be engaged, and the customary period of not less than twenty-four hours allowed for the principals to put their affairs in order.

"But Colfelt was eager for an early meeting. He felt certain that if the military authorities got wind of it, even though we are not in an actual state of war, they would forbid Holcombe's participation. He proposed to carry it through in any event, but he didn't relish the idea of court-martial. It was obvious to all of us that with a man of Holcombe's temperament a peaceable settlement was out of the question. As a matter of fact, I had hoped for an early meeting. With your devilish imagination, and your nervous temperament, I knew that the ordeal of a delay would count heavily against you. But I withheld my immediate consent and made it the basis for negotiating a concession in your behalf.

"That granted, we proceeded at once with the formalities. Holcombe wrote a proper and dignified cartel, which was presented by Colfelt after his departure. I accepted it for you under the power which I hold to transact your legal affairs—again very irregular—but accepted by mutual consent. Your cousin Bull-Smith has agreed to serve as your acting friend. He is a pompous ass, but if he knows anything at all it is duelling. He has figured, and with credit, in an extraordinary number of affairs."

Peter looked up sharply. "But why not you, Uncle Pierre?"

"I am ruled out on the grounds of consanguinity. And besides—" Suddenly the pose of disinterested adviser that Chardon had held so successfully went to pieces. The carefully schooled muscles of the face quivered and contracted. He rose and stood facing the fire, his back to Peter. His words sounded as though they were being torn violently from some part of his living organism. "Besides, I couldn't endure it."

After a moment he crossed to a table where a tray was placed every evening with decanter and glasses, poured and gulped a glass of neat brandy, and returned to his old position, fingers resting lightly on the table top. "We have arranged to meet at sunrise tomorrow."

Peter drew out a large double case watch and sprung it open. "It is two o'clock now." Then, after a moment, in a voice that was not quite steady and that left his sentence suspended in silence, "In four hours."

Chardon proceeded in a hard, controlled voice: "I must say, Peter, you handled the affair admirably. Had you let the moment pass without striking him, you would have had to challenge eventually. I think he counted on that. It would have given him the option, and he would have selected dueling pistols. This is not his first affair of honor, you know. He has something of a reputation."

"Then it's not pistols?"

"I named the Lindsay pocket piece as the weapon. It took them by surprise. They protested at once that it was not customary. This I admitted, but as the rules merely specify a smooth-bore piece with a barrel not over nine inches in length, my position was technically secure. I told Colfelt candidly the reason for my choice. You are not a shot. Holcombe has a reputation with the dueling pistol. Holcombe is a sportsman. I merely contended that this would give you at least the shadow of a chance, and then, since I had conceded an early meeting, they consented. Later I agreed to the use of the double-barreled type. It was a necessary compromise to avoid the aspersion of hiding behind an inadequate weapon. Under the terms of the encounter, the pistol may be emptied as rapidly as possible upon the signal to commence fire. Then if there are no casualties, and the customary question is put and answered in the negative, the arms may be reloaded for another exchange."

Chardon had now achieved complete self-possession. As though to punish himself for his moment of weakness, he went on ruthlessly: "As a matter of fact, the piece carries a fairly heavy ball—forty to the pound."

He reached into the skirt pocket of his coat, and said with a show of casualness, "It's a rather handy arm, lighter than the Smith and Wesson, and can perforate an inch plank at fifty yards." He produced the pistol and passed it to Peter. "Are you familiar with it?"

Peter smiled wryly. "You know I'm not, sir." He turned it over awkwardly in his hands.

"They are *le dernier cri,*" Chardon said. "Just appeared on the market on the strength of the new war fashions. Practically every man in the Hall tonight had one on him. They must all be playing soldier, even those in civilian dress. But by good fortune it seems that Holcombe is unfamiliar with its use. He shoots only the heavy, long-barreled piece, and the change in balance will disconcert him. You are blessed with a quick eye and knowing muscles." He paused and looked at Peter closely. "Are you tired?"

Peter got up and stretched his arms in a broad gesture. "No," he said, "not at all. And anyhow, sir, I couldn't rest."

"Very well. Go upstairs and get into black trousers and a white shirt, and meet me in the cellar. Cæsar will be there with coffee, and I propose by morning to make a shot of you."

For three hours Peter stood firing at a white smear the size of a man's head, that Cæsar had painted on the bricks at the far end of the cellar. At his side stood the negro, tearing cartridges open with his teeth, ramming the charges home and capping the nipples, loading while Peter fired a companion piece.

There was a technique for receiving and holding the

pistol, and at first this worried Peter, switching his mind back to the trivial details between discharges. Chardon would grasp the piece by the end of the barrel and pass it to him. He must take it with the left hand by the middle of the barrel, then present the butt to his right hand, grasp it, and stand with the muzzle pointing to the ground at his right. As soon as the piece was in position, Chardon would ask, "Are you ready?" then give the word. Peter would fire one barrel, cock, and fire the second as rapidly as possible.

When Peter had mastered the mechanics of handling the pistol, Chardon stopped him. "That will do," he said. "Your form will pass muster. Now you must learn to shoot." Then he explained that there were two types of shot employed. Of these the drop shot was the quicker, the rise shot the surer. "We will concentrate on the rise," he told him. "If Holcombe uses the drop he will probably get his fire in first, but not knowing this small arm, his success will be uncertain. You must school yourself not to be shaken by the sound of his report if it comes first."

Chardon demonstrated the mechanics of the shot, and the firing recommenced. It was astonishing how soon repetition reduced the unusual to the commonplace. The monotony of the performance acted like a sedative; the machinelike regularity of the loader—the laconic precision of the commands—the report in the confined space like a bright blade of sound flung from the barrel to ring against the silence, then hurled back again and again, blunted and broken by the low groined arches of the masonry.

Once a face appeared at the single low street window,

eyes and sudden teeth in the candle shine, then the slap of the terror-stricken feet dwindling away in the distance.

Toward morning it commenced to have a definite effect on Peter's nerves. Candle flames liquefied and flowed like spilled wine. It called forth a distinct effort for his eyes to draw them up again to the points of the tapers. His right hand gave the distinct impression of belonging to someone else. He marveled impersonally at his power to direct it. At its proper place in the ritual the voice would say, "Fire!" The hand would be there before him. His whole being would fly into focus upon the mechanism that lay in its fingers. Then it would burst into life, and a chip would fly from the wall at the end of the cellar.

Relentlessly the machine drove him on. The white blob on the wall commenced to take form. Between its two candles, it was changing into the lineaments of a human face. He noticed it after one discharge, and tried to brush it away when he took the next pistol from Chardon. But when he turned to fire again, it had gained form; it had leaped from the vague into the definite. It was Holcombe—mocking, sinister. The candle flames splayed out on either side of it, flowed together and became the first faint yellow of the dawn. Now against the light Holcombe stood silhouetted in detail. The light brightened. A silver thread that lay to the right surged out of the night mists and became the Ashley River with its familiar shore line dark against a shrouded west.

The feeling of detachment that he had experienced towards his firing hand spread through his whole being.

The scene projected itself sharp and detailed upon his retina. He saw, from outside of himself, his obedient body standing facing Holcombe. It had all taken place since his uncle had handed him the pistol. Now he waited for the word that would shatter the picture and set him free.

Then it came roaring through space. He saw Holcombe's pistol go up and blaze, and with the returning rush of consciousness felt the spasmodic contraction of his own finger upon the trigger.

He lurched back against the wall. His body felt shattered, empty. His fingers opened and dropped the pistol. Chardon was looking into his face. Cæsar was offering a cup of coffee.

"He got me, Uncle Pierre," Peter gasped.

"Nonsense, boy. Pull yourself together. Your last slug would have taken him full between the eyes. I'm proud of you." He turned to Cæsar. "Put the horses in the carriage," he ordered, "and meet us at the yard gate. By the time Mr. Peter finishes his coffee we should be on the move."

CHAPTER XIX

PETER did not know that any living habitation could be so quiet as the city was that morning. A heavy motionless fog filled the streets. The air, warm with early spring, seemed to sag with suspended moisture. The clop-clap, clop-clap of the trotters fell muffled and dead upon the cobbles. At the intersection of Broad and Meeting streets, the vehicle swung over toward the Ashley River and Peter noted the forbidding mass of the guard house on the left, and opposite, a vague suggestion of soaring columns where St. Michael's portico lifted into the murk. In the upper air the bells sang the quarter hours and struck six, and the voice of the watchman, as remote and impersonal as Fate, reached Peter with the ironic assurance that all was well.

The horses trotted steadily northward. Behind the fog, daylight began to climb into the sky, suffusing the murky atmosphere with a vague half-light, punctuated at regular intervals by blind street lamps distinguishable only as faint yellow auras in the universal gray. Presently, there was a sense of space—a feeling of freedom from invisible but oppressive barriers, and they knew that they were leaving the houses behind them.

Cæsar pulled the horses up sharply and peered to the left, then turned and wheeled the vehicle between the massive gateposts of the Washington course. To Peter came, sharp and distinct, the course as he had last seen it.

223

The grandstand to the right, a blaze of color in the clear sunlight. "Gwine to run all night, Gwine to run all day. Bet my money on the bob-tailed nag, Somebody bet on the bay." Albine hurtling her big overgrown colt's body, with black Bedo resplendent in red and white crouched monkeylike on her withers. The roar of the crowd as the Carolina horse passed Planet in the stretch. Damaris—a sudden, inexplicable, desperate nostalgia. That had been his day—he had belonged.

And his story of the race! He had known it was good because it was a part of him that he burned out of himself on to the sheets of paper; because of the price that it had cost him. And now, he wondered, was it going to be his last big story? The idea did not frighten him, because all through the night he had been steeling himself to meet it, because he deliberately made it a subject for abstract speculation, examined it, turned it over in his mind. And if it was,—if the vision that had come to him in the cellar had been prophetic and not merely a projection from overstrung nerves,—what then? He had traveled a long way spiritually from the conventional belief of his fathers. The Episcopal heaven and hell were in the discard. But he believed that somewhere in the complex mechanism that was labeled Peter Ashley there burned the spark of immortality. He had known so many moments when, with body weary and brain lax from the exhaustion of thinking, he had stepped suddenly across the threshold into a new dimension, and for a brief moment had touched the universal. The things that he had written then throbbed with life. They were the very few things that he had kept. He had sometimes wondered whether death might not be as simple as that.

Merely stepping over a threshold from an opaque into a lucent medium, with scarcely a break in the progression.

Chardon's voice, unnatural, metallic, under its rigid control, broke in upon his reverie. "I should have let your father know, of course, but there wasn't time. Is there anything that you would wish me to tell him——?"

Peter finished the sentence for him. "—if I don't come out of it? No." Then after a moment, "Do you know, Uncle Pierre, I think he'd be enormously proud, after a while. I've always been something of a humiliation. And since I've come home I've been harder than ever to explain—with the war and all, and Wake at the head of his own company. Now I may go down as the family hero. The story will be sure to end: 'Yes, by God, sir,—blood will tell!' "

The words were spoken without bitterness, and Chardon marveled at the boy's courage. "There's your mother And—" tentatively—"Damaris."

"You'd have to see them, I suppose. Women expect it. It would be damned trying, Uncle Pierre,—but you would know what to say."

The carriage rounded the corner of the long stable, and before them lay the field. The others had arrived and were standing motionless in the thinning fog. Two grooms stood near, holding the reins of several saddle horses, and an ambulance, with the driver hunched over in his seat, loomed ominously in the murky air. Cæsar pulled up the horses and looked over his shoulder for orders. "We'll wait here, Cæsar," Chardon said. Then he turned to Peter.

"This is as far as I can go with you. The rule excluding a close blood relation from the field is a wise one, and I must abide by it. But there would be little that I could do for you in any event; my offices as advising friend have terminated, and now your cousin Bull-Smith will assume command in his capacity of second. There is one point that you must keep in mind, and that is that his authority is supreme. From the moment that you step upon the field, he becomes the custodian of your person and your honor. You are to remain his pliant and submissive subject. If, after one exchange of shots, a decree of satisfaction is effected, he alone will be the judge of what concessions are consistent with your honor. I could not leave you in better hands. Your cousin has negotiated a number of affairs with great success, but he is a strict disciplinarian, and if you attempt to impose your own views upon him, in violation of the code, he will doubtless exercise his prerogative and march from the field."

A burly figure detached itself from the group in the center of the field and came toward them. Chardon said, "Here comes your second now. Go and meet him and I will send Cæsar after you with the pistols."

Peter got out of the carriage and the eyes of the two men met. Chardon held out his hand and Peter clasped it. "God bless you," said the older man, and Peter replied steadily, "Thank you, sir." Then he turned and walked toward the approaching figure.

Major Trapier Bull-Smith presented a perfect example of the English squire type. He had ridden to the rendezvous, and in his doeskin breeches and boots, he would have needed but to change the color of his coat to appear as much at home against rolling downs as he was on the flat, unbroken levels of the Carolina Low Country.

His ruddy face was flanked by graying mutton chops. His eyes were shrewd and kindly. He took Peter's hand and enveloped him in a warm reassuring smile.

"I'm proud of you, my boy," he said in greeting. "And I'm proud to be of service to you. And by God, sir, I wish that I had been at the Hall last night to see you cast that bounder's insult back into his teeth."

Peter thanked him, and added, "This is all new to me, you know, sir. You'll have to tell me exactly what to do."

"Exactly," approved his friend. "That's the proper spirit. I am here to do all the worrying for you. You have only to keep your head clear and your hand steady. I have been sounding the captain's friends. Nothing will be acceptable but an abject apology, and so we have no recourse but to proceed with the first exchange."

They reached the group of gentlemen. Day was coming rapidly now, and the dawn wind had set the fog moving. There were now present, besides himself, six men: Holcombe, Colfelt, Bull-Smith, two gentlemen who had accompanied the seconds to load, and another whom Peter immediately recognized as Dr. Vardell. He was glad of that. He remembered the rotund little surgeon and had always liked him. He was associated in his mind only with childish stomachaches, clean astringent smells, and peppermint lozenges. It was difficult to connect him with the grim practice of surgery. His presence gave him faintly something of the old childhood sense of security. The major and the boy lieutenant busied themselves at once with the preliminaries. First the major stepped off ten paces, then Colfelt verified the distance, marching very erect and self-important, turning with a snap, and saluting.

Peter stood watching them with intense mental concentration. If he could hold his mind unswervingly on externals, he knew that he could carry it off. A single moment of introspective weakness, and his emotions would be out of hand. He held the fingers of his right hand open before him—not a tremor. It was miraculous, the power of the human will to batten down the primal instinct of fear, and hold the flesh to the mark in the face of possible annihilation. The realization that he had that power infused his body with a sudden warmth of pride and self-confidence. He lost the sense of futility that had been bred of the night's vision, the feeling that what was to transpire had already been written. In its place came a heightened sentience, as though he had tapped unknown reserves of mental and physical power —what might eventuate ceased to be of importance. He was concerned only with the vital, immediate moment.

"Peter." The major's voice came to him, not as an interruption of his mood, but as a part of it.

"Yes, sir."

"We have decided to proceed. We'll have no sunrise, thanks to the fog—but there is enough light. Are you ready?"

And again Peter heard himself replying, "Yes, sir."

The turf was springy under Peter's feet—a jessamine that had preëmpted a scrub oak drenched the air with perfume. The fog was lifting. At the zenith there was already a faint hazy blue shot with gold from the early sun. The light was good, the visibility absolute, with no misleading highlights and shadows.

The major said: "As we are not using dueling pieces, we have not tossed for a choice of weapons. Each of you will use his own. They have been compared, and are identical. You have won the toss for position. We have decided that the line shall run north and south. Have you any choice?"

Peter saw two small stakes driven in the ground about thirty feet apart. He stepped decisively to one of them. "This will be my station," he said.

Holcombe had been standing at a little distance. His back was turned, and he was telling an amusing story to Dr. Vardell. He deliberately finished, made his point, and laughed a shade too boisterously. The doctor did not respond. His look said plainly that he considered it in execrable taste.

Holcombe walked over to his station, turned and faced them. The loaders presented two pistols to each of the seconds. They approached their principals. Peter found himself going through the routine of accepting the piece and carrying it to the proper position at his side. The doctor, and the seconds, each of whom had retained a pistol, took their places at a point halfway between the firing stations and well to one side, out of the range of fire.

The major spoke. "You are familiar with the procedure. Lieutenant Colfelt will give the word. He will count: one, two, three, fire. At the word 'fire,' you will open fire, discharging one barrel then cocking and firing the second barrel." He turned to Holcombe. "Are you ready, Captain Holcombe?"

"Ready."

"Are you ready, Mr. Ashley?"

"Ready."

"They are ready, Lieutenant Colfelt."

The young officer, heels together, head up, commenced, the high, tense voice jerking at the nerves of the watchers: "Prepare to receive the word." Then, "One, two, three—" At the last moment Peter's eyes had instinctively turned toward his uncle. Now, at the count, they swung an arc, recording with instantaneous and agonizing accuracy, the river, the stable, the group of watchers—Holcombe.

"Fire!"

Peter's hand went up. Contracted. There was a single explosion. Instantly Peter knew that he had escaped. He thought that Holcombe's piece had failed to fire. Then he saw that the barrel was smoking and that Holcombe was cocking the hammer for the second barrel. He realized that they had fired together, and that both had missed. Panic touched him as he clawed his own hammer back and heard it click. It passed as he raised his arm. Holcombe was using the drop shot. His pistol swung and cracked. Peter's answered like an echo, and again he knew that death had passed him by.

With an oath Holcombe flung his pistol down. Colfelt stepped forward and retrieved it. Major Bull-Smith addressed Colfelt: "Your principal accepted the Lindsay piece as the weapon. You should caution him against an unbecoming display of temper on the field."

Peter started forward. The major's voice was sharp, peremptory: "Principals will remain at their stations." Then he turned to Colfelt and in the stilted phraseology of the code said: "Our friends have exchanged shots. Are you satisfied, or is there any cause why the contest should be continued?"

Instantly Colfelt gave the reply: "We have been deeply

wronged, and if you are not disposed to repair the injury the contest must continue."

Peter strained to catch the reply. He was almost out of earshot of the low-spoken words. Then the major's voice reached him, raised on a note of finality. "As the custodian of my friend's honor, we have no recourse but to a second exchange."

Colfelt saluted. "Very good, sir."

The major said, "We shall proceed at once. Do you care to witness the reloading?"

Colfelt replied in the negative, and the loaders retired with the arms.

And now for the first time Peter noticed that quite a group had assembled in the vicinity of the carriages. He saw a figure detach itself from the mass and advance at a ponderous dog-trot; then he recognized Proctor Gordon. He was laboring under great distress, and when he joined the seconds he was breathless from his exertion.

"Gentlemen, gentlemen!" he panted. "I beg of you. This is deplorable, really deplorable."

The seconds waited, eyeing him with thinly veiled hostility. Presently he was able to explain. He had come to offer his services as a mediator. He was a conscientious objector to the institution of dueling, and in accordance with a new and none too popular custom had so advertised himself in the papers. This rendered him immune to challenge, and was assumed to qualify him as a mediator. Gordon's declaration had required moral courage. It was a step that could be taken only by one of unquestioned honor and a reputation for fearlessness without incurring the scorn of those who adhered to the code.

No one doubted Proctor Gordon's sincerity, or his courage, but his interference was tacitly resented.

The seconds listened to him in a sort of guarded silence. It was obvious that, with Holcombe's attitude in the matter, no peaceable settlement was possible, but neither Major Bull-Smith nor Colfelt was willing to have it said that he had closed a door that might have opened a way to the saving of bloodshed. That was the sort of thing that people would fasten upon, and repeat to a man's disadvantage. In the end they gave grudging consent. There was nothing for it but to march their principals from the field and parley.

The major took Peter by the arm and commenced to lead him to the group at the carriages. The nervous tension that had sustained him during the firing had passed. Under the guiding hand, his body moved heavily. A single thought had taken possession of his mind. He was going to have to go through with it all again. Then suddenly he realized where he was going. He couldn't face people now. Good God! couldn't the major see that? He stopped in his tracks. The hand urged him gently forward. "Come, come, stiff upper lip, you know. You won't have long to wait."

Peter cried desperately, "But I want to be alone. I've got to be alone."

The major's face cleared. "Oh, certainly. I thought that your mind would be diverted."

They started back. Under the following scrutiny of the crowd they crossed the field, and came to a broken paling fence at its farther boundary.

Peter said, "I'll wait here, sir."

The major gave him a hasty pat on the shoulder. His

face was preoccupied. He turned to go, then over his shoulder he threw his enveloping smile. It seemed to Peter to be empty and meaningless. It called for completion by an appropriate platitude, and the major added perfunctorily, "I'm proud of you, my boy, proud of you."

After a moment Peter seated himself on the grass and leaned his back against the fence. In the distance he could see Holcombe in animated discussion with two men in Confederate gray. In the center of the field Proctor Gordon, Dr. Vardell and the seconds drew together into a small, gesticulating circle. His glance picked up the group at the carriages. For a sickening moment he had the fear that his uncle would come to him. That he would separate himself from the others and commence the interminable journey across the field, that he would keep coming on and on like a man in a nightmare, and never arriving. Then he knew that Chardon would understand. Would know that he had to be alone.

The sun lifted over the eastern fog bank and drenched him in warm humid radiance. He was surprised to see how high it was. They must have been on the field for an hour. It was like a crucifixion. They could keep a man hanging between life and death for hours, the issue, even the man himself, forgotten in the interminable intricacies of the code. A tide of self-pity invaded his being. He let go, and sank voluptuously into its depths. He saw himself in a sharp exterior visualization sitting alone on the young grass, with the Low Country sky springing from its flat horizons and swinging its stupendous arc over his head. He saw himself waiting utterly alone while Destiny in the persons of Proctor Gordon and the two seconds moved laboriously through the ritual of the code toward the moment that would mean life or death.

And now, like the major, he realized that the offer of his well-meaning friend was little more than a senseless interruption, a protraction of this agonizing waiting. For he knew that Holcombe had come to the field with the intention of killing him. He decided that had it not been for Chardon's foresight in the choice of weapons he would already be either seriously wounded or finished once and for all.

Now the fear of death, that he had kept resolutely at bay during the night of intensive preparation and the moment of crisis on the field, invaded his mind. It lay like a great shadow from horizon to horizon. And under it his thoughts came and went in a vague twilight. He saw how utterly he had ceased to be a free agent, how inexorably the forces that had precipitated him into existence in this particular spot on the globe had reassumed the direction of his destiny from the moment of his return, how worse than futile had been his resistance.

When he had left Damaris three nights before he had told himself that given time he would win. But she had not let him see her again. And now Holcombe was waiting for the final shot. He asked himself dully why the man should be so inexorable. His own private convictions could be of little actual concern to him, certainly not a matter of such moment that he would put his life in jeopardy.

Then in a flash the situation became as clear as day. Holcombe had seen Damaris since his visit. She had been too proud to let Peter know that she loved him; she was too high-spirited to forgive him so readily for his desertion of her; but she had told Holcombe. His attack at the club had been Damaris' answer. It was in perfect character with his rival that he should have acted in exactly that way. Even his friends admitted that at times he was a little mad. The girl had become an obsession with him. The code had given him his chance.

Instantly Peter's mind cleared. His nerves steadied. He sprang to his feet, acutely conscious of the physical world, of the earth beneath him, quickening to the rhythm of spring. From an adjacent myrtle bush a pair of cardinals broke with a sudden beating of wings, and circled toward the sun in a nuptial flight. Far on the eastern horizon the three spires of the town were needle shafts of fire under the morning sun. He took life again squarely between his two hands. He was himself again —Peter Ashley—and he was fighting not over the meaning of a certain word—but for Damaris.

The conference was over. Peter saw Proctor Gordon return to the group at the carriages. Major Bull-Smith was coming toward him.

They met, and the major said: "The conference was useless. Holcombe's second was determined. We have only wasted time." He looked closely at his principal, and was evidently satisfied by what he saw in Peter's face.

The pistols were ready. The preliminary formalities had burned themselves into Peter's brain. When he took the pistol it was with a sense of complete familiarity.

Then Colfelt's voice, the words rushing past in the silence to the climax—"Fire!"

On the exact tick of time that Peter's pistol jerked with its recoil, he felt his body lurch under the impact of a blow, blunt, stunning, like the kick of a horse, delivered squarely upon his right breast. His fingers opened, and in the ringing silence he heard the soft thud of his pistol on the turf. Instinctively he bent toward it. A wave of nausea engulfed him, warning him that if he stooped, he would not have the power to rise. He straightened up, his feet braced wide apart. Out of a swirling nebula the form of Holcombe surged into his vision, the one fixed object in a world that raced in stupendous circles behind him. He was cocking for the second shot. Peter's thoughts were erratic, confused. An idea would be snatched up and hurled away through space. But at the sight of Holcombe, his consciousness rallied. His faculties centered on the hands that held the pistol. He saw the thumb on the hammer drawing it up.

The simple process seemed to take an eternity. The thumb slipped, groped its way back. The right hand grasped the barrels. The left got the hammer, lost it again, became frantic. Peter's gaze remained fixed on the hands, groping now like those of a blind man. And behind this preoccupation with externals, some deep consciousness kept warning him to keep his jaw muscles locked against the warm, salty pressure at his lips, to hold his breath, to stand erect and wait.

Then suddenly, when he had reached the limit of his endurance, the weapon flew clear of Holcombe's hands, and the man pitched forward on his face. Instantly the forces that Peter had held at bay closed upon him. From a dead center he was swung out on a great soaring arc that ended in blackness.

CHAPTER XX

CÆSAR had set breakfast on a small table before the library fire. Flounder, and hominy, thin slices from one of the Wakefields hams. Presently he would return with waffles, and would chide his master for leaving the food untasted.

But Chardon knew that he could not eat. He replaced the silver covers on the dishes. Then he poured a cup of black coffee and raised it to his lips. His hand shook so violently that the dark liquid spilled, staining the white linen of his shirt. He replaced the cup, and subjected the hand to a long scrutiny. He could not control the tremors. Presently he made his hands into two tight fists and jammed them into his coat pockets.

He fancied that in spite of the distance to Peter's room and the heavy planking of the floor, he could still hear irregular, strangled breathing. Behind the screen of familiar objects that his vision marshaled before him, he could still see the desperate conflict of which Peter's body was the battleground. He marveled again, as he had done through the interminable hours of the past day and night, during which he had never left the bedside, at the tenacity of human life, at the stubborn, almost ruthless persistence with which the unconscious functions of the body refused to surrender. The agonized flesh could show the white feather, the tired heart at the limit of its endurance could pray for peace, but the deep rhythm that

237

animated it maintained its forward swing, holding death at bay until the hour set for the ultimate capitulation.

He thought of Dr. Vardell, who had come to relieve him and who was sitting now at Peter's side, watching as he had watched, each inhalation, wondering whether the reservoir of the boy's splendid vitality would hold until the crisis had been passed, or whether it was decreed that the bright stream should falter and ebb out on the next strangling breath.

Vardell, when all was said and done, knew no more about it than he did. He could patch up the broken mechanism, he could deaden pain that became unendurable, and then, like himself, he could only wait the whim of an unknown power that worked a blind and senseless system. Life. Chardon had seen it fight with the ferocity of a tiger over the body of an aged and spent wastrel, and fling it against its own desire back upon a world that had already counted itself well rid of its burden. And he had seen it snatch the beautiful, the young, the proud, quick with the passion for living, and hurl them into the dark oblivion of death.

He thought suddenly of his own homecoming after the war. He had entered this room knowing of Bella's death. Then they had said the words of confirmation. He had vowed then that he would disarm the enemy; that he would never touch life so closely that its severance could wound him again. But that, too, was not a part of the plan. Life was too cunning for that. Life always had another hostage ready. Links must be forged so that they could be broken, but the chain that bound you was continuous. He had lost Bella. And he had been given Peter. And now——

He heard steps in the hall—Cæsar's measured tread and a quick light footfall. The door opened and Damaris crossed the threshold. Cæsar closed the door, and his departing tread sounded from the hall.

For a moment Damaris stood without movement. Chardon saw that she had come without a bonnet; that under her blue-black hair her face showed with the dull whiteness of chalk; that her eyes were larger and darker than he remembered them, and that they kept asking him something over and over.

He said, "Yes, he's alive."

Damaris sank upon a chair beside the door, and hid her face in her hands. Her hoops, forgotten for the moment, ballooned grotesquely before her, showing slim ankles, petticoat ruffles and the lace of her drawers. Presently she commenced to cry softly.

Chardon's impulse was to leave the room. In his state of emotional exhaustion he was moved only by a desire for escape. He had nothing more to give. He wanted only to be left alone, to save himself at all costs for Peter. But Damaris started to speak, and he knew that he must stay.

She said brokenly, "They didn't tell me. All day yesterday Mama pretended to be ill, and kept me by her. And this morning I heard the servants talking. They said that he was—they said that he was——"

Chardon crossed to where she was sitting, and dropped a hand on her head. "But he isn't, my dear. And now you must take hold of yourself."

He went to the dining room and returned with a glass of sherry, which he made her drink. She stopped crying and sat looking dumbly up at him, her handkerchief pressed to her mouth.

"Dr. Vardell is with Peter now," he said. "We hope to pull him through."

After a moment she said, "I suppose you'll say that I'm to blame."

"My dear, I am both too gallant and too fond of you to say any such thing."

"But you'll think it, just the same."

He had nothing to say in reply.

"You must say something," she cried at last. "I can't bear this."

"Suppose we call it fate," Chardon suggested.

She sprang up and came toward him. "You can't be like this, Uncle Pierre," she cried. "You've got to help me—help us. I'll tell you what it was. I had to be sure. You see, I've been fooled before. I wasn't sure of myself. I knew Peter was different. That if I told him that I loved him, there would be no turning back. I had to be sure of myself to protect him. And so I sent him away to think. But I couldn't make Captain Holcombe stop coming. Then I knew. And I told Captain Holcombe. He was terrible. I saw then what he was. But I never thought——"

Chardon took her hands and looked down into her eyes. "And now?"

Her hands tightened on his in sudden frenzy. "If anything happens, Uncle Pierre, if Peter goes—I'll die."

Chardon took her into his arms, and held her silently for a long moment. Then he released her.

She seated herself on a low stool beside the fire and

looked up into his face. "You're going to help me, aren't you, Uncle Pierre?"

"My dear," he answered, "you have very nearly restored my faith in a divine providence. You are an answer to prayer."

"Tell me about it," she begged. "Tell me how it happened."

"I can't. It was too horrible. Your father can tell you. Poor Proctor. He did what he could. But I'll say this: the lad was magnificent. No one realized that he had been hit until he fell. He kept his feet with a ball through the lung. He kept his chin up, waiting for the final shot. In justice to Holcombe I must say that I am sure even he did not realize it, or he would not have struggled to fire again."

"Was Captain Holcombe badly hurt?"

"Not seriously. The bullet ripped his scalp and stunned him. He lost a great deal of blood, but he will soon be out again."

"It is all too horrible," she cried. Then, after a moment, "Uncle Pierre, you must help me. What can I do now?"

Chardon stood looking down at her for a long moment. He was struck again by the change that had come over her, by the depths of pain in her eyes. And suddenly his heart went out to her because he knew that he, himself, had failed the boy. That, blinded by love, and hoping that he might be spared, he had forgotten that no man can stand between another and his destiny. That he had remembered only that his own tragedy had grown out of war, and had forgotten that it was as inevitable that Peter should go in eventually as that he had long ago obeyed his own blind impulse. He realized how unhappy Peter had been since his return, and how each step had led on towards the catastrophe. And he saw that if he would repair the damage, he must give the boy up. That in this brief prelude to destruction Peter must be brought into harmony with his world, that into it he must compress all of his passion for living, his love of beauty, his realization of love. He looked down into Damaris' face and said gently:

"If we pull him through, you can marry him, my dear, then you can send him away to war."

Damaris started to speak, but he held up his hand for silence. She took it in both of hers, and sat regarding him, her face quick with emotion, and her eyes never leaving his.

"I have been blind," Chardon went on. "I confused my need for him with his need for me. I forgot that I was old, finished. And that he was just beginning. You need each other now, while you are what you are."

"But, Uncle Pierre," she cried, "when the war is over he'll come back."

"They never do," he answered sadly. "Not when they're like Peter. Something in their semblance may return, but it's never the same. But you mustn't think of that now. You must think only that you have each other."

Damaris clung to his hand and said, "Oh, Uncle Pierre, I want to do so much for him."

"In giving him yourself, you are giving him everything, and when he leaves you he will carry your image in his heart—a talisman to fight for." Chardon was silent for a moment, then said in a musing voice: "Man is a strange creature, Damaris,—strange, yet simple. And still as primitive as Adam. You may lash him to war with a patriotic ideal. But in battle he forgets all of that. He must have a symbol to fight for. Something that he can compass with his imagination. With me in Mexico what I always saw in the moment of danger was Bella and the children. They had nothing to do with Mexico. And if I had stayed home I might have saved them. It was as illogical as that, as ironical as that, and yet without them I could not have driven my body into imminent peril of death.

"In my company there was a man, a simple fellow and a devout Catholic. He had been given a story that Mexican soldiers robbed and desecrated churches. He told me that what he always saw in battle was a boot-heel fouled with manure stamping the fire from an altar candle. He fought like a fiend. And later I heard that he had died with Davy Crockett at the Alamo."

He stopped speaking, and stood looking down into the fire.

After a moment Damaris asked softly, "May I go to him now?"

Chardon's retrospective mood vanished instantly. He apologized for keeping her so long and left the room. In a moment he was back again. He said: "His room is at the head of the stairs. Vardell is there. Peter will not know you, but go for a moment and see him. Then come back and wait here for me. I am going over to talk to Proctor."

And while Damaris was standing beside Peter's bed, while Archibald Holcombe lay at the infirmary, his scalp ripped by a bullet that had very nearly bled him to death, Major Trapier Bull-Smith was standing before the fire in the St. Andrew's lounge, facing a half-circle of eager attentive faces.

"I'll admit, gentlemen," he was saying, "that it was rather a nice point. Gordon got farther with his proposals than I had at first thought possible. Colfelt finally agreed that his principal would retract his insulting epithet, if Ashley would apologize for the blow. I naturally refused to consider a mere retraction as against an apology. Gordon pointed out that while a spoken word was something that could be retracted, a blow that had been struck could not be withdrawn, and that I should accept. I admit that I was sensible of the gravity of the situation, but my friend's honor was in my keeping. I would have been derelict in my duty had I conceded to an apology without an outright apology from Holcombe as well, and to this Colfelt would not agree. There remained no recourse but to a second exchange. It was, as I have said, a nice point. As nice a matter of decision as had occurred in my experience upon the field."

CHAPTER XXI

PETER lay inert under the weight of a great languor, conscious of the fact that he no longer slept, yet unwilling to open his eyes upon a world that was waiting to storm in and repossess itself of his being. His room was on the top floor of the building; facing east, and looking over low intervening roofs, it commanded a view of the harbor. He had grown to hate the picture that he knew was waiting there, the window framing its square of water, with Fort Moultrie jutting in from the left Fort Johnson from the right, and Sumter just enough to the right of center to throw the composition askew and inspire him with an insane desire to break up the silly pattern and rearrange it. It could be done so easily. One only needed to reassemble it upon the seesaw principle with Sumter in the middle of the board holding the two side masses in balance. He remembered vaguely having explained this over and over to the patient but somewhat blurred form of Dr. Vardell. He had tried to get into the doctor's stupid head that Major Anderson had nothing to do with the question of war. The whole business would right itself if only they had sense enough to see that the composition was out of balance and correct it before it was too late. Damaris had understood, but what could the two of them do against a world full of lunatics, who were bent upon self-destruction?

Minutes passed, and Peter slowly became conscious of the fact that for some reason unknown to himself he had ceased to care. It was no longer of prime importance. If it was destined to go on forever like that, badly out of drawing—well, he must face it, get used to it. It probably wouldn't matter much anyway so long as Damaris understood. He braced himself for a moment, then opened his eyes. He lay perfectly still and stared incredulously.

There was the same rectangle of window, but the forts were gone. What he saw now was a foreground of vivid green, a background of soft blue, and against the latter what appeared to be an army of gigantic captive balloons, colored a warm copper and swaying gently in a flood of early sunlight. "Professor T. S. C. Lowe, constructor and aeronaut of the mammoth airship *City of New York*, will make spectacular ascent in his balloon *Pioneer*." But Peter knew that the professor needed only a single balloon for his ascent, not an army of them. At least he ought to know, because he had reported the professor's spectacular feat for the paper yesterday; or was it a thousand years ago?

The effort to place the assignment properly in time worried Peter, and he closed his eyes for a moment. When he opened them again, the balloons had stopped swaying, and each was resting solidly upon a massive support. Then suddenly he recognized them. They were the great live oaks that dotted the Wakefields lawn, bronze in their brief magnificence of bloom. Beneath them across the young grass drifted a flock of sheep, and above them stretched illimitably the tranquil blue of the St. John's sky.

One by one, as he lay there, his senses awakened. After sight came hearing, sounds, the clear whistle of a cardinal, the determined reiterations of a bobwhite down in the canal woods, the good sound of human laughter, and a far snatch of song from the kitchen:

> "My Ole Mistis promise me
> When she die she set me free.
> She lib so long, an' she die so po'
> She lef' me hoein' de cotton row."

Odors then, stinging Peter's eyes with unreasoning nostalgic tears, and as quickly banishing them. Wisteria, and roses, pouring their perfume along the morning sunshine to drench the room with fragrance.

Something was happening to Peter, something that he could not explain, would not try to, something miraculous, to be accepted simply and without question. In the deep springs of his being there was quickening movement, life, spreading, gathering momentum, singing in his arteries, giving his body an odd buoyance, drawing him upward. He placed his hands beside him, and lifted suddenly to a sitting position. It ended in a flash of pain that took him in the side and dropped him gasping on the pillows. Then Peter remembered everything.

It came to him as memory always did, in a series of sharply visualized pictures that flashed backward in proper sequence to the moment of Holcomb's shot. The interminable ride from town with Dr. Vardell sitting beside him in the ambulance, and another place that held sometimes his mother, sometimes Damaris. Damaris, on back down the series of flashes, always there.

Her hand that he would take when the doctors came to dress his wound. She would let him carry it down into the black gulf with him; then, when the voice came echoing down into the abyss telling him that it was over for today, he would close tightly upon the slim fingers and they would lift him gently and firmly up into the sunlight again. He remembered distinctly the day when she had told him that she would never leave him. And he had believed her implicitly. But now in this changed environment he experienced a moment of hideous doubt. Perhaps she had told him that only because she knew how much it meant to him, that she would hold him tight until he was out of danger, then let him go. He remembered how in the early days before the duel she had been like water, flowing brightly away between his grasping fingers.

He was seized with a sudden uncontrollable panic. He had to know the truth at once or he couldn't go on. He called her name once, softly. There was no answer. The clear assured whistle of the partridge was a derisive note flung into the silence to drive him to frenzy. He drew a deep breath and winced at the pain, then it left his lips in a shout.

"Damaris!" he called. "Damaris!" again and again, his hand beating futilely against the sideboard of the bed.

The door opened and she stood on the threshold, her eyes wide with terror. She was wearing a dressing gown. He had never seen her without either her hoops or her voluminous habit. She looked so slender and girlish that for a moment he did not recognize her. Then she ran toward him and he knew her. She took his head to her breast in a swift fierce movement, and held it pressed there.

"I thought I'd lost you," Peter sobbed. "I thought I'd never see you again. I thought you'd left me."

She pressed her cheek to his, fiercely, as though she would weld their separate flesh into a single inseparable body. "I'll never leave you," she whispered, "never. And if you ever go away from me, you'll carry all of me that matters away with you. If it's the war. If you're in torment again, you will know that I am there every single minute. And when you come back, if it isn't until the end of the world, you'll find my empty shell here waiting for you to fill it."

Peter exhaled on a long shaken sigh, and relaxed suddenly in her arms. Damaris sat cradling his head between her breasts, rocking very gently back and forth. Her gaze was fixed on a point beyond the open window, beyond the great copper globes of the oaks. From time to time she paused in her rocking and flung a single word of defiance at what she saw out there. And the word was, "Always."

Peter's recovery at Wakefields was little short of miraculous. In town there had been those first few days of agonized suspense while they had all watched in fear of a fatal hemorrhage. Then, with that danger past, the progress had been steady but discouragingly slow. Now, back at the plantation, each passing day marked a distinct advance. Scartissue seemed to build visibly overnight, obliterating the cleanly healing wound. It was as though, with his return to the land that he had first known, he had sunk hungry roots into the soil, and spring in its rush through the swamps and across the fertile fields had found them and had set his veins racing with resurgent life.

After remaining for only three days with his patient, Dr. Vardell thought it safe to return to town, leaving Peter in care of the neighborhood physician, Dr. Chouvenou, a cousin of the Ashleys and an intimate and frequent visitor at Wakefields, and this change in physicians was a good thing for Peter. Vardell was associated in his mind with all that he had been through in town, and much as he liked and trusted him, his presence kept old hurts smarting. And Peter wanted to forget everything that lay behind the morning when Damaris had given herself irrevocably into his keeping.

That morning he had closed a door on the past and stepped with her into a new and different world. And yet the world in which he now found himself was not a new one for Peter. It was rather the one to which he had been predestined. Sooner or later that strangely self-contained, highly individualized and, it must be admitted, rather smugly complacent spot shown on the early maps as the Parish of St. John, was sure to claim its own. Those of her sons who were cursed incomprehensibly with an ambition to be other than a Carolina planter would leave. The driving power of that alien urge would determine the duration of the absence. It never meant a permanent separation from the community, and those who remained at home knew this. It was axiomatic. Each generation had repeated the lesson. Had driven it home.

Youth with a fire in its heels would ask its patrimony, speak solemn good-byes into faces that would answer with indulgent smiles, and turn from the sandy St. John's road into the highway that led to town. The cousins, the aunts and the uncles would thereafter refer to the absence as a visit to town, to the North, abroad. The young master's room would always be kept ready. The small negro who had been given to him as a playmate would always remain John's, or Tom's, boy. His filly would become a mare, the mare would foal, and the colt in time would as likely as not capture the Pineville sweepstakes. The winnings would go half across the world to the rightful owner. There was no such thing as escape, for, in the minds of his relatives at least, the ultimate return of the wanderer was based upon unanswerable logic. He came of a race distinguished for its sound common sense. That faculty would in time convince him that the Parish of St. John's was the most delectable spot on the globe for human habitation. The farther he went, the more great capitals he visited, the more overwhelming the evidence.

Once when Peter was in England he had received a letter from his Uncle Porcher of Burnt Savanna Plantation, in which he said: "Like you, I wanted to find out for myself, and after wide travel I arrived at the conclusion that of all the countries upon the globe the United States was preëminently the most desirable; of all the states South Carolina stood far in the lead; and of all sections of South Carolina the Parish of St. John's is infinitely the most superior. It was not, however, until my return home that it was borne in upon me that Middle St. John's, in which God in His Wisdom has seen fit to cast our lot, is so obviously superior to the upper and lower divisions of the parish that I have always tactfully refrained from comparisons for fear of embarrassing our neighbors."

The day after Peter's return, a negro rode in before breakfast with a hot plate containing a stack of hominy waffles made by the old Lifeland receipt. His Aunt Maria remembered that Peter had liked them especially when he had visited her eighteen years before.

The first day that he was able to leave his room and was basking in the sun on the broad south piazza, he heard the discreet shuffle of a bare foot upon the planking and turned to meet the eyes of a tall and magnificently set-up negro. He recognized him at once as the slave whom he had helped to purchase at the auction. He smiled up at the man.

"You're looking well, Washington. How do you like having three masters instead of one?"

His visitor smiled gravely. "I ain't gots no complaint, Mas' Peter," he conceded. He stepped forward and presented a note; it said, in a clear bold hand:

"Dear Peter:

We're glad you're back at home, and know you must have enjoyed your visit abroad. Charles and I are so happy over your return and your recovery that we want you to accept our shares of the boy, Washington, in celebration of the event. We find that he makes an excellent stable man, and suggest that you put him to work on Starling and get her ready for next season's racing.

Affectionately your cousin,

Bert Lawrence.

P. S. The title has been sent to the courthouse for recording."

Peter handed the note to Damaris who was sitting near with her sewing. He gave it to her with a laugh, but suddenly and inexplicably his throat contracted, cutting it off abruptly. These people were doing something to Peter that he hadn't counted upon. Aunt Maria with her waffles, and now Charles and Bert; and the others, Wake, his mother, Thomas Ashley, the doctor. He told himself that his illness was responsible for these moments of surrender to his emotions, but in his heart he knew that this was not so. There were still occasional flashes of the old faculty of seeing himself from the outside—few now, and not welcome, and when they came he saw what was happening. He was letting go.

The protracted ordeal of the duel, his wound, had given him a short cut to that fatalism which sooner or later comes to every soldier who has been long under fire. His experience had brought him sharply a realization of the impermanence of life, the fragility of human happiness, the ridiculous futility of arguing with Destiny. He had Damaris. He was utterly happy. He was flowing again into the narrow but irresistible current of the parish life. The course that he had cut for himself, that had led him into other lands, other levels of thought, was now a faint trickle behind him. It was good to lie in the sun with the deep tides of his being flowing smoothly and of their own volition into the warm and genial stream. It was a good thing to have friends, to know love, to be understood.

He was awakened from his brief reverie by the shuffling of a calloused foot on the piazza floor. The negro was waiting, his body relaxed, his gaze fixed upon a buzzard that was spiraling down out of the blue into the canal woods. With a quite human sense of triumph, Peter remembered that Washington had belonged to Holcombe. Now Holcombe was out of the picture. It was strange that after winning Damaris, Fate should bring him his rival's servant as well. "Holcombe, poor devil," he thought, "how he must hate me." The idea of being hated stimulated him strangely. It made him feel arrogant. He said to the negro:

"You used to belong to Mr. Holcombe, I hear. They say he was kind to his people."

The man's eyes were wistful; he said, with his gaze still upon the circling vulture: "He been uh good mastuh."

Peter said with slight irritation, "Well, you belong to me now. Do you know horses?"

Washington answered eagerly, "Dat I does, suh. Mas' Archie——"

"Go to the stable," Peter cut in, "and tell Daddy Paul to turn Starling over to you. Polish her up well and give her an hour's gentle exercise. But before you start, bring her around to the front. I want to see you handle her."

It was the first time Peter had ever given an order to a servant of his own. He felt that something more was expected of him. He attempted the exact shade of affectionate irascibility that his father always employed: "Now get a move on you, you damn rascal."

But Washington did not respond with the customary grin. He saluted gravely and departed.

Peter said to Damaris, "I wouldn't be surprised if that boy had a sullen streak in him." But in his heart he knew that this was a libel. He knew that he had missed the exact shade of feeling in what he said that would have kept it from being abusive. In short, that he was an amateur, or worse, an alien, and that Washington had let him know that he knew it. It left him, oddly enough, with the feeling that he was going to have to make good with his own negro. If Wake had said that, Washington would have taken it. He wondered irritably if he had not been wasting a lot of time during the past dozen or so years. He looked at Damaris and saw that her eyes were dancing. She got to her feet and came to stand beside him. He regarded her expectantly. This was not the new serious Damaris who had given herself to him. It was the laughing elusive girl who had mocked him in town. It filled him with a new sense of possession to see her standing there.

She said, "It's a rare pleasure to see you at home again, Mr. Peter Ashley, and since you have a negro yard of your own, I am going to celebrate your homecoming with a valuable present. I shall bestow upon you a fine, loyal, and well-trained woman. Her name is Virginia, and I will have her delivered post haste from my own yard in town."

Peter opened his mouth to protest, but a quick, surprisingly strong hand was pressed upon it, forcing his head back into the pillows.

"Not a word, Mr. Ashley, not a single word," Damaris ordered. "You remember that the doctor left me in charge, and his orders were that you were not to talk unless I gave my permission. You've had quite enough to say for this morning, and now I shall have to insist upon your silence."

CHAPTER XXII

THEY were lyric days for Peter Ashley, those days of his convalescence, when, freed from the tyranny of thought, he gave himself over without reservation to life. They were days filled with beauty, color, movement, and a gaiety so sustained, so universal within the narrow limits of the neighborhood, as to gild the crowded hours with a glamour tinged with unreality.

Peter was riding again. Not Starling; he was not yet a match for her explosive vitality; but his mother's mare, a single-footer as steady as the Church of England. He would escort Damaris on what he described as introductory tours. Beyond the overgrown ditch of the old Santee Canal lay the tract that Thomas Ashley had promised him for his own. He would come back and break ground perhaps next season, but certainly not later than the winter of 'sixty-three. The house would be large, square and plain, after the manner of Wakefields, with an eight-foot basement, and broad steps leading up to the piazza. Under the piazza there would be a place for children to play. It would be floored with deep cool sand, and there would be two long joggling-boards against the wall. Next winter when the crop was laid by, Thomas Ashley would send the men to the saw-pit and they would commence to rip out the lumber.

The first time he crossed the canal with Damaris, they pulled their horses up involuntarily beneath the far-flung arms of a giant live oak, and stood looking out across the cleared land which lay fallow and drowsing under a heavy noon sun, toward the grove of oaks where the house would stand. From far away came the ring of an axe on oak; otherwise the silence was absolute. Their hands found each other, and locked. There was nothing that Peter could say. The moment was too big, too pregnant with the future. Behind the barriers of speech he thought, "Ours. Our children's." And then across the open field shimmering in sun, among the distant oaks, he saw, like a desert mirage, the house come trembling into being, standing foursquare behind the dense green, and through the interstices of the branches, the bright noon radiance refracted from new shingles. For a moment it trembled in the heat, then was gone. He lifted Damaris' slender hand to his lips, palm up, and kissed it. Looking out across the sunny field Damaris whispered, "Always."

Another day they broke through heavy woods into a small bay filled with low scrub and surrounded by pines. A sense of the familiar baffled Peter for a moment, then it came home to him suddenly. This was the place where his first and last fox hunt had ended. He started to tell Damaris about it. He laughed in the silent woods.

"It was a great joke on me," he said. "They've never let me forget it. They'll be telling you sooner or later. I always could ride, you know. I was the first here. The scrub was full of dogs. I could see their tails threshing, and the clearing was ringing. Until then I had always thought that a tonguing pack was the most beautiful music on earth. Then I was right on top of them. The fox had stopped fighting, but he was alive, and he looked right into my eyes. Blood was all over the leaves. I was off in a second into the midst of it. The fox was still looking at me, and I saw him die. Then the others came and found me crying like a baby and being very sick. They laughed at me and I hated them." He stopped speaking for a moment. His face was white under its new coat of tan. He said: "But of course, that was a long time ago."

Damaris' face was averted. Peter could not see what she was thinking. After he had finished speaking, she said on a hard little note of affirmation,

"Of course, that was a very long time ago." She turned and looked into his face. Her eyes were frightened. She said sharply, with finality, as though he had made a statement which had provoked in her a desperate necessity to argue, "But you're a man now. You wouldn't mind seeing—It wouldn't hurt you to look at——" Then suddenly her mood changed. She looked up at him and gave a short reckless laugh.

"Come," she called, as she swung her horse and gave him the spur. "We're wasting time. We'll be late for supper, and that will mean being late for the Belle Isle dance. And I'm bound to have you there and flaunt you under the noses of the local belles."

No time for contemplation now. No time to be lonely. Emily Ashley surrounded by her committee of ladies and a small army of sewing women was completing the uniforms for the Mounted Rifles. A field near the house had been cleared for a parade and practice ground. Wake, in high boots and higher spirits, was all over the place giving orders, and bringing in any number of fellow officers and men to breakfast, dinner or supper. Men who, to Peter's surprise, went out of their way to express their liking and admiration for him. They seldom spoke directly of his duel with Holcombe, but they let him know that he had behaved as a Middle St. John's man should have behaved, and they rejoiced with him in his successful courtship.

And under it all, like the foundations of the structure that was being builded, Thomas Ashley was driving the labor to the limit in the cotton fields. Out before day with his overseer and drivers, waking the clean well-kept fields to the young life that would break later into leagues of white fiber, furnishing the Confederacy with the sinews of war and forcing the world to kneel and pay tribute.

Peter found himself listening for the familiar parish names, getting an especial pleasure when he heard them. The French Huguenot names with their clear silver ring: Chouvenou, Gendron, Ravenel, Couturier, Gourdin, Gaillard, Bisseau, Dutarque; and the English, resonant as struck bronze: Irvine, Oliver, Whitfield, Broughton. The plantation names too had their own music—some French, some English, like the families who founded them: Lifeland, Mattessee, Burnt Savanna, Somerset, Tower Hill, Belvidere, Woodlawn, Belle Isle, Stuarton, Bluford. Names that were lovely, but that meant more than merely a lovely sound against the ear. Names that meant: "Well, Peter, how's the side? Well enough to let you ride over for supper tonight?" "By the way, I'm sending over the bay filly for Damaris. She's too fine a colt to go out of the family." "It's wonderful having you back to stay, my boy." Names that meant long evenings on broad moon-drenched front steps, the warmth of friends, and above in the shadowed depths of the piazza, the older people rocking, talking, faintly swaying white forms in the blue darkness, glowing cigar-ends. Roses and tobacco smoke blowing by in alternate waves, then mingling poignant and bitter-sweet. Under the high stars: "Juanita," "Spanish Cavalier," "Nellie Gray," "In the Gloaming." Then, with the boys in their saddles, "Auld Lang Syne."

Then, full-bodied, resonant, sustained, swelling suddenly up and possessing the night, the voice of the swamp. The voice that those who are bred within its sound never hear until they go away, and then listen for always in their dreams until they return.

And so it was at home that Peter found at last his escape from reality, his brief sanctuary, his moment of complete happiness. And yet those who knew, who were old enough and wise enough to read the future from the record of the past, could have told him, had they been unkind, that the peace that brooded over the wide fields was deceptive; the gaiety that never slackened, an ominous portent. St. John's: The hip pocket of the commonwealth, that in a flash could exchange the flask for the pistol; that had raced and danced once before, until a certain Sir Peter Parker had arrived off Charleston Harbor with a British fleet, and that had then taken the saddle and ridden down out of their fastnesses, carrying with them two excellent cotton planters, one a large bluff man called William Moultrie, and the other a modest little gentleman of French Huguenot extraction by the name of Francis Marion.

CHAPTER XXIII

MARCH, mad month in the maddest of years. Up in Washington, Buchanan, "The Property Man," has handed the lighted fuse to Lincoln, and has dropped gently into oblivion. Lincoln, the untried, the unknown, standing amid the babel of advice, the pull of opposing wills, with his single immovable idea: "The Union must be preserved."

But time is racing now. The fuse that he is holding must presently be stamped out or its fire will reach Fort Sumter and detonate the waiting charge. Shall Anderson be reinforced? Shall Anderson be withdrawn? The old question, but no longer to be evaded. And the world watching, waiting, holding its breath, for the word.

In Montgomery, Davis and his cabinet are facing a delicate problem. The central government must assume command of the military forces at Charleston. And Charleston is known to be difficult. The task calls for a soldier, but it also requires something of a diplomat, and, emphatically, a gentleman. And the God of Battles that smiles with such inspiring indulgence upon the new Confederation presents them with Pierre Gustave Toutant Beauregard. Beauregard, great-grandson of Jacques Toutant-Beauregard who, under Louis XIV, had been in command of the flotilla to the Province of Louisiana, and on the distaff side direct descendant of François Marie Chevalier de Reggio, royal standard bearer under the

Spanish domain. Oh, most emphatically a gentleman, but a soldier as well—hero of Chapultepec, Cerro Gordo, Vera Cruz, and late commander of the military academy at West Point.

March fourth. General Beauregard arrives at Charleston and assumes command of the military forces. On the fifth, he appears publicly with Governor Pickens and his aides at a performance at the Charleston Theater. Little Misses Fanny and Julia dance and sing. A competent cast performs *The Lady of Lyons*. But the sensation of the evening is the glittering presence in the proscenium box, and Charleston, remembering Jacques Toutant-Beauregard and François Marie Chevalier de Reggio, feels safe in taking the general unreservedly to its heart. Overnight he becomes the fashion. Ladies denude their gardens and convert headquarters at Institute Hall into a bower. Lads who have patiently cultivated fierce and warlike beards trim them down without a quiver to the Beauregard mustache and goatee. Huguenots with one accord forget that the general is a Catholic, and remember only that he is French.

But Beauregard is now in seclusion at headquarters, facing a stupendous task, opposing order to chaos. Martial law is declared for the island defenses. There are no longer champagne punches and parties of laughing and delicately stepping ladies among the tents. Leaves are canceled.

March twelfth. By special correspondent of the *News and Courier* at Washington, "It is unofficially announced that the President favors withdrawal of Anderson from Sumter."

March eighteenth. "It is now generally conceded that within a few days Sumter will be vacated."

In his private office at Institute Hall, Beauregard takes the newspaper in his slender long-fingered hand, smiles his slow skeptical smile, and orders an extra draft of five hundred slaves to rush the work on the forts. That night, up the river, sledges ring on spikes until morning, where they are sheathing the floating battery with railroad irons.

On March twenty-ninth, the Reverend Charles Cotesworth Pinckney ascends to his pulpit in Grace Episcopal Church and delivers his Sunday morning sermon. The church is crowded to the doors. The rector is known as a man of independent thought. He says what he pleases; and that, within limits, is right and proper, for is he not a man of God and a Pinckney? But with the announcement of the text, the congregation begins to have misgivings. Protected by his cloth, and by that monopoly of vocal expression which the Church bestows upon its priests, the speaker at once likens the South to Nebuchadnezzar whom, because of his pride and vainglory, God had reduced to the level of a beast of the field. He points to the fate of the Chaldean Monarchy, the Roman Empire, the Greek Republic, and, because they had been slave-holding civilizations, likens them to the Confederacy, and predicts a similar disintegration; and lastly, under the intoxication of his own oratory, he utters the ultimate blasphemy: He says that cotton cannot be depended upon to force the world to kneel and pay tribute to the South.

The congregation leaves in silence. The affair is neither infuriating nor amusing, but actually distressing. It is remembered that brilliant mentalities sometimes go like that. But after all, it is a matter to be handled by the family. The Pinckney connection is large and well-to-do, and what steps should be taken as to the care of their unfortunate member is a matter for them and not the community. Decidedly the proper attitude is that of tactfully ignoring the fact that a sermon had been preached at Grace Church on the morning of March twenty-ninth. And should anyone who had been present during the distressing exhibition chance subsequently to meet the rector, it will be well to hold the conversation to the subject of his choice collection of early roses.

On April second, the Honorable Louis T. Wigfall, late United States Senator from Texas, having decided to remove the seat of war from Washington to Charleston, arrives with his lady, and quarters himself at the Mills House. With his passing, Washington must seem strangely quiet, for the Senator's private campaign at the Capital has been violent and sustained.

One by one the other Southern Senators and representatives had abandoned the fight as hopeless and left for their homes. Their deflection had only stiffened the resistance of the redoubtable Texan. Of tremendous physique, inexhaustible vitality, and known as a fearless and deadly duelist, he had set himself the task of destroying the hostile government at its source by the sheer power of his oratory. It was said that he never slept. Hour on hour the tremendous mellifluous voice poured its broadsides of invective into the ears of the exasperated but powerless Senators. At night he would pursue them to their clubs, and there, holding them with his fierce magnetic gaze, he would deliver a verbal chastisement that so exhausted them that, when he left in the morning fresh and vigorous to carry the fight back to the Senate chamber, they were incapable of following him. There was a half-hearted suggestion that he be arrested, tried for treason, and hanged, in the somewhat forlorn hope that he would thus be silenced. He laughed in their faces, told them that they were Yankee shopkeepers and poltroons, and that for his part he was done with them. They could consider themselves dismissed. He now had more important business before him. He would go to Charleston and attend to Major Anderson.

On the third of April the Senator appears at headquarters. He is wearing varnished top boots and huge Texas spurs. About the senatorial frock coat is tied a broad, red, tasseled sash, and through this is thrust a sword. In his hand he carries his black plainsman's felt hat, and his magnificent leonine head is bare to the spring morning. Inside the building he discovers that a number of aides have attached themselves to his person and are assuring him that the general is busy and is seeing no one. He brushes them from his sleeves, enters the private office and announces to General Beauregard that he has arrived. When he emerges he is Colonel Wigfall, and a duly appointed aide to the commanding general.

It is evident that Beauregard has remembered that he is not only a soldier and a gentleman, but upon occasion a diplomat as well. But it is not unlikely, as the door of the private office closes upon his magnificent newest colonel, that he feels somewhat as though he has reached out and closed his hand upon the tail of a flaming comet.

It is probable that at no other time in his life Beauregard was as completely in harmony with his destiny as he was during those momentous days at Charleston. There was an element of mystery. In a community where the refusal to drink with a friend had been known to provoke a duel, he declined with charming courtesy, but absolute finality, to indulge in ardent spirits. He spent much time alone, working out his plan for the investment of Sumter, and the engineering genius that had lifted him to preëminence in Mexico came into full flower.

As to whether or not he desired war, we have only to remember that for six hundred years his forebears had distinguished themselves upon the field of battle and that, at that particular moment, should hostilities eventuate, he stood practically unrivaled upon the threshold of the supreme command. It is not likely that these circumstances would have conspired together for the creation of an ardent pacifist. He knew that President Davis and his cabinet did not desire war. He must have known that President Lincoln did not desire it. Had he been consulted as to his views, he would doubtless have replied that it was not the province of the soldier either to believe or to disbelieve that a war was imminent —but to be prepared. And to this end, under the grave formal elegance of the man in the private office, there drove steadily forward all day and most of the night the irresistible momentum of a superb engineering machine.

It may have appeared that, knowing the reluctance of Montgomery to precipitate the effusion of blood and finding himself in Charleston which already considered itself at war, his position would have been embarrassing. But it was singularly the reverse. He was scrupulous in his dealings with the Confederate command. In every decision he deferred to Davis and awaited instructions. And he was in complete harmony with the Carolinians. He must have understood their temper completely. He surrounded himself with a group of aides taken for the most part from civil life, and incongruously attired in black frock coats, sashes and swords. They represented the flower of the commonwealth. Statesmen, orators, men of high courage, very great gentlemen, arrant individualists, they were, with their latest recruit Colonel Wigfall, the comet to which the general had attached himself and the Confederate States of America, while he kept flashing his full and punctilious reports out across the void toward Montgomery.

In Washington, on April *seventh,* Secretary of State Seward sends his famous message to the Confederate commissioners through the person of Associate Justice Campbell: "Faith as to Sumter fully kept. Wait and see."

On April *eighth* the papers contain official announcement that Lincoln had already dispatched his messenger to Charleston to state that Fort Sumter would be relieved peaceably or by force. The *Powhatan,* first vessel of the flotilla, had put to sea for Sumter on the *sixth.*

And now, dramatically, the moment has arrived. Destiny has leaped beyond human control. It remains only for those in authority to preserve a decent reluctance, to write into the record those final brief dispatches by which each side hopes to convince posterity that the other is the aggressor.

In Charleston the excitement is terrific. For two days the crowds never leave the bulletin boards.

The newspapers bombard them with headlines:

"Washington, April tenth. Special correspondent to The Courier reports: Lincoln's policy coercion and war. Fort Sumter to be relieved at all hazards. Anderson to open on Batteries. Four light draft cruisers have already sailed with troops."

"Montgomery calls for three thousand troops from each state."

"Leaving Columbia for Charleston: The Governor's Guards, Columbia Grays, Congaree Riflemen."

"The Berkeley Mounted Rifles, Capt. Wakefield Ashley in command, have arrived and are encamped north of the City Boundary."

Orators thunder invective:

While the South has been listening in good faith to the promises of Seward, while Lincoln has pretended to consider Anderson's peaceable withdrawal, the Yankees have been deliberately playing upon the credulity of the South and making ready for war. Davis is openly criticized. Does he expect Charleston to sit calmly by until the arrival of reinforcements for Sumter?

But Beauregard will not be stampeded. He dispatches Colonel Chestnut and Captain Lee to Anderson with a demand that he surrender, and offering him the opportunity of evacuating with all supplies and a fifty-gun salute to his flag. Anderson refuses but states that he will be starved out and have to vacate in a few days if, in the meantime, he has not been battered to pieces.

General Beauregard confers with Montgomery and submits: "If you will state the time at which you will evacuate Fort Sumter, and agree that in the meantime you will not use your guns against us, unless ours shall be employed against Fort Sumter, we will abstain from opening fire against you."

At two-thirty A.M. April twelfth, Anderson replies that he will vacate by noon on April fifteenth, should he not receive prior to that time "controlling instructions" from his government or additional supplies.

The Confederate command, knowing that "controlling instructions" are already on their way to Fort Sumter, and that the relief flotilla is expected momentarily off the bar, sees in the reply a continuation of the tactics that have been employed by Washington, merely a postponement against a more complete preparedness.

At three-twenty A.M. on April twelfth, the final dispatch crosses the harbor toward Sumter:

"To Major Robert Anderson,
United States Army, Commanding Fort Sumter.
Sir:

By the authority of Brigadier-General Beauregard, commanding the provisional forces of the Confederate States, we have the honour to notify you that he will open the fire of his batteries on Fort Sumter in one hour from this time.

We have the honour to be, very respectfully,
Your obedient servants,
James Chestnut, Jr. Aide-de-camp.
Stephen D. Lee, Capt. S. C. Army
and Aide-de-camp."

CHAPTER XXIV

CHARDON had been sleeping badly of late, and on the night of April twelfth he had retired early, hoping for rest before that early hour at which he always abandoned the struggle as hopeless. But clearly this was going to be one of his bad nights. He would doze off and immediately his thoughts would return to Peter, waking him to sharp and painful consciousness, and to the question of whether he had been right in again taking a hand in the boy's affairs.

That day when he had abandoned all claims in favor of Damaris had been a turning point for Peter. The weeks that had passed since then had proved his wisdom. The boy had in that short space of time achieved a happiness, a complete harmony with life that, he knew from his own brief idyl with Bella, could compensate for anything that the future might hold for him. There would always be those days to which he could retreat when future reality should become unendurable.

But now time was hastening and the reckoning could not be far distant. And no one was looking beyond the immediate moment. It had been tacitly assumed that when Peter had fully recovered he would enlist in Wake's company. This Chardon saw plainly would mean the horror of the actual front, and with his understanding of Peter's temperament he still believed that this would mean Peter's annihilation.

It had occurred to him that somewhat of the horror might be averted if he could secure him an assignment with the local headquarters, and could succeed in inducing the boy to accept it. It had been easier than he had expected. But his own part in it left him with a sense of shame, because for the first time in his life, he had equivocated upon the subject of his personal convictions.

Chardon had known Beauregard in Mexico, and had no difficulty securing an audience. The general greeted him guardedly until he learned his mission. Possibly he feared that his old associate would insist upon an appointment as aide. But he could use a staff messenger, and Peter could be sent to him at once. Then came the moment that Chardon could not remember without flinching. The general had assumed that his former fellow campaigner was as ardent a Secessionist as he, and that he was prevented from enlisting only by his wound. Chardon was afraid of weakening Peter's chances, so he consented by his silence. After all, it was for the boy.

When he was leaving he said with a show of casualness, "By the way, general, my nephew has been wounded recently. You'll remember that and not try him too arduously at first."

Beauregard enquired the cause of the wound, and Chardon told him of the encounter with Holcombe. The general regarded him with his grave, charming smile, and remarked: "Ah, I see. Another Wigfall. If I don't appoint him, I suppose he'll call me out." Then he had shaken hands with Chardon and showed him out.

Peter had not been difficult. A chance for immediate action. Middle St. John's slapped him on the shoulder and told him what a lucky fellow he was, gave him an impromptu dance, and the following day, accompanied by Damaris, and followed by Washington on Starling, he drove to town and reported for duty.

Chardon must have finally dozed off, for the pounding and the incessant clamor of the front doorbell had him out of bed with his heart thudding, before he could collect his faculties. Then the noise shifted to the yard gate, and he heard Wake's voice demanding that Cæsar open the street door and let him in. The windows of Chardon's room were open and through them came the damp heavy pressure of an east wind. The sky was overcast, and when he looked down into the street he could distinguish nothing. But up out of the night came the sound of low, excited voices, and the shuffling of feet.

He heard Cæsar's tread, then the front door opened and closed. Boots took the steps two in a stride, rang strong and vital on the corridor, and paused before his door. Then, with "I'm coming in, Uncle Pierre," Wake was in the room. He was carrying a lantern that he had taken from Cæsar. The light, hanging low, showed Chardon military boots and gray breeches. Above, in the fainter, reflected glow, he saw the face of his nephew, flushed, eager, excited.

Wake said, "Hurry and dress, Uncle Pierre. We're opening on Sumter at half-past four."

Chardon, shivering in his nightshirt, answered testily: "You are, are you? Well, come in and close the door."

"But you don't understand, sir. I have some of the boys from the Rifles here, and we're hoping that some of the ladies will join us. I hope you don't mind, sir, but I'm having Cæsar open the trapdoor to the roof. We want to be there for the first shot."

Something in Chardon wanted to cry out. Wanted to warn the boy that war was not, after all, a gala festival. But, as he often did when deeply affected, he sought concealment in irony.

"Perhaps," he suggested, "you had better send orders to Beauregard to hold his fire until you have your gallery arranged and your ladies seated. It would be a pity to have them miss the first act." Then his manner changed. He asked sharply: "Where's Peter?"

"I don't know," Wake told him. "He's on duty tonight. That's how we got the word so promptly. He knew when Colonel Chestnut sent the last dispatch to Anderson, and he sent Washington out to the camp on Starling to tell us to come down."

He stood a moment looking at his uncle, then said, "I hope you don't mind us coming here, sir. It's not going to last long, you see; we had to hurry. Someone said ____"

"Yes, yes, I know. You'll probably be breakfasting in Washington. But get along to the roof now, with your friends, and I'll join you as soon as I am decently covered."

Chardon lifted his head and shoulders through the trap and looked about him. Clouds, heavy with moisture, hung low and dense. A wind from the Atlantic drove steadily westward over the roofs. It had body, substance, and when it flung its weight against Chardon, his footing became uncertain on the ladder.

But he was immediately sighted by the group of men

who were gathered about the lantern on the flat roof of the rear piazza. Lawrence and Wake were at his side in a moment. They lifted him out lightly, as though he had been a child, to the secure footing of the roof. Their tenderness and solicitude embarrassed him, as, each holding him by an arm, they conducted him across the short distance to the group. His bad leg always stiffened up while he slept, making his lameness more apparent. He was impelled to say with dignity: "You needn't carry me. I am fully capable of maintaining my own footing."

They laughed indulgently, and Wake said, ridiculously, "Of course you are, Uncle Pierre. I'm just hanging on to you to keep from being blown off the roof."

The half dozen soldiers greeted him with exaggerated courtesy. In the darkness, with the light of the lantern thrown upward from the floor, they looked like young giants, and the air was charged with their released animal vitality. By comparison Chardon felt old, done for. When he responded to their greetings his voice sounded to him high and uncertain, like that of an old man. For the first time, he experienced a pang of jealous animosity toward youth and the world that it so confidently claimed for its own.

He pulled himself together, and fell back to familiar ground, welcoming them to his home, and summoning Cæsar to bring up a decanter and glasses.

He noticed then that lights were coming up on adjacent roofs, and from one to another excited voices were calling across the darkness. The de Sassures had assembled quite a party. He could see hoop skirts swinging in the wind like large bells, and negroes were bringing up chairs and rugs for the ladies.

Presently the Gordons and Alicia Pringle arrived. Damaris kissed Chardon in silence, and slipped an arm through his. They stood a little apart from the others, saying nothing, their eyes staring out into the darkness. Cæsar came with decanter and glasses, supplied the guests, and retired.

Wake was standing by the lantern, his watch in his hand. Chardon had seen him often with that look of concentration on his face, as he stood timing the start of a race on the Pineville track.

"We've only three minutes to wait," he announced. "It is four-twenty-seven." A great silence had fallen over the roofs. From the street came the sound of hurrying feet, but no talk.

Wake's voice came wire-tense in the stillness,
"Time."

Minutes passed. The suspense became unbearable. Feet shuffled. Alicia Pringle cried, "I can't bear it!" Chardon, with his finger nails pressing little pains into his palms, stood motionless, his gaze focused on the spot in the night where the fort stood waiting.

The boats of the night patrol were coming in. He could see the flares moving toward the town, bright gouts of blood on the water, with smears drawn from them toward the shore.

A sudden flash on James Island. An audible cosmic sigh from the town, lost after a moment in a deep, flat report. From the mainland a spark hurtled up into the night, executing small rapid circles as it swung up and over the harbor in a wide arc, descended, seemed to hover for a split second, then burst into flame. A rending report struck the low clouds and was hurled downward.

Behind Chardon a voice said facetiously, "There goes a pill that even a Black-Republican stomach can't digest."

"Ah," Chardon thought, as he recognized the voice as that of a neighbor who was given to studied witticisms, "he's had that ready for a month."

And now the narrow streets that lay dark between the downtown mansions leapt from silence to sound. Through their confining channels torrents of humanity set out toward the water front. Doors slammed. The hooves of the night patrol rang on the cobbles, slowed down. A peremptory voice demanded passage. Voices, excited laughter, rose to the roofs. Chardon, peering down, saw in the gray half-light a world in flux, pouring out over the White Point Gardens and massing solidly along the sea wall.

Then the noise was drowned by a tremendous explosion on James Island. That would be the old frame building that had screened the Howitzer Battery, and that was scheduled for demolition as soon as the engagement commenced. To the northeast, Fort Moultrie went into action, her great guns slashing the darkness with blades of flame. So familiar was Chardon with the location of the various defenses that even in the masking blackness he had no difficulty identifying the batteries as they went into action. From Moultrie the contagion spread to Cummings Point, and thence back across the harbor to the Floating and Enfilade batteries, with the intervening stations filling in the gaps, until the harbor lay, a wide crescent of fire, the two horns resting on Sullivan's and Morris islands, and the opening toward the sea.

The sound became deafening and continuous. You could no longer say, "There goes Moultrie" or "Now the Iron Battery is in." Caught between the low ceiling of cloud and the floor of the harbor, separate explosions were hurled back and forth until, augmented by the constantly increasing fire, they merged into a concerted roar that rose and fell like a hurricane surf but never let up into a definite break.

Dense clouds compounded of smoke and the acrid fumes of burning sulphur and saltpeter commenced to drift across the town. They discomposed the ladies, and they could be seen retiring from the roofs to the clearer air below stairs.

At times, a number of shells bursting together over Sumter would illumine the forbidding mass that lay unresponsive under the rain of metal.

At five-thirty Anderson made his first acknowledgment, scarcely more than a taunt flung into the teeth of his assailants. From his upper-tier two guns were discharged at Moultrie, then the fortress sank again into silence.

At seven, dramatically, Sumter entered the engagement. Looking from his vantage point, Chardon saw the fort surge up in the thinning dark and stand in silhouette against a gray and haggard dawn. Then suddenly the inert mass broke into life. Fire leaped from every embrasure. The barbette guns crowned the fortress with flame. The detonation was terrific. In the gray half-light, forms on the neighboring roofs seemed to reel under the impact.

In the second that followed there was almost silence. Chardon caught a phrase from "The Star-Spangled Banner" and raised his field glasses just in time to see the flag go up over the cloud of smoke that was obscuring the fort.

Damaris had not gone below when the other ladies had abandoned the roofs. She had remained beside Chardon, at times resting on the chair that Cæsar had placed for her, now and again rising and slipping her arm through that of her companion. During the three hours of that first watch, neither spoke. By her failure to mention Peter's absence, Chardon judged that she knew that he was on duty, but he refrained from any comment that might confirm her fears, or that, by putting his apprehensions into words, might increase his own sense of impending disaster.

It was just after Sumter opened fire that René Berrenger arrived. Some inner sense that always functioned where Peter was concerned warned Chardon before René spoke. He turned quickly to meet him, to warn him that Damaris was present. But before he could reach him he was surrounded by a group of excited questioners.

Yes, he was just from headquarters. He had been given four hours off for sleep. As if he wanted to sleep now! Some fellows had all the luck. There had been some change in plans that necessitated the delivery of dispatches to one of the batteries. The choice had lain between Peter and himself, and Peter had got it. René sighted Chardon then, but, full of his grievance, failed to recognize his signals.

"It was on your account, confound you, sir,—excuse me, sir," he blurted out. "The general said you were a gallant soldier. That Peter had a tradition to live up to and he was going to be given a chance."

It was too late now to stop the young fool. Of course Damaris had heard. Wake asked René if he knew the station to which Peter had been sent, but he couldn't tell him. They had been damned secretive about it. And of course he didn't know when he might be expected back. The boat might be caught by daylight and have to stay if the route lay under Sumter's guns.

Chardon returned to Damaris. She was sitting as he had left her, but as he approached he noticed an uncompromising rigidity about the little figure, as though the instinct to turn and look into his face were being held under deliberate control. He said with a good show of casualness, "Peter's off with dispatches, and you needn't feel alarmed. There is probably very little danger."

She looked up then. Her face was white, her composure absolute. She shook her head in negation, took his hand in hers for a moment, then turned her gaze back to the harbor with its cross play of fire that was growing pallid now in the gathering light. Chardon urged her to go home, but she only shook her head again. He had not heard her voice since she had arrived at a little after four o'clock.

He sent for Proctor Gordon, who had gone below with his wife and had missed René's arrival. When his friend reached the roof they conferred, and Gordon went to Damaris.

"Come, little one," he bade her. "It's time to go home and get some rest."

She got up then, meekly, like an obedient small child, and preceded her father from the roof.

And now with a fine rain setting in, their ears deafened by sound, and eyes unable to penetrate the heavy atmosphere, the crowds commence to leave the water front for the bulletin boards uptown. For blocks about the offices of the *Mercury* and the *Courier* the streets are packed with humanity. At headquarters there is no such thing as censorship of news. And this is proper, for, after all, this is Charleston's war, and who should be informed if not Charlestonians! Bulletins are rushed from Institute Hall to the papers, and are posted simultaneously on both boards. Analyzed, they have little of value to impart, but the temper of the crowds is such that each announcement is endowed with momentous significance and is hailed with appropriate cheers or hisses.

8 A.M. Opening shot fired from Howitzer Battery by the venerable Edward Ruffin, chivalric Virginian who had volunteered with the Palmetto Guard.

9 A.M. News that Stevens' Iron Battery and Floating Battery are breaching south and southwest walls of Sumter.

11 A.M. Iron Battery great success. Shot glance from sheathing like marbles thrown by a child on the back of a turtle.

12 M. Messenger from Cummings Point reports two guns dismantled on Sumter.

12:30 P.M. The rifled cannon recently received from England and the first to be used in America proves a marvel of accuracy, the whirling projectiles playing a large part in breaching of Sumter's walls.

1 P.M. Two guns in Stevens' Battery temporarily disabled, but great havoc being wrought in return. Estimated wall of Sumter will be breached in two hours.

1:30 P.M. Three steam vessels reported off bar. Doubtless relief flotilla for Sumter.

2 P.M. Capt. R. S. Parker reports Moultrie and Enfilade Battery giving good account of themselves.

2:30 P.M. Stevens' Iron Battery most formidable. Effect of Dahlgrens and 64-pounders terrific. Clouds of brick dust and mortar rise from fort as the "shot hiss on their errand of death."

3 P.M. Southwest wall of Sumter reported breached.

Nine o'clock Friday morning found Chardon and Wake standing in the rain before Institute Hall. Neither the prestige of the older man nor the uniform of the younger had been able to win them admittance to the building. Only staff officers and messengers were allowed to pass the sentries.

There were surprisingly few people about. The policy of giving out news from the offices of the papers had concentrated the crowds away from headquarters. Those who were waiting in such cover as they could find in adjacent doorways were, Chardon surmised, like themselves, facing the realization that War, while a master showman, was a prompt and inexorable bill-collector.

Across the street he saw his cousin Bull-Smith, taking the weather in stolid indifference to discomfort, and he remembered with a pang of pity that his booming relative had two sons on Morris Island. Certainly there was no bluster about him now, as he stood waiting for news in the sulphurous drench of smoke and rain, with the shattering concussions from the harbor rocking the unclean atmosphere about him.

At eleven René Berrenger appeared for duty. Wake and Chardon fell upon him eagerly. He promised to return at once with such news as he could gather. It was half an hour before he descended the steps and approached them. His face was grave. Chardon gripped his stick, and stood waiting.

"He's still out," René told them. "No one seems to know where he was sent. It was some private mission of the general's." Chardon's questions elicited the additional information that Peter had gone out on the dispatch boat *Antelope*. That the boat had returned and been sent up the river out of the range of fire, and that Peter had not been aboard when she had touched town on her way up.

"But you needn't have the slightest fear for Peter," René assured them, a trace too hastily. "I have it on good authority that no casualties have been reported."

Chardon thought with a sinking heart that Beauregard was much too good a general to post losses at the beginning of an engagement. Wait until there was a victory to show for it, then publish the cost.

They stationed a servant near the Hall, and René promised to send any word that came in. Then with no end that could be served by waiting longer they turned their steps downtown.

At seven Friday evening the fire slackened, then settled into a routine of a discharge every twenty minutes. There was no wind, and the air, loaded with smoke and moisture, pressed heavily and muffling upon the town. It produced a silence that was singularly lifeless, and across this three times in every hour came the blam! of a discharge from Moultrie, caught up and hurled back like an echo from one of Sumter's barbette guns.

Looking back, Chardon always remembered this ominous interlude as the most trying phase of the engagement. It was like that period following the delirium of fever, when one lies counting slow heartbeats, and waiting for the crisis with its verdict of life or death.

In the streets now there was no laughter, no noisy boasting. The roofs were deserted. Night fell before its appointed time. By seven, the darkness was an impenetrable wall that circled each separate light, isolating families from the sustaining presence of their neighbors, destroying that confidence which is bred of crowds, and without which only the truly courageous can face destiny. In looking back Chardon always recalled that time with an involuntary shudder, for he knew that it was then that the Dark Angel had first touched the spirit of his beloved city, prophetically, with a hovering wing.

By eight o'clock a small company had assembled at the Chardon residence. The spirit of the gathering was different from that of the early morning. Chardon could scarcely believe that this was the same day as the one on which he had stood looking at Wake while watch in hand he was counting off the minutes for the opening gun.

Proctor and Mrs. Gordon were there, and Damaris; Thomas and Emily Ashley, who had heard the guns and had driven down, arriving just before dark; Wake, and Chardon. Cæsar had made them comfortable in the master's room, from the windows of which one commanded a limited view of the harbor. There was a tea table with a cold supper, a decanter of sherry and one of brandy, and a bowl of ice from the last ice schooner down from New England.

The room, which was large and square, was a perfect expression of its owner's personality. Its unencumbered spaciousness gave it a suggestion of austerity, and against this each article of furniture and decoration stood revealed in its intrinsic and appropriate beauty. And in everything there was a looking backward, in the air a distillation of the long past. The floor was bare save for a small India rug before the hearth and a sheepskin beside the bed. The bed itself was one of those tremendous structures with a trundle bed beneath it, and a flight of four steps beside it for the master's ascent and descent. It was of some very dark wood, and was covered with a smooth linen spread. Its black and white mass gave the room dignity and presence. It was more than a place to spend a night and from which to arise refreshed in the morning. It was the source, the present, the future. The great bed above, the trundle bed for the children below: wedlock, childbirth, old age, death, and again wedlock, each completed cycle linking into one which was just beginning, transmitting something that was as intangible as it was priceless, and which even Death on his inevitable rounds was powerless to seize and hold.

Between two of the windows stood a Sheraton chest, and against the opposite wall a massive highboy of the same period. Chardon had made but one change in the room when he commenced to live there with Bella. He had brought from Naples one of those small shrines which stand imbedded in the wall beside the entrance of the humbler homes, a plaster Mother and Child crudely colored by some primitive Italian craftsman. This had been set into the wall above the bed. It probably held little or no religious significance for Chardon, but there was something about its simple sincerity that had appealed to him. Cæsar always lit a candle in the small sconce that stood beside it when he retired for the night, and it served as a night light for the room. At first the family had viewed the little figure with suspicion, and had jokingly called Chardon "the Papist," but with the passage of time it had been accepted as one of his eccentricities and forgotten. Tonight the candle was lit as usual. With the exception of the candelabra on the tea table, it was the only light in the room.

No one seemed to be hungry. Under the candelabra the crystal and silver lay in an orderly pattern of high lights against sleek dark mahogany. Wake had been rattling ice absently in an empty glass. Ashley broke a long silence with, "For God's sake, stop that noise."

Emily Ashley was tatting, the small precise circles of the fancywork falling from under her busy fingers and coiling upon her lap. At each stroke, the small bone shuttle struck her wedding ring, and so absolute was the silence that the sound was plainly audible, insistent, cadenced, progressive, like the ticking of a watch. Although she could tat as well in the dark as the light, she kept her eyes lowered to her work. But from time to time she would raise them, and stare over the heads of the others at the Madonna brooding in the flickering candlelight over her bambino.

Damaris sat looking out of a window. She was fanning herself with an ivory fan that Peter had given her. The slow, unfaltering rhythm made Chardon think of a mechanism that someone had started and had forgotten to stop. At each discharge of the guns, a slight shudder ran through her body. She was perfectly composed, and for the first time Chardon noticed that she was wearing rouge. He wondered whether it was customary, and was only now apparent against her pallor, or whether it was a brave front she was putting up. He wished that she hadn't. There was something of her behind it that had been extinguished, and that made it seem strangely incongruous.

They had just got word from Berrenger. At six-thirty Peter had not returned, and René had been unable to discover his whereabouts.

At eight o'clock a rush of clean cold rain passed over the town, setting the stagnant air in motion, and purging it to a momentary clarity. Lights emerged from the murk. It had been assumed that with the coming of night and the tide at the flood, the fleet would attempt to enter and establish contact with Anderson, and a heavily augmented harbor patrol was out. The red and yellow of petroleum flares, and the harsh white of calcium burners, kept passing and repassing in the outer harbor, and streaming along the horizon in a continuous line. They reminded Chardon more than anything else of a distant water carnival. And in the moment that preceded the shattering report of Moultrie's cannon, he was in Venice again, with Bella beside him, and his heart was big with that first utter ecstasy of possession, and their future was a faint delirious perfume from a blossom beyond the Atlantic, open on its stem and waiting to be plucked.

The report hurled him back into the present. And there sat Damaris with Peter's fan, and her eyes fixed on the moving lights, and the pitiful bravery of her rouge. And somewhere out there Peter was waiting for the next attack. And this was reality, the thing from which he had fled twenty years ago, but from which there is always only a respite, never escape.

He rose from his chair and filled a sherry glass, then he crossed to where Damaris was sitting and presented it to her. She looked up and their eyes met. Then she drained the glass and returned it. He was turning away when she caught his hand and pressed it silently to her cheek. Then she let him go and resumed her vigil.

At ten, a violent rain storm commenced, and simultaneously the bombardment was reopened. The effect was spectacular in the extreme. From horn to horn the crescent of fire bore down on Sumter. The upper dark was latticed by a cross fire from the mortar batteries, the shells taking the air like giant rockets, curving, hovering, and exploding over the fort. At times the sheeted rain would obscure details, and illuminated by the explosions, lie over the mass of Sumter with an effect like that of vapors flung upward from a caldron of molten ore.

For hour after hour the bombardment continued with unabated fury, with Anderson replying from every gun at his command. Then, just before dawn, it commenced to slacken. The wind veered to the westward and blew strong, tonic and unsullied from the St. Andrew's fields. It tumbled the clouds neck and crop out over the Atlantic, and swept the harbor clean. Dawn was a taut crimson back drop against which the fleet showed in spidery outline. Then the sun lifted, wet and shining, and deluged the bay, the forts, the town with light.

Instantly the mercurial spirits of the old city responded. Trap doors banged open and the roofs commenced to take on life. The scattered spectators along the sea wall were joined by returning crowds refreshed by a few hours' sleep. Judge Magrath was back with an April rose in his lapel.

Chardon noticed that some of his neighbors were preparing to breakfast informally on their roofs, so that they need miss nothing that was taking place, and thinking that the invigorating upper air would prove refreshing to the ladies, who had been resting below, he had Cæsar carry up a card table and a few chairs, and tell Daphne to prepare a light breakfast.

At eight o'clock, with only a desultory fire taking place, it became apparent that Fort Sumter was on fire. A dense smoke rose from the ramparts into the sky, hanging there like a great thunder cloud with exploding shells vibrating like lightning at its heart.

Excitement along the sea wall and on the roofs ran high. Telescopes and field glasses were leveled upon the fortress, and those who were fortunate enough to possess them reported to avid bystanders. A fantastic rumor ran from mouth to mouth that Anderson was signaling to the fleet to enter the harbor and come to his assistance. Jeers followed. "Poltroons if they stay out." "Yes, but Davy Jones' locker if they attempt to enter." Then one of Sumter's barbette magazines exploded, hurling débris and dense white smoke upward, and proving the genuineness of the fire.

By ten o'clock the fortress presented the appearance of an inferno, belching dense clouds of smoke and sheets of flame into the sky, while the Confederates poured a terrific cannonade into the structure. One by one Anderson's guns had ceased to reply. But at the height of the conflagration a spasm of firing broke from the fort. Only five guns were engaged, all that Anderson had left in commission. It was a tremendously gallant gesture. Sumter was dying, but dying with its boots on. Instantly the Confederate fire ceased, and after each discharge from the fort a burst of cheering went up from the encircling batteries.

Chardon, standing on his roof, heard the cheers, a slight, silvery note in the brazen clamor of war, a spontaneous tribute to a gallant opponent. One by one Sumter's guns fell silent as the flames drove the gunners back. Then when the last one was abandoned, the Confederates resumed the offensive, attempting to hasten a conclusion that had now become inevitable.

CHAPTER XXV

AT twelve-forty-five Sumter's flag was shot away. An adjacent Confederate battery had been gunning for it since daybreak, and at last a ball had passed cleanly through the staff, carrying away its upper half and plunging the colors headlong into the smoke and flame.

Now, shoot away the flag in the midst of an engagement and you have a hero. The situation is as inevitable in its cause and effect as thunder and lightning, and like lightning there is no telling where the bolt will strike. The master brain that has built up the elaborate plan of attack will be forgotten. Of the scores of soldiers who are standing in the vicinity, there are doubtless dozens whose courage is equal to the emergency, but who are destined never to emerge from the obscurity of the mass. But somewhere near by there is always one whose brow has been shaped by Destiny to wear the laurel wreath. He may never have distinguished himself before; he may be destined immediately after to return to his native obscurity. But in that fleeting, white-hot moment the event and the man are fused into a single glorified symbol. The populace has its darling, war its justification, history its hero.

And up to this point the battle of Fort Sumter had been desperately in need of a hero. The engagement had presented a magnificent spectacle. Confederate cannon had pounded their way through the walls of the fortification, but except under the stimulus of the actual firing the items posted upon the bulletin boards would have made pathetically sterile reading.

And then suddenly the moment—and, inevitably, the man. But not, as might be supposed, the Union soldier who was groping through the flames to find and replace the fallen colors; not General Beauregard, whose genius had created the elaborate system that had produced the situation; but one whose temperament, personality, and appearance had so supremely prepared him that instinctively he gathered the moment to his breast and made it his own: in short, Colonel Louis T. Wigfall.

General Beauregard had stationed the doughty colonel with General Simons on James Island, probably concluding that the temperament of his aide better fitted him for the dangers of the bombardment than the more delicate task of conducting negotiations with Anderson when the fortress should fall, as inevitably it must. And the colonel was at his post on James Island when the flag went down. General Simons was away at the time. General Beauregard was five miles distant at headquarters, and—the moment had arrived. It was obvious that Anderson could not hold out in his present dire straits, and before he should attempt to replace his flag was the psychological moment for offering him an opportunity to surrender.

With that complete independence of spirit which is characteristic of those who are cognizant of their own greatness, Colonel Wigfall determined to act at once. The fact that the bombardment was at its height and that only by a miracle could one hope to reach the fort alive merely added that tang of adventure without which duty to the colonel was always an unappetizing morsel on the tongue.

At some distance behind the batteries, out of the range of fire, the negro laborers were stationed during the engagement. Had they exposed themselves, they would have been punished, for the companies using them were financially responsible to their owners in case of their loss, and they represented a heavy cash liability. It was accordingly the custom during action to station them at a safe distance, and such repairs as were necessary under fire were made by the private soldiers.

Into the midst of the recumbent blacks strode the terrifying figure of the colonel. With the thunders of the bombardment behind him, his great eyes under their shaggy brows lit by excitement, and his sword flashing, he must have seemed the incarnation of Africa's great god, Mabiali Mundembi. With an utter disregard for expense, he ordered two negroes who would have fetched a thousand dollars each, to precede him to the beach and take their places at the oars of a waiting skiff. When the party was on the point of embarking, Private W. Gourdin Young approached and volunteered to accompany the colonel. Young was a modest hero. He materialized, was given a seat in the stern, and was immediately lost in the glare that beat about him from the presence that placed itself before him, and that towered sword in hand above the cowering blacks.

From the point at which the skiff left the shore it was impossible to see the diminished flag pole on Sumter. It was also impossible for most of the Confederate batteries to see the skiff, and they continued to hurl a terrific fire over the fort and into the water that the colonel must traverse. Behind the receding boat, the James and Morris Island Batteries saw what was happening, ceased firing, and fell to cheering.

But the colonel was as oblivious in that moment to the cheers as he was to the hail of metal. Life had risen on a tedious crescendo of duels of words and affairs of honor, to this transcendent moment of realization, and the death which rowed with him in the skiff was not the lugubrious companion of the storybooks, with his narcotics and mumbled prayers, but a very good fellow indeed who held to his lips the ultimate, the supreme intoxicant.

The colonel had affixed his pocket handkerchief to the end of his sword and held it aloft as the skiff advanced, although in the smoke and the spray from flying projectiles it could not possibly have been visible from the fort. To his two oarsmen he must have presented a terrifying spectacle. His hair, which was thick and raven-black, fell almost to his shoulders, and his eyes of a golden-brown color gave under the heat of emotion the illusion of dilating and glowing like those of an enraged lion. He was wearing his red sash, and his huge Texas spurs, and at regular intervals he would wave his bared sword with its pocket handkerchief flag, and send his enormous voice roaring toward the fort with a demand that it surrender.

From time to time a ball would take the water immediately before the advancing bow, causing the skiff to rock violently and deluging the occupants. At first when this happened it produced a temporary paralysis in the oarsmen. They would fall forward in a babblement of prayers and entreaties, addressed impartially to God and the colonel. But if centuries of servitude had taught the negro anything, it was to accept the inevitable, and after the initial shock they settled with a frenzy of physical effort into their task. Under the arch of the colonel's legs as he balanced himself Colossus-wise in the skiff, they could see the peaceful shore line of James Island receding into distance. At their backs, as they bent to the oars, annihilating thunders roared, but they kept at it; there was no way out but through, because it had become obvious that even their last resort—that of reminding the gentleman tactfully, yet with a becoming blend of modesty and pride, of the fact they were worth a thousand dollars apiece—would fall upon deaf ears. It had evidently pleased the gentleman to go on a perfectly magnificent bust, and there was nothing for it but to row.

In town at headquarters the game of war was proceeding quite according to schedule. With Anderson's surrender imminent, Beauregard had summoned his staff to a conference. It was important that an immediate decision be reached as to the terms upon which Anderson would be allowed to evacuate. There was every disposition to treat Anderson like the soldier and gentleman that he was but, after all, he had invited the battle by remaining, and he had been vanquished.

When he had been asked to vacate peaceably three days before, he had been offered the opportunity of marching out with all supplies, flags flying, band playing, and with a fifty-gun salute to the flag. Now, obviously, since he had remained and fought, the terms must be somewhat modified. The people expected it, and it was their right. It was finally concluded that the original terms should stand with but one exception. The flag would have to do without its fifty-gun salute.

With his skiff half full of water but, miraculously, no casualties, Colonel Wigfall finally reached the narrow beach from which the wall of the fort rose precipitously. At the moment their keel grounded, Anderson blew up his barracks in the hope of stopping the fire.

The detonation caught them with a physical impact so terrific that it was stupefying. They stood dazed for a moment, while a shattered heaven poured its débris down upon them. Then, when the universe rocked back to its balance, the colonel bade his crew await his return, and left them, to parley with Anderson. The negroes promptly turned the boat over and crawled beneath it, and Private Young demonstrated the superior courage of the Caucasian by seating himself fully exposed upon its upturned bottom.

While Wigfall had been in transit, the Stars and Stripes had been replaced upon the ramparts, and at this signal of defiance the Confederate cannonade had broken out with redoubled fury.

It was now that the colonel faced his greatest danger. He knew that his only hope of making his presence known to the defenders was to skirt the northern face of the fort to a small door at the rear. He did not hesitate a moment. His progress was of necessity very slow, for the tide was well in and the strip of beach was narrow and cluttered with unstable heaps of débris. Above him the wall was giving way under the merciless pounding, and from time to time landslides of masonry came crashing down the fifty-foot drop. Into the wall above him, roundshot crashed, dull, metallic, like blows from a sledge in the hands of a Titan.

At last he turned the corner and came out on the western face of the fort, which was covered by his own battery. They must have picked him up at once with their glasses, for a distant cheer penetrated the din, precipitating him into that state of exaltation for which the profession of soldiering has no adequate term, and which we can convey only by borrowing from the vocabulary of the poet his magnificent and all-embracing "divine afflatus."

In that moment Colonel Wigfall became omnipotent. The destinies of nations lay quiescent in the hollow of his hand. He strode to the nearest embrasure and met the gaze of a smoke-begrimed soldier. Even after he had spoken, demanding to be shown into the presence of Major Anderson, the man stood goggling at him, frankly skeptical of the evidence of senses. Finally, at the colonel's repeated demand, he disappeared and returned presently with an officer. Then the door was unbarred and the colonel strode majestically within.

Twenty minutes later, at exactly one-thirty on the afternoon of April thirteenth, to be historically accurate, Colonel Wigfall, the "Lion of Fort Sumter," emerged from the fort and returned to his skiff, and simultaneously, high on the ramparts, a white square climbed the flag pole and flattened in the breeze.

And now, at headquarters, the moment that had been so eagerly awaited, and for which plans had been so carefully prepared, had arrived. With the flag of truce proclaiming Anderson's unconditional surrender, Beauregard dispatched Major Jones, Colonels Manning, Chestnut and Chisolm, and Surgeon-General Gibbes to Sumter with the conditions of surrender upon which they had agreed.

In town the crowds waited in breathless excitement, all eyes fixed upon Sumter's flag pole, from which presently the flag would descend to make place for the Confederate colors.

But the God of Battles, whose delight is the anticlimax, continued to withhold their great moment. Finally the flag appeared to move. A cheer rose, then hung suspended. The movement had ceased. It was not until Sunday afternoon following Anderson's evacuation, that simultaneously the Confederate flag and the Palmetto banner took their places above the vanquished fortress.

But in the meantime, behind the locked doors of headquarters, there was the very devil to pay. After what must have seemed an unconscionable absence, Beauregard's representatives returned. It was immediately evident that they had encountered unexpected difficulties.

In the general's private office, the truth came out. Anderson had received them with the utmost courtesy. They had exchanged greetings, and for a moment or two talked of this and that. There had been a slight pause, then Anderson had asked that his compliments be conveyed to Major Stevens upon the performance of the Iron Battery. Finally the visitors had touched upon the surrender, and stated the terms dictated by General Beauregard. It was then that the bomb had exploded in their midst.

Anderson had regarded them with amazed incredulity, and had informed them that he had surrendered twenty minutes before to Colonel Wigfall. The colonel had been very gallant and magnanimous, and had given him to understand that the terms would stand as they were before the engagement, including the salute to the flag. Anderson had assumed that Wigfall had come as the representative of the commanding general, and had accepted the terms. Of course, now, if Beauregard chose to repudiate Wigfall, and specify other conditions—well, that would be another matter.

And so there they sat in Beauregard's private office, hesitating in the face of the alternatives. Either they must eat crow and let Anderson salute, or they must repudiate the colonel and stand the consequences.

And while they hesitated, the colonel himself became the deciding factor. Surrounded by an escort of cheering soldiery, he arrived in the city to be met by the populace, and accorded an ovation of earth-shaking proportions. Acceding to the demands of the crowd, he allowed himself to be hoisted upon an improvised stand, and in the midst of an awed hush carried them with him step for step upon the thrilling adventure. No one remembered Beauregard now. No one gave a passing thought to Jefferson Davis and his cabinet. All afternoon the cheering crowds followed the colonel from place to place, and as the hours passed, the reiterated recital grew in power and glory, for the gallant senator-soldier was never one to insult a gentleman by refusing proffered hospitality, or to turn a deaf ear when urged to speak by a cheering constituency.

Finally, as evening approached, in response to the demands of a throng that packed Meeting Street from wall to wall, he appeared for a moment with his lady, upon a balcony of the Mills House, and the ovation rattled the windows of a room a block away in Institute Hall where Beauregard and his aides were closeted with their problem. Immediately, and with one accord, they arrived at a decision.

The eating of crow, especially to one of General Beauregard's temperament, was of course a singularly unpleasant experience, but the alternative of approaching "The Lion of Fort Sumter" at this particular moment with a public repudiation had suddenly become unthinkable.

At seven-thirty Major Anderson received a communication from Beauregard, informing him that the general "very cheerfully" acceded to his request for a fifty-gun salute to his flag.

CHAPTER XXVI

WITH the approach of evening, the Gordons, who had gone home earlier in the day, returned to the Chardon residence. They were all back now. Emily had remained indoors all day. Thomas, Wake, and Chardon had just returned from their last unsuccessful visit to headquarters.

They had been caught in the crowd that jammed the street under Wigfall's balcony, and looked exhausted and disheveled. Thomas and Wake were showing the strain badly. There were deep shadows under their eyes, and their faces, so alike always, had aged together and whitened under their tan. Chardon's stock was awry, and a button was missing from his coat. He had reached the point at which nervous excitement gives place to complete exhaustion, and looked on the verge of collapse.

They were assembled in the drawing room. Damaris, seated on a sofa between her parents, raised her eyes to Chardon, and her lips parted in a brief, mechanical smile of welcome.

Chardon said, "We can learn nothing. Beauregard and his staff are locked up in headquarters. Everything is at a standstill. No word has been given out even as to when Anderson will evacuate."

Damaris said, "Some of our boys are already up in town. I saw some of the Cadets from Morris Island.

They called out that there had been no casualties in their battery."

Thomas Ashley's voice, overemphatic almost to the point of argument, flung out: "That's what I've been telling you. Of course there's nothing official yet, but it's all over town that there have been no losses. There can't be a rumor like that unless it has some foundation."

Wake said, into the ensuing silence, "By the way, René and Alicia have announced their engagement. We met them together on the way home, and they told us. They're going to be married at once."

Damaris answered: "I hope they will be very happy"— her voice faltered a moment, then she added steadily— "always."

Cæsar appeared, to announce supper. He had opened the door, shuffled his foot to attract his master's attention. No one noticed him and he cleared his throat discreetly. It was very still.

Then suddenly the silence was shattered by the slamming of the front door. In the room everyone jerked erect. Boots rang staccato on the piazza floor, on the planking of the hall. In the doorway Cæsar's jaw dropped, his eyes widened, then he was nearly thrown off his balance, and Peter was there in the middle of the room with Damaris in his arms.

It was a great occasion, that supper. Chardon had gone himself to the cellar and brought up half a dozen of the Oliviera Madeira that had been gathering cobwebs there when he and Bella were married. It lay under the candles in the slim glasses like little wedges of amber fire that from time to time might flicker low but that Cæsar never allowed to expire.

They all sat and listened while Peter talked, and Chardon had ample opportunity to note the change that had come over him: how unaffectedly emotional he had become, how unquestioningly he accepted what he was told, how complete had been his escape from the tyranny of reality. His old habit of starting a sentence impulsively, then arresting himself and pondering his words, was gone. He talked with an eager, unstudied impetuosity. He seemed young—years younger than the boy who had come to live with Chardon after Mexico. Damaris sat next to him, in one of her rich silences, and her eyes never left his face.

He said: "The other fellows at headquarters are so jealous of me, I am going to keep out of their sight until my leave is over. It was wonderful luck, and I owed it to you, you know, Uncle Pierre. The general selected me on your account. I carried dispatches to the Floating Battery, and my orders were to wait there during the engagement. It was wonderful being in the thick of it, and getting an idea of what war is really like.

"Sumter's shot struck the sloping irons. You could hear them ring, then see them vault over your head and fall into the water behind you. At first we were all excited, and started scoring hits, but you'd be surprised how soon the boys got used to it. You might doubt me, but I pledge you my word, after the first couple of hours, as soon as the gunners were relieved they would sit in at hands of bluff and euchre, and the games kept going all day."

He paused and laughed excitedly. "I never cared much for gambling, you know. Betting on a race, yes, but not cards. But I sat in with them. I had beginner's luck,

I guess." He drew a handful of silver dollars from his pocket and let them fall heavily on the table before him. "There. How's that for a morning's work?"

He went off at a tangent: "You know, of course, there were no casualties on either side. Yes, that's official. And you heard, I suppose, what Anderson said when he heard. It is the sort of thing that entirely changes your conception of war. Major Jones gave him the news when he went out on seeing the flag of truce. Anderson grasped his hand and exclaimed devoutly, 'Thank God!' —and mind you, we're supposed to be his enemies. Major Jones extended General Beauregard's congratulations on the fact that Sumter had experienced no losses. They say the two of them sat there like two gentlemen at a club. By God, it makes you feel proud, doesn't it?"

Peter was tremendously enthusiastic over Wigfall's exploit. Captain Tucker, with whom he had left headquarters, had taken him into Mills House on his way home and introduced him to the colonel. Peter launched into a detailed account of the spectacular harbor excursion.

Chardon, sitting at the foot of the table, unnoticed, forgotten, sipped his Madeira absently and watched his nephew as he rattled on. He shrewdly suspected Beauregard of having deliberately sent the boy to the Floating Battery as a kindness to himself, and as a means of breaking Peter gently into the game of war. It was the sort of surprising little personal courtesy that, knowing the general, he might have expected.

But he wondered now whether it had actually been a kindness. Whether the comfort of a present illusion was worth the terror of the ultimate tragic awakening. The

Battle of Fort Sumter! Good God, it wasn't a battle at all. It was little more than an exchange of civilities between gentlemen; a bloodless duel with pistols fired into the air. Commanding officers thanking God that their enemies had been spared! War was never war until men had been taught to hate.

His gaze shifted to Damaris. Ah, there was a difference. Damaris knew. The women were always the first to learn. She had been a girl forty-eight hours ago. Now she was a woman who was already letter-perfect in her part. She had learned how to wait, and she knew what waiting cost. In her eyes as she looked at Peter there was a grave and complete attentiveness to all that he was saying, but there was something more, a desperate, insatiable hunger for him, a hunger that she must feed now, every moment, against the coming of starvation.

It was as though she already divined the tragic truth that Chardon knew so well: the fact that after a war they never come back. If it pleased God to be very lenient, there might be a Peter who would return, who would come back to her arms with undiminished devotion. But he would never be this boy, sitting there beside her with the glory of youth upon him, and his faith like a bright, unfleshed blade in his hands.

And Chardon found himself wondering if after all life was worth it—if its few moments of ecstasy compensated for its insensate cruelties. And then he remembered Bella, and he knew that it was worth the price. He knew that life, in the final analysis, for Peter as for himself, was not a matter of three score years and ten, but of a succession of years of anticipation, and a receding vista of regret, and that between these two there stood that moment which was life in actuality. It may be a few years—a few days—hours—but that was of little consequence. It was not a matter of duration, but intensity. It was not the long journey that counted, but the altitude of the particular peak that you had scaled together. He had had five years with Bella. Peter and Damaris were standing now upon the heights. It was worth it. They had not been cheated.

The thought came to him that they must be married at once. He blamed himself for not urging it before. Now, while happiness was in their hands, they must know it in its completeness. They must live together before the inevitable hour of parting. He determined to suggest it at once, while he had both families assembled. He would insist upon the day being set. He was suddenly in a fever of impatience. Peter was telling them about the new rifled cannon. It had been a sensational success. They had got the jump on the Yankees there. Now they must run as many in from England as possible before the Yankee fleet could interfere.

Chardon rapped with his glass for silence, but his interruption went unheeded. He was on the point of speaking up, when the door opened and Alicia and René entered. Chairs were pushed back and the young couple was showered with congratulations.

But there was something that René had come to tell them. After a moment he managed to make himself heard. Boats from the fleet were visiting at Sumter. "It's a great sight, with all the signal rockets and flares," he said. "You oughtn't to miss it. Can't we adjourn to the roof?"

Then for the last time they all stood together on their

lofty lookout, with the soft spring stars hanging low over their heads, and the land breeze sweet, clean and earthy about them, and watched the final nocturnal scene of the drama as it played itself out into darkness and silence against the east.

Sunday afternoon: Out at Sumter everything was in readiness for the evacuation. Luggage and movable equipment were stored in the boats. Officers and men stood at attention. General Beauregard had absented himself, feeling that his presence might prove embarrassing to Major Anderson, his old friend and former instructor when he had been a cadet at "The Point."

Above the waiting soldiers, the Stars and Stripes floated languidly in the soft air. Upon the ramparts a cannon had been mounted, and the crew stood in readiness to fire the mooted salute. The band crashed into "Yankee Doodle." An order rang out, and the gunner applied his fire. With a terrific detonation the cannon exploded, killing the gunner instantly and wounding the remainder of the crew.

But the flag had not gone unhonored. And Colonel Wigfall had remained unchallenged as the gallant and magnanimous hero of the occasion. And if it had pleased the high gods to jest at the expense of a certain obscure gunner, it was not for the survivors, standing there still sound in life and limb, to question their immemorial right.

CHAPTER XXVII

JUNE at Wakefields Plantation. The season had been unusually cool, and as yet there had been no threat of fever, so the Ashleys had broken their rule and remained. But tomorrow the house would be closed, the family and house servants would leave for Pineville. There would be no incentive to remain longer, because today the Rifles, now encamped upon their old parade ground, were leaving for Virginia.

In his old room that overlooked the great lawn, Peter lay very still so as not to awaken Damaris. They had been married now for two months, but still every morning when he opened his eyes he was struck dumb at the miracle of finding her there beside him. It was not yet day, and a late moon, out behind the house where the fields stretched away to an unobstructed horizon, touched the great oaks with frosted silver and trailed enormous shadows after them across the lawn. Monotonous, cadenced throbbing, the swamp sounded its immemorial nocturne.

This would be his last hour like this, alone with Damaris, alone with himself. After this there would always be the boys around, Wake, Bert and the rest, and action every day and all day until his muscles would ache. No time for thinking then. It was strange how little he minded the prospect. There would be the pain of awaking alone, and these precious moments when he lay motionless, watching for Damaris' eyes and her first drowsy smile, would be gone for a while, but except for that separation the prospect of going gave him no great concern. He knew war at first hand now, and he had no fear.

He must have changed mightily in the last three months, he thought. What an annoying and argumentative fellow he must have been. What a prig he must have seemed to poor old Archie Holcombe that night at St. Andrew's. It was not surprising that he had called him out. He supposed after all that Uncle Pierre had been responsible for his false start. From the beginning he had encouraged him to exalt the importance of individual opinion. Then, when he had come home with his head full of theories, and no first-hand knowledge of actual conditions, he had let him go ahead and make rather an ass of himself.

But on thinking it over, he decided that he oughtn't to blame Chardon. He should have realized sooner that the horror of war had become an obsession with his uncle; that the death of Aunt Bella and the children had become confused in his mind with the actual fighting, and that his judgment was not to be trusted.

For his own part, he was fully satisfied with his ability to take care of himself. Hadn't he been under fire for forty-eight hours? Hadn't he had the guts to stand up and take Holcombe's bullet? Of course there was that old squeamishness at the sight of blood, and the hideous habit of feeling the suffering of others like nausea at the pit of his stomach, but he supposed he'd get used even to that in time. He knew the worst already, and after all it would soon be over. He'd soon be back again to take up his life in earnest.

Beside him Damaris stirred in her sleep. Her arm was thrown out over the light counterpane, and Peter saw the fingers open slowly, like the petals of a flower unfolding to greet the dawn. He slipped his hand into hers, and their fingers intertwined. She smiled in her sleep, and turned her face toward him on the pillow. Her breathing was a faint stir of air on his cheek. He was shaken by an impulse to crush her suddenly in his arms. But passion gave place immediately to an almost paternal desire to protect her. Today would bring the ordeal of parting, and he must let her sleep as long as she would.

He wondered how soon they would be together again like this. Next winter, perhaps, in time for Race Week. Race Week—he was bound to have Hercules train Starling. Washington would take good care of her in Virginia, and if old Herc could have her for even a month before the meet, she'd be good for the Hutchinson stakes at least. He'd carry Damaris down to stay with Uncle Pierre and no doubt the old gentleman would give a ball in her honor.

Some day he and Damaris would live there. Uncle Pierre had said that it would all come to him when—but he'd rather, of course, think of Chardon as being there always. God! he was a great gentleman, when all was said and done.

Then there'd be his own broad acres, his negroes, and the new plantation house. Ashley would have the construction well under way by Christmas. A planter. Peter smiled. He'd never make a planter. He knew that perfectly well. But good old Wake would look after practical details for him, and get him a good overseer, and then he could get back to his writing. There would be long visits from the others, Henry Timrod, Paul Hayne, Basil Gildersleeve, even Simms maybe, when the fever of war had burned itself out of their brains.

There was that old idea of his about reviving *Russell's Magazine*. That would be first on the list after getting settled. The old book store crowd again! By God, they'd make Charleston the intellectual capital of the Confederacy. They'd like Damaris. She was such a good listener. He saw her then at the far end of a long table, smiling to him down the aisle of faces, and his heart grew big with pride of her.

Later there'd be children. Children playing on the joggling-boards under the piazza, going down to town with them for the season and the fun of seeing Starling run. Children growing up into men and women, replicas of Damaris and himself, making their début at the St. Cecilia Ball, marrying, linking cycle into cycle as his generation was doing.

But in the meantime—war. The word drove into his consciousness like a metal wedge, swift, keen, incisive. He resisted it consciously, as he always did now. Why dwell upon it? Why theorize? Theories were for those who had nothing at stake. As for himself, for St. John's, for South Carolina, they had created a life that was completely satisfactory, that had beauty, harmony, dignity, continuity. It was theirs. They asked only the right to enjoy their own, undisturbed. At the thought of outside interference he experienced a dull resentment that was something quite new to him. They had always been their own masters, and by God! they'd continue to be.

And if they had to fight to keep what was theirs, to assure their children's future—well, it was a job to be done, and for his part with as little fuss and fury as possible, but with every ounce of power that he possessed. And when it was over—Damaris—home—beauty—life.

Out beyond the open windows the lights were changing. The moon had dropped below the western fields, leaving the live oaks to stand, ominous black masses, in a swimming gray nebula. On the lawn the night mists that had lain in low well-defined strata commenced to stir, to lift; then they went streaming up to meet the dawn that was changing rapidly to violet and from violet to rose. From the canal woods came the whistle of the first partridge, and then, suddenly, shattering the silence and filling the world with beauty and terror, the clear sure notes of reveille went spiraling up to greet the day.

The sound lifted Peter from the bed and carried him to the window. In the early light he could see the camp springing to life. In the distance he heard Wake's voice, clear, authoritative. A horse neighed shrilly, another answered. Then there were many voices, calling, giving orders. The men had slept in their clothes. They were going to show St. John's how quickly a crack outfit could be on the march. They would give the home folks something to remember, to brag about when they were gone. While he watched, tents started to come down, and the wagons commenced to arrive from the stable. By God, the Rifles were top notch. He thrilled with possessive pride. He was suddenly tremendously excited. He must get dressed and go down at once. He turned from the window.

Damaris had got out of bed and was standing in the middle of the room, watching him. She was looking at him curiously, as though he were a stranger. Their eyes met, and she said hesitantly, as though doubting his identity, "Peter?"

At the touch of her small, lithe body, something seemed to give way suddenly inside of Peter. Of the two, it was he who clung, she who sustained. It was his voice that shook as he said:

"It won't be long, darling; it can't be."

And hers that answered steadily: "No, my beloved. Not long, and then we'll have each other—always."

Chardon stood in the press of St. John's folk on the Wakefields piazza waiting to bid the Rifles "Godspeed." Since early dawn the families had been arriving, and the lawn was dotted with buggies, buckboards, and even an occasional family coach, each with a groom at the horses' heads. Servants were passing coffee and toasted waffles. The atmosphere was charged with a bright, forced gaiety, and drenched with perfume from the bouquets that the ladies had brought to throw.

Chardon wished they had not brought flowers. For the young they might signify romance, love; but for the old, who had seen too many of their fellows lying under their impersonal solace, they were too perilously close to death.

Surrounded by the shrill tense chatter of the women, and the obvious chaffing of the older men, he felt strangely alone and deserted. He needed at this moment desperately to be taken out of himself, to forget that Peter was going; and crowds always drove him to introspection. If he could get away, be alone, not actually see the boy go, it would not be half so difficult. But he must wait. He had promised Peter to be there beside Damaris when they rode by. Behind him someone was quoting in a bantering voice:

" 'I could not love thee dear so well, loved I not honour more.' "

It switched his mind to poetry, to the group around the fire at Russell's in the old quiet days when he used to carry Peter there and let him listen. It seemed like only yesterday as he stood visualizing the scene, and yet already they were scattered. He mustn't dwell upon that. There was little comfort in that memory. But he could not let it go; he had invoked something that hung there just across the threshold of his consciousness, something elusive, but that yet insisted upon his notice. Timrod? Hayne? Simms? and then the others. He tried them all. Then in a flash he had it—Legare—J. M. Legare. He had forgotten about him. He had died in 'fifty-nine. He had written some good poems, but already, with the intervening excitement, he had become vague, shadowy, a figure of the past.

But there was something that he had written, something germane to the present moment. At last Chardon was out of himself. He tried to remember, to open his mind to the small insistent voice. Then it came to him, the title and the closing quatrain of a poem, "The Reaper":

> *"Dawn in the meadows of the heart.*
> *The birds sing out a last refrain,*
> *And ready garnered to the mart,*
> *I see the ripe and yellow grain."*

He had been tricked. Tricked by the God who endowed poets with the gift of prophecy. The words kept ringing in his brain. Above him the dawn of a strange and hazardous day was spreading in the familiar heavens; and in the meadows of the heart, dawn upon what unguessed miseries.

He was fumbling for his handkerchief, telling himself that he mustn't be seen like this, that he was an emotional old fool, when an arm was slipped through his and he looked down into Damaris' face. She had come through. No breaking there. She was wearing the look of calm serenity that he knew so well. It was Emily's look. It could face partings, death even, without a tremor. It pulled Chardon up, gave him back his self-control. She led him gently through the crowd to the piazza rail, and they stood silently, arm in arm, waiting.

Presently they heard them coming, hooves muffled by the sandy road, voices, the rattle of equipment, sudden thunder as they crossed the bridge over the old canal. Then they came into view around a bend in the road, taking the first rays of the sun full upon their faces.

Wake was at their head, mounted upon a magnificent roan. Then came the trumpeter with his bugle against his hip. Men and horses were in high spirits. It was beautiful to see the handling of the nervous, high-strung mounts. Only those born to the saddle could have held them to the rigid military pattern.

Chardon and Damaris found Peter at the same moment. The men were riding in column fours; he was in the first row, second from their end. His eyes were shadowed by the visor of his cap, but Chardon caught the flash of his teeth as he smiled at them. There was something gay and debonair and poignantly young about him. He sat Starling jauntily and there was, Chardon thought, already the beginning of a cavalry swagger in his bearing.

There were to be no final leave-takings. Good-byes had been said after the dance last night, and it was not the way of St. John's folk to flaunt private emotions in public. But now from the direction of the deserted camp, where the wagons were getting under way, came the strains of a spiritual, and against it the rise and fall of unrestrained wailing. Africa was bidding good-bye to its men after its ancient custom. It made it terribly hard for the assemblage on the piazza. Chardon felt Damaris' hand tighten on his arm. About him the chatter of the women jumped to a higher key. The men laughed a shade more boisterously.

An order rang out; the trumpeter sounded a call and the company swung to a long single line facing the piazza, then came to the salute. On the piazza there was a surge of color as the ladies flung their bouquets. The line of horses reared and pitched. Eyes front, not a muscle above the waist moving, the men brought them back to statuelike immobility. The piazza cheered and applauded. Swinging from their saddles, the men retrieved the bouquets, thrust them under belts and into the mouths of rifle holsters.

A call sounded; four round full notes in a momentary and pregnant silence. The column formed again. The months of preparation were over. They were actually leaving for the seat of war. Out across the vivid green of the lawn, under the great live oaks, the column moved, plunging into shadow and again out into a dazzle of morning sun. Two centuries had gone into the making of the little cavalcade. Axes had rung in the primeval forests, plantations had grown and spread, life had provided itself with its necessities, then had clothed itself in an appropriate and individual beauty. There had been a time for work and a time for play. There had been a spaciousness about the days. Room for youth to ride untrammeled under the high St. John's sky, to love in privacy, to beget, to know the unrestrained laughter of children. And, at the last, room for a man to grow old gently and, still loved, to pass into the graveyard on the land that his feet had always trod. And down the years always, like the wand passed from hand to hand of runners in a race, the tradition of gentility, hospitality, loyalty to one's own.

And now they were at the gate that let into the highway. Chardon saw the column halt, and back across the distance that they had gone came a snatch of song.

"The birds sing out a last refrain."

They were in the highway now, forming again for the march, beautiful lithe bodies flowing in rhythm to the antics of their thoroughbred mounts, drenched in a flood of June sunshine. But to Chardon the glory that lay about them was not that of high summer, but the light which slants long-shadowed across an autumn field.

"And ready garnered to the mart,
I see the ripe and yellow grain."